Crush at Thomas Hall

Book One of The Thomas Hall Series

Beth Sorensen

Contents

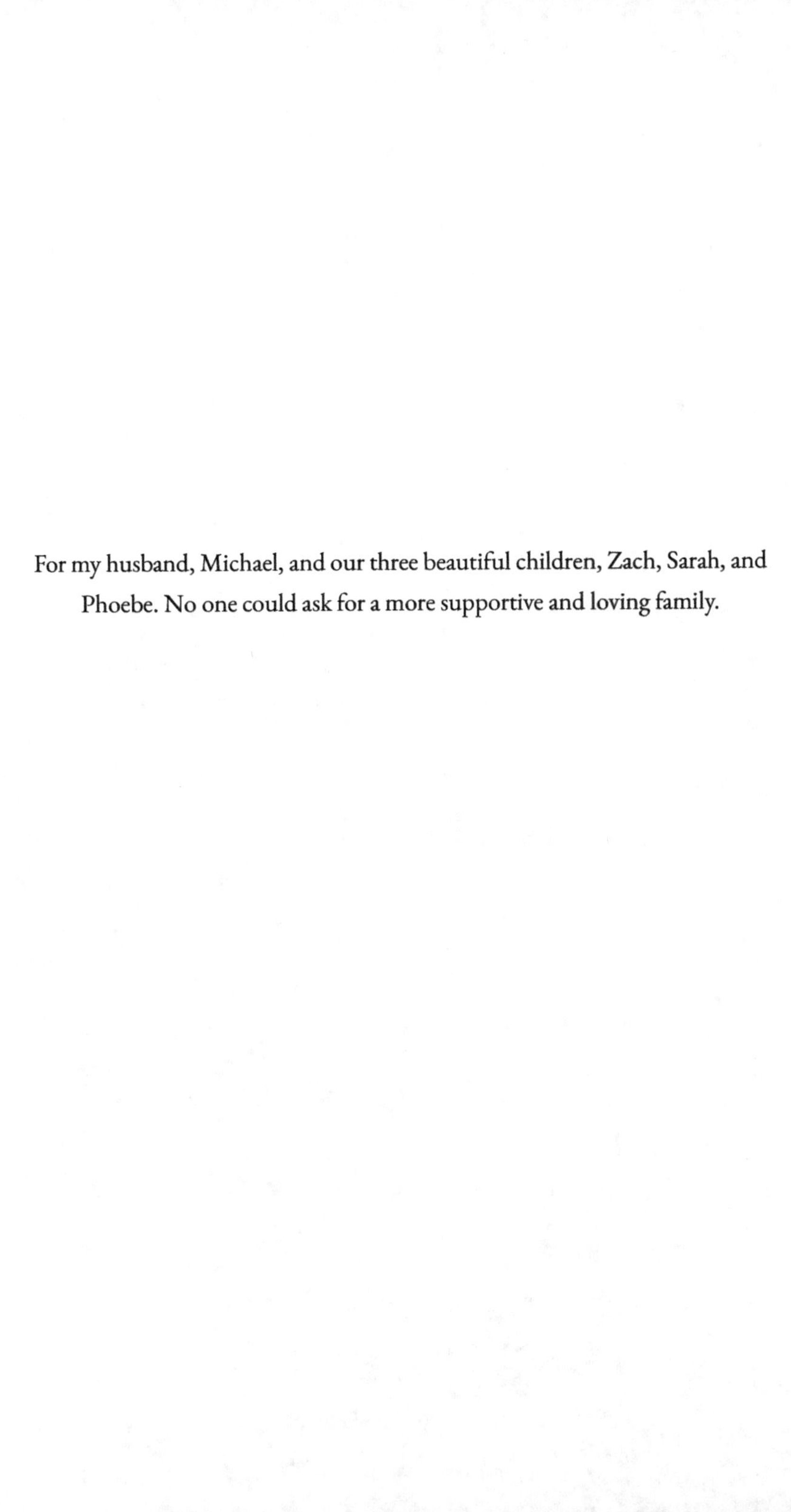

For my husband, Michael, and our three beautiful children, Zach, Sarah, and Phoebe. No one could ask for a more supportive and loving family.

Chapter One

I PRIED MY EYES open to blinding white light and it took a moment of blinking to adjust to the fluorescence. This wasn't the last place I remembered being. The wine cellar was dark, damp, and smelled of sweet wine and mold. But this place was bright, sterile, and smelled of death. I could taste the pungent smell in my mouth. I scanned my field of vision, only to see a multitude of people in lab coats and scrubs.

My chest tightened, and in a flash, I was twelve, sitting in an emergency room, waiting for the doctors to tell me what I already knew. My parents were dead. But that wasn't now. That was fourteen years ago.

I let my head fall to one side and saw Edward talking to a doctor. He was so handsome. Why had our first actual date ended like this? It was going so well too. His early arrival from Chicago was a pleasant surprise and we enjoyed a magnificent lunch with his parents before heading into town.

The movie marathon that followed had been exciting for multiple reasons. But after the movies was what I couldn't piece together. There was a walk. Edward and I talked about my future at Thomas Hall. Then I was in the wine cellar. There was something on the floor. Wine? No, blood. And—

"Senior?" I needed to know he was okay. When I tried to sit up, I felt as though someone had put a meat cleaver through the back of my skull and the nurse next to my bed stopped me from moving.

"Darlin', can you tell me your name? Do you know where you are?"

The nurse had fire engine red hair. I looked at her and tried to speak, but all that came out was a broken whisper. "Cassandra Martin. A hospital?"

"Very good. Do you know what day it is?"

"Thursday night, maybe Friday morning. Middle of the night."

"Good." I heard the nurse say to someone that I was lucid. I tried to sit up and get a better view of what was going on around me, but once again, the nurse stopped me.

"Darlin', you need to rest yourself. You've been through a lot. You were hit in the head multiple times and have a concussion. You have three fractured ribs and a laceration from broken glass in your side. You've lost a lot of blood. Now that you're awake, we need permission to continue treating you."

A broad-shouldered man who appeared to be in his early fifties leaned over me. He was wearing khaki pants and a navy blue polo shirt. I wouldn't have known he was a cop if it hadn't been for the police logo embroidered on his shirt. His salt and peppered hair was buzzed short, allowing his lagoon blue eyes to be the most prominent feature on his face.

"Someone tried to kill you. My name is Detective Brian Hayes. I'm the Willow Creek police detective assigned to this case. I need to talk to you."

The nurse interceded. "Not tonight, detective. She's in no shape to deal with you." She turned to me, needing answers. "Is it okay to continue treatment? Are you allergic to anything?"

"Yes, and yes. Penicillin."

"How allergic?" She was checking my blood pressure and the cuff was so tight that I felt like it would leave a bruise. I took a deep breath and my whole body hurt.

"Anaphylaxis. In less than twenty."

"Darlin', you really should be wearing a medical alert bracelet." It wasn't the first time someone in the medical field had said that to me. "On a scale from zero to ten, tell me your pain level."

"Nine. Eight if I don't breathe."

"Keep breathing. I'll go see what's been ordered for you."

"Ms. Martin, I need to talk to you as soon as possible." Detective Hayes stood up, dropped his card by the phone, and gave one to the nurse. He signaled Edward to follow him out.

Edward ignored the detective and leaned in toward me. His cocoa-colored eyes were bloodshot and the lines around them looked more deeply etched into his face than they had just a few hours earlier. Every hair on his head was out of place as though he'd run his fingers through it a hundred times. He was a disheveled mess, complete with blood splattered across the front of his shirt. He tried to fake a reassuring smile but couldn't quite make it happen.

"Edward?" I grabbed his hand and squeezed it tight in an unsuccessful attempt to let him know that I was fine.

"Yes, my love."

"Put on a clean shirt. I feel a little queasy." He managed a genuine smile and gently pushed the hair away from my face, untangling a piece that had gotten caught in my new earrings.

"Okay, Sweetie, I'll try to find one."

But I wasn't fine. The pain was excruciating and I couldn't catch my breath. I closed my eyes and tried to inhale. Before I slipped into unconsciousness, my mind drifted back to the day this began. The day Edward dialed the wrong number.

Chapter Two

It had only been ten days since the phone rang as I closed the front door. After a moment of debate, I walked back into the house and picked it up in the kitchen, just in case it was Sarah.

"Abbott Residence."

"Sarah?" The man on the other end of the phone line had a voice I thought I recognized.

"No. This is a house guest of hers. Can I help you?"

"Oh, I meant to call her office, my mistake. I must have dialed the wrong number."

"I'd be glad to take a message, if you'd like."

I scurried around, looking for a pad and paper to write down anything pertinent. Ever since Sarah and Michael moved into their new home six months ago, Sarah had begged me to come for a visit. It was a typical Georgetown townhouse: beautiful, red brick on the outside, and in need of serious renovation on the inside. They were systematically taking each room and renovating it. Unfortunately, the kitchen was one of the rooms that had yet to be remodeled, and the phone was an avocado green wall-mounted rotary model with a tangled cord, so I was trapped within the realm of its reach. After three kitchen drawers of failure, I managed to find an old dry cleaning receipt and a marker.

"Thanks. Would you let her know Edward called and that Crush Weekend will start the day after tomorrow?" I was having trouble deciphering the strange message in order to write it down. As I tried to process it, he began to speak again. "I just realized that probably doesn't make much sense. My family owns a winery about an hour southeast of D.C. on the Northern Neck of Virginia. Sarah does the bookkeeping for the winery, and for the last few years she and Michael have come down for Crush Weekend. It's when we harvest and crush the grapes. My family makes a party of it every year."

I scribbled the words Crush, Harvest Celebration, This Weekend, Edward.' I still couldn't place the voice, but I was now certain I knew this man. "Well, that does make things clearer. It sounds like fun."

"It is. You should come, too. You could ride down with Sarah and Michael. It's exhausting, but we always have a good time. Consider it an invitation, Miss ...?"

I knew this trick. My mother had taught it to me about a year before she died. It was a polite way to retrieve someone's name during a conversation. I found myself twisting the spiral cord of the phone around my fingers as I replied. "Cassandra, Cassandra Martin."

There was a long silent pause at the other end of the line. I wondered if he knew me. I thought I heard him slowly exhale and realized my own breath had become quick and shallow.

"Well then, Cassandra, I truly hope you'll join us this weekend. I'd be disappointed if you didn't."

"I'll see what I can do." While we were talking, I had nervously twisted my fingers so tightly into the phone cord that I was beginning to lose circulation in the tips of two of them. It was as if there was a bond between us, even though I was unaware of it.

"I look forward to meeting you again then," he said.

Again?

A short taxi ride later, I sat on the patio of a trendy bistro eating a roast beef and swiss sandwich, while Sarah devoured her bacon, lettuce, and tomato sandwich. It was a beautiful September day and Washington, D.C. was bustling along at a steady pace as cars and people maneuvered about. I usually enjoyed watching people, but I was distracted by other things. One of which was trying to remember where I had heard the voice of the man I had spoken to an hour earlier.

Sarah attacked her meal as though she had not eaten in days. "C.C., you're the smartest person I've ever known. I mean you're a genius. You have a Ph.D. in Cartography, but you won't drive a car into town, even with a GPS map from a company you interned with? It just doesn't make sense to me."

"I haven't driven in over six months and I don't think Washington is the place to start again. The cab wasn't that expensive. Besides, you know I hate to drive."

I looked down at my plate. The sandwich was delicious but my appetite was gone. My jet-lagged mind wasn't interested in food. Jet lag is funny like that. Your body is so in tune with where you were that it fails to recognize where you truly are. However, knowing it was lunchtime in my present time zone, I picked at the warm roast beef hanging out the side of the sandwich.

"Okay, I'll give you that one, but, I still can't get over how great you look. I thought you needed to be committed when you took off on this world trek of yours, but you look so peaceful. And so much thinner."

"I guess I finally figured out that eating doesn't solve all of your problems, but it sure is a fun way to drown them." I said.

Sarah laughed as she wolfed down the last bite of her sandwich. I was already stuffed. I offered the other half of my sandwich to Sarah, but she opted to eat the fries off my plate instead, dredging them through the ketchup on her plate as she went.

"I'm sorry Michael couldn't join us, C.C. This is one of his favorite lunch spots. He's stuck with some new clients. We should take something back to the office for him."

I couldn't decide if she was telling the truth, or making excuses for her husband. Michael had been my husband's best friend. He didn't care for me the entire time Tony and I dated and had grown even less fond of me after we married, although I never understood why. But we both loved his wife, so Michael and I tolerated one another.

"You know, no one really calls me C.C. anymore. Oh, before I forget, one of your clients called the house this morning. He said his name was Edward." I waved the waiter over and asked for more water.

"Oh, Edward Baker. Why did he call the house?"

I rubbed my left temple with my index and middle fingers as I contemplated why that name seemed so familiar. "Dialed wrong. He meant to call your office, but he told me to tell you that 'Crush Weekend' starts the day after tomorrow."

Sarah's eyes lit up like they did in college when we would get invited somewhere fun. She leaned into the table towards me and grinned. "I love Crush Weekend."

"He invited me along too. Should I go or was he just being polite?"

"Oh no, if the Baker Family invites you to Crush, you go." She reached across the table and pressed the palm of her soft hand on top of mine. "It rates up there with an invitation to the White House. Besides, we'll have a fabulous time there together. Who knows, maybe you'll meet Mr. Right."

"No thanks. I've already done that once, and we know how that turned out." The waiter brought my water and I thanked him as he walked away.

"You know C.C., excuse me, Cassandra; you're too young to spend the rest of your life alone. Maybe it's time for you to start dating again. Just think about it, okay?"

Dating was the last thing I wanted to think about, but I knew what to say to keep Sarah happy. "I'll think about it, but not today. Tell me about this guy, Edward Baker, do I know him? His voice sounded familiar and so does his name, but I can't place him."

She lifted her hand off mine and began to speak. Sarah liked to gesture with her hands so much I had often teased her that if you tied her hands behind her back she wouldn't be able to hold a conversation.

"I don't think you've ever met him. But he is in the business and social section of the D.C. newspapers a lot. Who knows, maybe he's your soul mate." Sarah leaned back into her chair and began to laugh out loud and I smiled. When she regained her composure she told me a little about him.

"I'm sorry. As much as I'd like to see you find someone, Edward's not the soul mate type. I'm not sure he even has a soul. The only thing he's ever been in love with is his work. His idea of a romantic evening is working late."

"How would you know?" Sarah and Michael spent some time living apart about a year ago and I had always wondered if either strayed from their wedding vows.

"I've heard talk from his staff. I guess that's the price you pay for becoming the CEO of your family's company at thirty-two."

"That's a lot of pressure. Running a family business. He sounds devoted." I said.

"That's not devotion C.C., that's being a workaholic."

"I've never met anyone that matches that description." But still, I wondered why I recognized his voice.

Washington D.C. has two major problems: crooked politicians and poorly designed road networks. I came to the realization that the latter of the two was the more serious problem the next evening when the three of us headed out to the winery. The trip, which shouldn't have taken more than an hour, turned into a three-hour odyssey involving Thursday night rush hour traffic and rain.

I hated the rain. The thunder rolled across the fields lining the road and the lightning, while seldom, struck hard and sharp as the bright white lines made their way to solid ground. I wanted to curl up in a tiny ball and disappear until the storm passed. Some storms bothered me more than others. This one disturbed me more than any in a long time and I knew why. It was the road. It was dark, wet, hilly, and winding; much like the one my parents and I were on the night of the accident that killed them both.

Michael drove and Sarah read over some files from work, occasionally looking into the back seat to check on me. She was one of the few people who understood the effects of a storm on my mental health. As we crept along Route 301, I tried to keep my mind on other things. I contemplated whether I had made the right decision coming back to the States with the thought of not traveling anymore. After all, I had no home to return to. I wasn't even certain my job was still available at the university or if I even wanted to live in Ohio anymore. And just to fill any gaps in my thoughts, I kept drifting back to the sound of the familiar voice on the phone the day before.

By the time we reached Thomas Hall Winery, it was late into the evening and the three of us were exhausted. The rain had finally stopped and it was pitch dark. When we got out of the car, I could not help but to notice not only a syrupy sweet smell in the air but also how quiet it was. It was nice to hear the frogs and crickets peacefully singing, as opposed to the traffic and sirens of a big city.

The main house was lit by floodlights. It was a beautiful old plantation-style mansion. Unfortunately, the details of the exterior were hidden in the shadows. I looked forward to the morning and viewing the house in the full light of day.

We were greeted at the front door by a butler and his assistant. The butler was a short, thin man with gray hair. I figured he was in his mid-sixties. His assistant was about half his age and a foot taller.

"Good evening, Mr. Abbott, Mrs. Abbott. Welcome back to Thomas Hall. It's been much too long since your last visit." It was apparent the butler had been in the States for years, but you could still hear his Yorkshire accent slip into his speech. The assistant took Sarah and Michael's bags and disappeared through the front door.

"I agree, Victor." Sarah was obviously fond of Victor by the way she shook his hand. Michael approached him in the same manner.

"Victor," Michael said as we moved toward the door. "I thought you were just supervising the staff these days. I'm surprised to see you out here."

"This weekend, everyone waits on the guests and family. I've been assigned to Edward, Jr. and one other person."

Sarah turned and introduced me to Victor. "I'd like you to meet one of our dearest friends, Cassandra Martin."

"Ah yes, Edward told me you might be bringing someone special." Victor stopped, smiled, and gently shook my hand. He took my bags and then continued to lead us into the house. "He told me that if you were half as beautiful as you sounded on the phone, I should put you in the best room in the house. I think I will put you in the Elizabeth suite. Not only is it our best guest suite, but it is right across from the Abbott's regular rooms.

Michael's face puckered in response as if he'd swallowed a bug. "Edward didn't really say that, did he?"

Victor guided us up a grand staircase as he continued. "When was the last time you saw him, Mr. Abbott?"

"It's been a while, at least six months."

"He's changed." The tone of Victor's voice shifted. I'm not sure how or why, but it made a distinct impression. "Over the last few months, he's undergone a strange metamorphosis, you might say. It's as though he finally realized his life was missing something."

"Why?"

"I'm surprised the two of you haven't heard all of this. I thought everyone knew. Edward went on a business trip about four months ago and he hasn't been the same since. Apparently, he fell in love with a girl he met on the trip, but now he can't find her. He's gone as far as to hire several detectives to figure out where she went."

"Edward? Love? Seriously?"

"Mr. Abbott, you are a man of many words tonight." We all burst into laughter as we realized the usually talkative man had been stunned to the point of one-word sentences.

Somehow, during our brief conversation, Victor had not only led us upstairs but also hung up all of the clothes in my bag and turned down the sheets. As he headed out the door, presumably to lead Michael and Sarah to their room, Victor turned back to me and smiled, "Sleep well, Miss Martin. The upcoming days will be busy ones."

However, I didn't sleep well. I tossed and turned, but it was by no fault of my accommodations. The mattress was so soft it was like laying in a cloud. The sheets and pillowcases were scented with lavender and were as soft as the mattress. Even with a wonderful place to unwind, I was fighting jet lag and my mind was too full to sleep. My thoughts from the car ride stayed in my head long after the storm was over. I was still contemplating the decisions I would need to make soon about my future, along with the vaguely familiar voice on the other end of the phone.

Chapter Three

Why is it that the moment you drift off to sleep, the alarm clock goes off? I had fallen asleep sometime after one in the morning and it seemed like a split second later, the alarm clock buzzer was screaming at me and it was seven. I rolled out of bed and looked around as sunlight began to fill the room. I was still tired but knew the only solution for jet lag was to battle through the desire to sleep and live within the current time zone's parameters.

The room had a strange sweet smell I couldn't place. It wasn't lavender or sugar. I had noticed it last night when we arrived at the main house. The heat of the morning rays seemed to intensify it and its source puzzled me.

The Elizabeth Suite, as Victor had referred to it, was three rooms. The first was a sitting room, tastefully decorated in the Colonial Williamsburg tradition, and had a small bar that not only contained various beverages and snacks but also a small microwave and coffee maker. As I explored the bar, I was happy to discover a chest containing a variety of teas, including my favorite, ginger peach. So I heated some water in the microwave and made myself a cup.

The second room was the bedroom and dressing room. While the sitting room was by no means small, the bedroom was twice its size. It was decorated in the same style and was very formal, like something from a historical museum. While I had never lived anywhere as lovely as this suite, I felt very comfortable, almost as if I were home.

I walked over to the closet with my tea in one hand and opened the door. I removed a pair of jeans, a clean t-shirt, tennis shoes, and underwear and moved it all into the last room of the suite: the bathroom. With the morning light streaming in through the window, the room seemed even larger than it had the night before. I had lived in apartments smaller than this room. It had two sinks, a garden tub, a walk-in shower, and a sauna. In the middle of the room were a chaise lounge and a small, round table. I laid my now empty teacup on the table and stripped off the t-shirt and undies I had slept in the night before. Ten minutes in the sauna and a hot shower later, I felt refreshed and ready for whatever the day might bring. I brushed my teeth, got dressed, and went back into the bedroom to put my shoes on. My bed had already been made and a large basket with a purple bow sat at the foot of the bed. Attached to the bow was a hand-written note:

> Miss Martin,
> I hope you found your first night at Thomas Hall enjoyable. I had Victor put together a basket of things you might find useful during your stay with us. The entire Baker family looks forward to meeting you at breakfast.
> Sincerely, Senior

I was not used to receiving gifts, especially from strangers, and I felt overwhelmed by my host's generosity. I wondered if he was this generous to all of his guests. I reminded myself to thank him as I carefully untied the bow and opened the cellophane that encased the basket to find a bottle of sunscreen, a purple Thomas Hall Winery fleece jacket, a bottle of the vineyard's Chardonnay, two beautifully etched wine glasses, and a pair of gardening gloves. It was a bit cool in the house, so I put on the jacket, rubbed some sunscreen onto my face and neck, stuffed the gloves into the jacket pocket, and headed out of my suite.

When I knocked on the door to Sarah and Michael's room, there was no answer. I opened the door just enough to poke my head in, only to find they were already gone. I thought it was unusually rude of them to bring me somewhere

I knew no one and then just leave me on my own to make my way to breakfast. I looked around their room from the doorway. It was a smaller version of mine, only with no wall dividing the sitting room from the bedroom and decorated in hues of burgundies and greens.

I glanced up and down the hall. I wished I had paid more attention to the maze Victor had led us through the night before. After a few wrong turns, I found my way to the main staircase. It seemed strange that the staircase would be hard to find as it was majestic in stature with its white marble stairs and mahogany handrail. When I reached the base of the staircase, a young maid guided me toward the other guests.

A large group of people had already gathered in the massive formal dining room. It looked more like the ballroom at the White House than a dining room, and I had the distinct impression it could be converted for a party at a moment's notice. The three chandeliers were equally spaced across the ceiling and the floor was covered by large Turkish rugs. But the highly polished cherry wood peeked out from between the carpets revealing their beauty.

The guests were eating a variety of items that all seemed to be made to order, as several waiters were attending to their needs. It was apparent these people all knew each other. Their conversations seemed friendly, continuous, and over-lapping. Sarah and Michael were nowhere to be seen. I froze for a moment and debated what to do next. I was not comfortable around large groups of strangers, and yet I was in a room full of people I had never met. I considered retreating to my room and waiting for familiar faces to arrive when a strikingly handsome man in his seventies with bright blue eyes and an amazing smile approached me and held out his hand to greet me. He limped slightly as though his left knee had worn out years ago and he had not bothered having it replaced.

"Miss Martin, good morning. I'm Edward Baker, Sr. Welcome to Thomas Hall."

"You know who I am?" I was surprised he knew me by name but was glad someone did.

"You are our only new guest this year, my dear. We have basically the same group of friends that come to stay with us year after year." He gestured to the others seated at the long, narrow oak table that could have easily seated twenty-four people at any given meal.

As we walked toward the table, I tried to find something appropriate to say. "Thank you for having me here, Mr. Baker, and for the lovely gifts as well. The jacket is wonderful."

"Please, call me Senior. Everyone does. Victor noticed last night that you might not have a jacket appropriate for the unusually cool morning we're experiencing. Besides, you make a beautiful billboard."

I looked at the floor and swallowed hard, trying to hide my embarrassment from the compliment. I didn't consider myself beautiful by any means. I had recently lost over fifty pounds, but I probably still weighed about ten or fifteen pounds more than I should have. If I had to choose, I would have said I was built like Marilyn Monroe, fleshy and curvy. Although I wished I looked more like Twiggy, thin and lean, the kind of body clothes hung beautifully from. In light of my fair complexion and once heavy build, I had spent most of my life looking like the "Stay Puft Marshmallow" kid.

"May I have your attention, everyone? I'd like to introduce you to Miss Cassandra Martin. She's the newest addition to this year's harvest." I found myself staring at the carpet, wishing I wasn't the center of attention. He turned to me, "I'll start at the head of the table and work my way around."

There were enough people at the table that as they were introduced, I wasn't required to make polite conversation with anyone, which was a good thing. I've never been the overly social type and making small talk, in particular, was always a strained and uncomfortable task. Senior introduced me to the Bryants, longtime friends of the Baker family; Dr. Charles Rice, Senior's physician; Judge Eugene Smith and his wife; and Kelly Fields, Edward, Jr.'s assistant.

Next, he introduced me to the younger of his two sons, Henry. Henry was a carbon copy of his father, with the same bright blue eyes and a broad smile. He was quite the gentleman and stood to greet me. As he shook my hand, I noticed he had already mastered some of the same sweet, inviting mannerisms of his father. Henry apologized for the absence of his wife as she was recovering from a migraine.

When Senior finished introducing me to Henry, he introduced me to the love of his life, Vivian. She was a beautiful woman, petite, thin, well-manicured, and every hair was perfectly in place. It made me wish I had done more than pull my hair back into a simple ponytail. Even in Khaki pants and a short-sleeved turtleneck, she had a regal look about her.

"Really, Senior. Haven't you tortured the poor girl with introductions enough? Come sit and eat something, my dear." She gestured for me to take the empty seat next to her. "My husband is so fond of beautiful, young women that he seems to forget they need to eat a good breakfast too." She was as spunky as she was beautiful. I immediately liked her and hoped I had made a good first impression.

Victor appeared from what seemed like nowhere and held out my chair for me. He took my breakfast order and quickly returned with ginger peach tea and white bread, lightly toasted with strawberry preserves. It was the same breakfast I had eaten nearly every morning since I was twelve years old.

Over breakfast, Mrs. Baker informed me that we were waiting for her oldest son to arrive from D.C., as well as the vineyard's wine master to return from the lab at the winery's production building. She gave me a condensed version of the importance of having the right percentage of sugars in the grapes to create a fine wine with the perfect alcohol content. I decided not to tell her I read three books the day before on the making of wine and one had delved into the importance of the sugars and how they break down within the process in great detail.

While I was finishing my last piece of toast, Sarah and Michael joined the rest of the party. They apologized for their lateness, claiming they overslept. I knew this was a lie, as they had left their room before I left mine. Something was going on. I must have had a curious expression on my face because Sarah leaned over and whispered, "I'll tell you later."

Suddenly, a young man raced in and yelled with unbridled joy, "It's time, everybody! Let's go make some wine!"

Some people are just a little too cheerful first thing in the morning. Not really being a morning person myself, I find this type of personality about as delightful as a dentist's drill and this man was no exception. The very enthusiastic human was Alex White, the vineyard's wine master. He was young for the business he was in, not much older than me in fact, and his youthful enthusiasm radiated throughout everyone in the room and the level of excitement amongst the guests quickly rose.

As everyone in the room began to leave the breakfast table and head toward the door, a man in his mid to late forties walked in. He was carrying a cup of coffee and chatting with Kelly, who had been introduced to me as Edward Jr.'s assistant. To say he was handsome was an understatement. He stood about six foot three and was broad-shouldered. He had a fabulous head of hair, which had been trained to stay in place, was well dressed, and looked strikingly like Senior, with exception of his height and eyes. He was several inches taller and his eyes were a warm chocolaty brown that could melt a girl's heart. I knew this man. We had met before.

The sight of him caused me to smile and I had to stop moving to catch my breath. It was then that Edward Baker, Jr. saw me. He dropped his coffee cup which smashed into several pieces on the marble floor of the foyer, causing those remaining in the house to stop and turn around. He ran his hand through his hair as he looked down at the broken cup, then looked back at me. I walked toward him, hoping he remembered me.

"Cassandra Martin." The corners of Edward's lips turned upward into a smile when he said my name. "I've been looking everywhere for you."

I was at a loss for words, but that was a pretty normal state for me. After a moment or two, I finally managed to squeak out a coherent sentence. "I thought your voice sounded familiar." I could feel my cheeks getting hot. It always happened when I blushed, which embarrassed me even more. I looked down at the floor. We both bent over at the same time and began to pick up the pieces of the coffee cup as Victor quickly mopped up the remaining liquid.

"When you told me who you were on the phone, I wasn't sure I should believe it."

He continued to stare at the mess he'd made. I could tell he was embarrassed by his momentary clumsiness so I smiled and tried to reassure him. I placed my hand on his bicep. When I did I felt his hard, chiseled muscle. It caused me to pause before I said, "Don't worry, I drop things all the time. Or have you forgotten?"

We looked at one another, both smiled and quietly laughed.

Edward and I met in the first class cabin of a United Airlines flight between Seattle and Chicago. A weather delay had left us sitting on the runway for forty-five minutes and the flight from Seattle to Chicago wasn't short either at just over four hours. He had been assigned the seat next to mine and asked if I'd like to split a bottle of wine with him. When the flight attendant handed me my glass, I dropped it straight into his lap. Luckily, he had carried his suit bag on board and quickly changed.

While it was unheard of for me to recover from such embarrassing incidents, he made me feel at ease and I enjoyed talking with him throughout the flight. As we drank, we discussed politics, love, family, books, everything and anything it seemed.

He talked a lot about his work. He was the CEO of a biotech company his mother had inherited. He normally would have used the company jet, but his pilot had the flu and was grounded in Seattle until he recovered. So he had opted for a commercial flight home.

I talked a little about my travels and where I was headed to next. He was very interested in the places I had been, why I had chosen them, and what I seen. There had definitely been chemistry between us but the timing was wrong and we both had other flights to catch.

Before I even glanced up, I could feel everyone's eyes staring at us. Even those guests who had previously left had returned to investigate why the others had stayed behind. Edward noticed we weren't alone as well and quickly helped me to my feet while he handed Victor the pieces of the broken cup.

Edward brushed the back of his hand against my cheek, pushing back a wisp of hair that had fallen loose from my ponytail. He had done the same thing just before he kissed that cheek in the Chicago airport.

I found myself praying that he would kiss me again.

Chapter Four

The walk to the vines offered my first daylight view of Thomas Hall. The house was a traditional plantation-style mansion built on the foundation that once held a similar house. I was disappointed it was not the original, as the architectural details I was hoping to see no longer existed on the white-columned home. Many of the large homes in the South were burnt down during the Civil War and then rebuilt at some point later. They were still beautiful but lacked the architectural elegance of the originals.

The grounds were superbly maintained with beautiful flowers lining the paths out to the fields, which were filled with rows and rows of grapevines, most weighted heavily with beautiful fruit ready for harvest. The syrupy sweet smell of grapes filled the air and I finally connected it to the same sweet smell I experienced in my room and upon our arrival. It seemed to infuse every pore of my body and I was certain I'd carry it with me long after the weekend was over.

As we walked along the path to the vines, I could feel Edward staring at me and the occasional glance at him confirmed it. The night we met I wasn't nervous at all, but now being so close to him again made my whole body quiver. I had often thought about the southern gentleman I had met that night. I wondered if our circumstances were different, if we would have pursued some sort of relationship. The problem was I couldn't remember his name. I was wonderful at remembering faces, but names tended to go in one ear and out the other. I'm so bad at remembering them that I had taken to keeping a journal where I could note people's names and when and where I met them. If I could remember their names long enough to write them down.

When we reached the vines we were to harvest, Edward and I somehow ended up at opposite ends of the same row of vines. And while I was glad to see him again, I appreciated the opportunity to have a moment to collect my thoughts.

The morning flew by and in doing so transformed from cool and foggy straight into a glorious sunny Virginia autumn day. Our morning began with a ten-minute lesson on how to properly use the sharp pruning shears to harvest the grapes without damaging the vines, followed by several hours of actually harvesting them. We sang songs in a variety of languages and laughed as we messed up the words. Between songs, we all talked amongst ourselves while harvesting grapes as the bright sun warmed the morning air. Everyone there seemed truly happy I had joined them this year and made me feel welcome within their close-knit group, even Dr. Rice, who I kept calling Judge Smith.

I occasionally glanced down the row of grapevines to where Edward was working. Nearly every time I did, I would find him staring at me and smiling. My hands felt hot and sweaty, and I removed the gardening gloves and put them in my jacket pocket. I couldn't decide if the cause was the steady climb in temperature or Edward's presence. It wasn't long before I found it necessary to remove my coat as well. When I looked down at the v-necked t-shirt I had chosen to wear, and I wished I had selected one that showed a little less cleavage.

Every time Edward would get close enough for us to start a conversation, one of us would be interrupted by someone or something. First, it was Alex. He was a nice-looking guy, but looked more like he should be shredding waves than making wine. He was tan, muscular, and had shaggy sun-bleached hair.

"Hi." He walked up behind me and gently moved my right hand, so the shears were in another spot on the vine. "Don't be afraid to cut a little further up when you take the bunch off. It won't hurt the vine and you'll have fewer loose grapes rolling around on the ground."

"Oh, okay."

He took my hand, with the shears still in them, to the next bunch of grapes and held my waist as he leaned in with me to pick the next bunch. I couldn't decide if he was trying to flirt with me or if he was genuinely concerned with the method of pruning I was using. But after a moment of analyzing the way he held my waist, it was clear he could not care less how I was harvesting the grapes.

"Thanks, I think I've got it now." I gently took his hand from my mid-section. "But I do have a question for you. I'm a little surprised we're harvesting today after last night's heavy rain. I know the rain can have a negative effect on sugar concentration levels. Was there a reason you chose not to wait?"

"Wow. Good question. No one told me you were so well educated in viticulture."

"I'm not, just a little light reading yesterday."

"Light, I doubt, with a question like that. We would have waited a few more days except for this," Alex leaned down and picked a leaf off a lower growing vine and flipped it over. It was covered in tan spots that were outlined in black. He didn't realize it, but everyone had stopped to listen to him speak. "It's a fungus, and its spreading fast. The vines have been treated, so the roots will be fine, but it attacks new growth. I'd rather take my chances on a weaker alcohol percentage end product than the grapes being overcome with fungi and completely unusable."

"Makes sense, thanks." I turned to go back to the task at hand when Alex stopped me by reaching out and clasping my hand.

"If you want to get a solid foundation on winemaking, try reading *The World Atlas of Wine*. I have a copy; if you want to borrow it, you'll have to come to my place and get it." Then he winked at me. The thought made my skin crawl.

I wasn't interested in borrowing anything from him. Besides, it had been the first book I read on Thursday morning. I released my hand from his and silently continued with the harvest.

Next, Senior worked his way over. It had taken him a while to do and I noticed he was repositioning himself in order to talk to me. So I made an effort, for the sake of my gracious host, to purposefully work in his direction as well.

"Cassandra dear, have you ever done anything like this before?"

"No sir. I was in France last spring and got to see the vines in bloom from a distance, but this is my first harvest."

"Ah, but you seem to be very well educated in vines. Where did that knowledge come from my dear?"

"I like to read a lot. Some people might even say to the point of obsession."

"Well, we have a wonderful library at the main house. Consider it at your disposal during your stay."

"Why, thank you. That's very kind of you." I reached over and put my hand on his elbow. "But I have a question for you as well. What do you think the best time of year is to be at a winery?"

"*This,* my dear, *is* the best time of year. Every Crush Weekend I get to see at my age is a blessing. And the best part is all of these beautiful women spending the day at Thomas Hall with me!" He made me smile. I liked Senior and wished I had known him as a young man. I thought about it for a brief moment as I went back to work while we talked.

"Senior, you are quite the charmer. I bet you were a real lady's man in your youth."

He laughed as he repositioned himself so the sun wasn't beating directly into his eyes and once again began to harvest the grapes.

"More than you know. And if you had been around in my youth, I would have followed you to the ends of the earth. As beautiful as you are, no wonder Edward's spent so much time trying to find you." I could feel my face get warm and hoped that if I ignored it, maybe the blush would just go away.

"Everyone keeps saying that, but I don't understand why. We just met the one time."

"I think you'll understand before the weekend is over, my dear." Senior stopped working for a moment as though he needed to rest. "So tell me, how do you know Sarah and Michael Abbott?"

"The four of us went to college together. Sarah and I were roommates at The University of North Carolina."

"The four of you?"

I felt like I had just swallowed a rock, and it landed at the bottom of my stomach. I had said four. Now I would have to explain.

It was then Victor appeared in the fields, along with numerous members of his staff carrying baskets containing jugs of water and lemonade along with fruit, cheese, and bread. Victor's timing was impeccable. Not only was I starving, but his arrival was enough of a distraction that Senior forgot about his question.

Victor's staff laid large picnic blankets between the vines and we all stopped working. I sat on a blanket with Edward, Sarah, and Michael and we devoured our mid-morning snacks. It might have been a good time for the two of us to reconnect, but Edward sensed I didn't want to have that conversation in front of Michael and Sarah. So instead, we talked about how sweet the plums were and debated the name of each kind of cheese. It was nothing more than polite conversation, but it was the same type of conversation that launched our delightful evening on the airplane. I'd forgotten how relaxed I felt talking with him and was glad to do so again. It was a strange mix of emotions. When we were face to face, I was fine. But thinking about talking to him made me feel like I was going to pass out.

It wasn't long before Senior summoned us all back to work. This was a job we returned to willingly, talking and laughing as we worked toward completing the task at hand. Not too long after our mid-morning break, Sarah and I managed to squeeze in a minute of conversation and I explained to her how I knew Edward.

"You're kidding me, right?"

"No. We just met the one time on that flight from Seattle to Chicago. Don't you think it's weird that he would go to the trouble to find me?"

"If it were anyone but Edward Baker, I'd say yes. But C.C. Edward is a very extreme person. If he does something, he does it a hundred and ten percent and he has an unlimited source of cash by which to achieve it."

"Is that a comment or a warning?" I stopped working to get the full scope of her response.

"A little of both." I was shocked that her answer was so monotone and to the point.

"But Sarah, I don't know what to say to him."

"Just be yourself. It seemed to work well when we took our break earlier."

"Easier said than done."

The nervous energy in my body had been building since the moment he dropped his coffee cup at the house and the more I thought about a conversation alone with him, the more my nervousness grew. I was certain I'd end up sounding like a blithering idiot the next time he and I had the chance to speak.

Then just before lunch, it appeared that Edward and I would finally get that moment to talk alone. Not that I had a clue what I was going to say to him. He had been looking for me for the last four months and all I knew about Edward Baker was that he had not only made me feel weak in the knees in the middle of Chicago's O'Hare Airport, but had also made me feel comfortable enough upon meeting him, a complete stranger, to tell him nearly anything.

He worked his way over toward me and was about to say hello when his cell phone rang. He stopped working, looked at the caller ID, and answered quickly. A wave of disappointment ran through me.

"Hey Clark, where are you? No way! You're kidding, right? Oh man, it won't be the same without you. Yeah, I know. Well, tell the hurricane I said hello." Edward laughed, causing his eyes to squint and a few little wrinkles to reveal themselves. I'd never really been attracted to men my own age. There's something about a little gray around the temples, which Edward didn't have, or a few wrinkles, which he had when he laughed, I always found attractive on men.

Edward finished up the conversation and told the person on the other end of the phone to call him in a few days and said his goodbyes. I stopped harvesting and turned toward him to give him my full attention.

"Sorry about that. It was a frat brother of mine. He and his wife were supposed to come up for the weekend but the hurricane that's heading toward Florida spoiled their travel plans. It's just as well I suppose. Victor had originally planned to put them in the Elizabeth Suite, but I understand that's become your bedroom this weekend."

"There's a hurricane heading toward Florida?" I could feel my heart skip a beat as I said the words out loud.

"It's been on the news for over a week, where have you been?"

I had forgotten that Edward was utterly unaware of my travels since our first meeting.

"Well, in the last couple of weeks, I finished up a stay in China, and then I was in Istanbul until Tuesday, then D.C., then here. I've either been too jet-lagged or too busy traveling to watch the news. I guess that's the downside of traveling. You tend to live in a bubble and if you're not careful, can isolate yourself from the world."

Edward looked at me, then smiled and asked the obvious question, "Exactly where have you been for the last four months?"

I wasn't about to tell him, or anyone else, the complete answer to that question. The thought of the answer alone haunted me. I bit my bottom lip, thought about the best way to respond, and shook my head.

"You wouldn't believe me even if I told you. But about this hurricane, how bad are they expecting it to be? My aunt and uncle live in the Keys. They're the only family I have left." I was worried, and it must have shown because he looked into my eyes, smiled, and brushed his hand against my cheek again. I was certain I'd melt like a stick of butter before the day was over if he kept doing that to me.

"Don't worry; it's barely a category one storm. They're just expecting some heavy rain and wind. Here, take my phone and check on them. I'm sure you'll feel better once you do."

He handed me his cell phone, stood behind me, and rested his hands on my shoulders while I stumbled my way through dialing my uncle's number. I had never used a touch screen cell phone before, and I found using it was an exercise in aggravation.

Edward's hands radiated a certain sexual energy that I was unaccustomed to and I could feel the muscles in my body tighten. I knew he had noticed my reaction because he began to lift his hands off my shoulders. I suddenly found myself doing something unexpected. I reached behind me with my free hand and softly pressed his hand back on my shoulder, and leaned my head against it.

All I heard when the call went through was a weird busy signal. I hung up the phone, turned around, and handed it back to Edward as I let out a quiet sigh.

"The house line is down and I don't know my uncle's cell by heart. It's in my address book back at the main house."

"We'll walk back to the main house and get it. I don't want you to worry about your family."

"No, it can wait until tonight. I'm sure they're fine." That was the great thing about my Uncle Fred. Even in the worst and weirdest situations, Fred always seemed to be just fine. My dad had been the same way. It was a family trait I felt had skipped my entire generation.

Edward was gently holding me around the waist at this point. I wasn't sure whether or not I was completely comfortable with this. I barely knew this man. But when I looked into Edward's eyes, I couldn't help but like the position I was in. From the look on his face, I thought he might even kiss me, but Henry walked up behind us and said, "Hey big brother, save the romance for later. It's lunchtime."

In the dining room, we were served a fabulous buffet of salads, sandwiches, pasta, wine, and desserts that would rival any five-star restaurant. I chose a chicken salad sandwich, baby carrots, and some strawberries dipped in chocolate. I was going to skip dessert but Sarah insisted that I try the strawberries. Once I was seated next to Edward, Victor came around and poured the two of us glasses of Chardonnay. It was the same wine we had shared on our flight. He didn't tell me the night we met that the wine we were sharing was from his family's winery. I looked at Edward and smiled. I knew he had asked Victor specifically to serve this to us.

Maybe I imagined it, but I felt like anytime Edward and I spoke to one another, at least half a dozen people would stop to listen. Luckily there was some light jazz being piped into the speakers of the dining room so there was no fear of total silence. He and I talked about the music, food, and wine. It was a safe topic of conversation and the other guests soon grew bored with us. He made me laugh when he commented on how little I ate. He was shocked when I told him of my weight issues as a teenager and assured me I no longer had such a problem.

When lunch ended, Edward turned to me and said, "I have to meet with Dad and Sarah about the winery's books this afternoon, but I'd like to spend some time alone with you before dinner."

I nodded quietly, but as Edward stood from the table, I reached out and grabbed his hand to stop him. When I did, our fingers intertwined, and I felt the energy from his body radiated into my hand, sending a slight shock through my body. When he turned and looked at me, I could tell he was happy with my unspoken request not to leave. Curiosity had finally gotten the best of me, and with a glass and a half of wine in me, I felt bold enough to ask.

"This morning, you told me you'd been looking everywhere for me. I have it on good authority that you went so far as to hire detectives to find me. Why?"

He reached into his pocket and pulled out a beautiful gold crucifix. It was my gold crucifix.

"How on Earth?" I clasped my hands to my heart. I felt my eyes begin to well up with tears. The necklace had belonged to my mother and I was devastated when I realized it had disappeared. "I lost that necklace ages ago somewhere between Moscow and Tibet. I thought I'd never see it again."

"No, you actually lost this necklace four months, two weeks, and three days ago. Just before my connecting flight took off, the flight attendant in charge of our cabin on the Chicago flight came on board and said she had found the necklace in my seat. I remembered seeing it on you. It must have fallen off as we were exiting the plane. Anyway, I told her it belonged to you, but I promised her that I would see that you got it back. I hope you don't mind, but I took the liberty of having the broken clasp replaced."

"You spent four months looking for me just to return a necklace?"

"Well, I did promise her I'd return it. And, to be honest, I wanted to see you again. You're not an easy woman to find, Cassandra Martin." The corners of his lips crept upward into a sexy smile. "That is until you show up on my front doorstep."

Edward walked behind my chair, slowly pushed my ponytail to one side, put the necklace around my neck, and secured the clasp. I closed my eyes and took a moment to enjoy his attentiveness. Then he leaned over and whispered in my ear, "I'll see you later." When I opened my eyes and turned around, he was gone. I let out an audible sigh that I'm certain everyone within a five-mile radius heard.

Victor, who had been scurrying around all through lunch, took a moment and sat beside me. "It may be out of place for me to say this, Miss Martin, but you do understand the reason he was looking for you had nothing to do with that necklace? He fell in love with you on that flight. He told his father that by the time he realized what had happened to him, you were gone. I would bet my retirement Edward knew exactly who you were the moment he heard your voice on the phone a few days ago. How else would he have known to put the necklace in his pocket this morning?"

I liked Victor. He seemed to know just when to chime in and fill in all the blanks. But before I could properly thank him, he was up and moving, along with everyone else who seemed to be heading out the door to harvest more grapes. I stood and moved to join them and was nearly at the door when Vivian Baker put her tiny hand on my shoulder and stopped me just short of the doorway.

"Oh, Cassandra dear, your face is already getting burnt."

I turned and looked in the oval mirror on the wall by the front door. My cheeks and nose were beet red. It seemed like no matter how much sunscreen I used, I was always either sunburnt or had just recovered from one.

"Why don't you take a break from the harvest and I'll give you a tour of the winery and the main house? Besides, I'd like to get to know you better."

Michael, who rarely commented on anything concerning me, said, "You know, C.C., it might be a good idea for you to stay with Vivian. You're the only person here who doesn't know the house or the grounds. And I'd hate for Sarah and me to have to explain to your uncle why his only niece resembles the product of a lobster crossed with a French fry!"

Laughter bubbled out of everyone remaining in the room as we all envisioned Michael's description and the conversation that would have to take place. While Michael was not always my favorite person, you could always count on him for a good laugh.

I agreed to join Vivian for the afternoon. It appeared that both Edward and Sarah wouldn't be returning to the fields, and they were my first choice of people I would want to spend time with.

I followed Vivian through the vast, modern kitchen to a side door that led us outside to a paved path with several white golf carts parked along its edge. Each cart had the Thomas Hall logo painted on it. She hopped into the first cart in the line and I climbed into the passenger's seat. This morning I had felt comfortable socializing with her, but knowing she was Edward's mother, caused a certain sense of nervousness to set in. As she drove, she struck up a conversation.

"Tell me something about yourself, my dear. Where do you live?"

"At the moment, I'm homeless. I sold my home a little over a year ago and I've been traveling ever since. I always wanted to see the world and decided it was time." This answer usually evoked one of two responses from people. Half of the people I would tell this to thought I had lost my mind, while the other half wished they were brave enough to leave everything behind and do exactly what I had. But I was emotionally unprepared for Vivian's reply.

"Traveling or running?"

I think I might have given myself whiplash when I turned to look at her. I had never given it any thought before, whether I was deciding how to rebuild my life or just running away from it, but her question struck a chord deep inside of me. It was the same feeling I had the night before, when I was trying to decide what to do with my future.

I had always been a firm believer in the old adage, Silence is golden. However, that Friday afternoon I found the silence Vivian and I sat in as she drove along the freshly paved driveway completely unnerving. Luckily for me, Vivian soon began to point out things that she thought were important.

As we moved along down the path, to the right of us were the fields that the main crews were harvesting. The field we were in was close to the main house and much smaller. The grapes were all the same though. They were Pinot Noir grapes. They are used for a variety of wines including Thomas Hall's latest venture, a sparkling wine. I had earlier read that true champagne was only ever made in a specific region of France and the rest is considered a sparkling wine. The majority of Americans do not really care about making the distinction and within the confines of Thomas Hall, everyone happily called their concoction champagne.

As we continued down the path, Vivian began to tell me about the houses to the left of us.

"About seven years ago, Senior and I sat down and redesigned the entire property. When we did we built these three houses, one for each of our children. While the main house is sufficiently large enough for anyone who wants to stay, we thought it might be nice for each child to have a place of their own. The idea was it would give them, their spouses, and children a place to unwind and relax. Henry and his wife are the only ones who live here full-time. I don't know if you're aware but, Edward has apartments in D.C., London, and L.A. It seems like he only ever uses any of them for work though." I could tell Vivian was trying to make her son look impressive, even though I was already convinced he didn't need any help. "Needless to say, dust bunnies spend more time in his house here than he does. This first house is his. The one behind it is Phoebe's."

"Phoebe? Have I met her?" I already knew the answer to the question, but I have often found that when you ask an obvious question, people tell you more than just the answer.

"No, but you will meet her tonight at dinner. She is my middle child and quite the hand full. But the poor dear is going through an ugly divorce and my beautiful grandchildren are caught in the middle of it. Unfortunately, they won't be joining us this weekend."

I shifted my body to face her and asked, "How old are your grandchildren?"

Vivian smiled. I knew I had earned some brownie points with that question and was beginning to feel comfortable around her once again.

"Noah is nine and Nora is eleven. They are quite the precocious pair. They remind me of Edward at that age."

I smiled and replied, "It's too bad they won't be here. I would have liked to have met them."

"I wish I had more grandchildren. Unfortunately, Henry's wife, Darla, is not fond of children. Their house is a little further around this bend on the left." I had not met Henry's wife yet, but Vivian's comment led me to believe she didn't approve of her youngest son not producing any grandchildren for her and Senior. "Cassandra dear, do you like children?"

"I don't like children, Mrs. Baker, I love them. That's why I didn't join the convent when I was fifteen. It's hard to have a houseful of children when you're a nun." I paused for a moment and thought about what I had just said. "Oh my God, did I just say that out loud?" I buried my face into my hands.

When I looked up at Vivian, she was smiling at me in a motherly sort of way.

"Until this moment, the only other person who knew I had even considered joining an order was Sarah."

"Well, my dear, I will make a deal with you." She put her hand on my shoulder for a moment then returned it to the task of driving. "I will keep your little secret if you stop calling me Mrs. Baker and start calling me Vivian. Okay?"

I smiled and nodded my head. As we rode along I enjoyed looking at the beautiful roses that were planted at the end of each row of vines. They were planted to act as a bug repellant for the vines and, according to everything I'd read, it was effective. Regardless of their function, the roses were magnificent shades of red, pink, and coral. The conversation began to stall so I kept it on a topic I liked, children.

"Does it surprise you I love children, Mrs. Ba--, I mean Vivian?" People had often told me I didn't seem like the motherly type. I thought it would be interesting to get her opinion on the subject.

"Not at all, I'm just surprised that you haven't found yourself a nice husband yet and started having those babies. As beautiful as you are, it shouldn't be very difficult."

I had to decide if I was going to tell her and if so, how much. I knew she would find out eventually, so I decided I might as well tell her at least part of my story.

"Well, to be honest with you, I was married once."

The golf cart came to a full stop. I'm certain she thought I was about to describe a big, messy divorce, as so many marriages end that way and she wanted to listen to what I had to say next with no distractions.

"We married after I finished school, Tony graduated the year before. We had been married close to two years when he died in a plane crash." That was the truth, just not quite every ugly detail. I figured it was enough for now. Maybe someday I'd tell her the whole story of my marriage to Tony, but not today.

Vivian now had a sympathetic look about her. She put her hand on top of mine. "Oh my poor child. I am so sorry. How long has it been?"

"A little over a year and a half ago." Talking about my life with Tony and his death always caused me to go silent. It all felt like a lifetime ago, and I wanted it to stay at least that far away from the present.

Vivian began to drive the golf cart again, moving toward what looked like a large warehouse situated on the opposite side of the cluster of buildings from the main house.

Moments later we arrived at the winery production building and parked the golf cart. Vivian walked me through to what seemed like a maze of doors into a single massive warehouse building. The building was well lit but it seemed dim after coming in from the midday sun. Inside the building, the pressing and production crews scurried about like field mice. Alex White was standing at the far end of the expansive room arguing with a tall, stick-thin woman. Vivian pretended not to hear their conversation as she led me around the building explaining what each piece of equipment did and its part in the wine-making process. However, the couple's voices grew louder and louder, making them hard to ignore.

"I told you, it's over!" Alex was trying hard to dismiss the woman, but she would have no part of it. "It was fun and all but you're married and I'm just not that into you." He walked away as to continue his busy harvest schedule but the woman followed him, taking quick, short steps in her high-heeled shoes causing them to make a distinctive clicking sound.

"It's not over, until I say it's over! You promised me and I plan on making you keep that promise!"

"I didn't promise you anything but a good time and I know I delivered on that."

"But it's all supposed to be mine. You, the winery, everything I've ever wanted."

Alex turned around to face her, but continued walking backwards. "Look, in case you haven't noticed, I've moved on."

"You think you have." The woman continued moving at a rapid pace and quickly caught up with him. "Sleeping with that little slut is not moving on, it's moving down the ladder. She's nothing but white trailer park trash. She had no shame when I walked in on the two of you in bed. What a disgusting cow!"

"Just remember, you grew up next to her, so if she's trailer park trash then so are –"

Before Alex could finish his sentence the woman slapped him across the face and stomped away, slamming the heels of her pumps into the cement floor. He just smiled, rubbed his pink cheek, and laughed. As the woman walked away she continued her rant.

"Everyone at this vineyard is warped! You don't know a good thing when it's in front of you, Senior won't die, and Edward's gone nuts over some non-existent girl. Somebody needs to fix all of you. All of you!"

Chapter Five

Alex appeared next to us, "Hello ladies."

Vivian looked at Alex with a look of general disgust and rolled her eyes. "Alexander, is there a problem?"

"None at all. I thought you would like to know we started filling the steel tanks for the chardonnay. We finished off the French oak barrels around lunchtime."

"Nice." There was a sense of irritation in her voice.

"Are you showing Miss ..., Miss ...? I'm sorry, I just realized I don't know your name." He smiled at me with that big eyed boyish look grown men get when they know they've behaved badly, or are at least hoping to in the near future.

"It's Cassandra Martin," I replied.

"Well Cassandra, Vivian may not have picked the best day to show you around. It's a real mess in here right now. I'd almost say it was dangerous." I hadn't noticed before, but as I looked around the production room was a sweet smelling, sticky mess. I imagined it was like that every year during the harvest.

The entire time Alex spoke he was looking at me and not so much at my face as my bustline. I resisted the urge to remind him my eyes were higher on my body. I was pretty sure that he was dreaming up some fantasy that involved him, me, a lot of grapes, and very little clothing. Odds were at his age though, that fantasy would have a different woman in it tomorrow. I was beginning to realize he might be the most dangerous thing in the room.

Vivian was literally biting her tongue at this point. She didn't like being told what to do by anyone, especially Alex. And I'm sure she didn't appreciate the fact that Alex was hitting on the girl that her son had just spent a lot of time and money to find.

"Well, we're about done in the warehouse anyway. Come my dear, I'll show you the wine cellars." She spun on her heels and turned her head back to look at me.

The conversation had grown tense. The two of them were in a power struggle and I was about to be put in the middle of it. Before I had the chance to move, Alex reached out, took my hand and kissed the back of it. The kiss was wet and sloppy, not the way a kiss should be given on the back of a hand.

"I hope you'll be here a few more days. You add a missing beauty to the winery. I think I would enjoy getting to know you better." He had that hungry look men get when they decide they want a woman. I couldn't decide if it made me nervous or nauseated.

This whole day was completely out of control. When I was in college I couldn't find a man who would give me the time of day, and today alone multiple men had commented on my beauty. Luckily, I had the good sense at this moment to think carefully about what I said before I responded.

"Perhaps we could talk at some point when you aren't so busy. I'd like to know more about your unique occupation."

Alex smiled and began to say something more but was called away. I wiped the back of my now slimy hand on my jeans.

I turned to Vivian and said, "He seems like an interesting person." I stopped there, knowing her response would speak volumes beyond her words.

"A word of advice my dear, stay away from him. That man is trouble on multiple levels."

"What do you mean?" I hoped I might find out what the problem was between the two of them was, but the answer was disappointing.

"Just trust me on this one."

I followed Vivian to the wine cellar which turned out to be a maze of tiny rooms that shot off of a massive main corridor. As we walked through what seemed like an endless cave, Vivian explained that the wine cellar was originally dug out just before the Civil War in an effort to help hide slaves trying to escape to freedom. It wasn't until prohibition it was converted into a wine cellar. As we were walking, I realized we were heading back in the direction of the main house.

"Do these cellars connect the main house with the production rooms?"

"You're a very observant young lady. They connect the two buildings. The family cellar is at the end here. That spiral staircase leads up to the kitchen."

By the edge of the stairs were cases marked champagne stacked three and four cases high. One of the cases was on the floor by itself and opened. I removed a bottle only to find it unlabeled. I turned to ask Vivian about the label, or lack thereof, but she was gone. I stood wondering if I should wait or go looking for her when the door at the top of the stairs opened and Vivian appeared with two champagne glasses. She flipped the light switch at the top of the stairs but it didn't work. She shook her head and carefully made her way down. As she did I wondered how she'd gotten past me and up the steps without my noticing.

When she reached the bottom, she smiled politely and handed me a glass. "I thought we might have some champagne this afternoon. It seems a shame to let it all go to waste since we can't let it leave the winery."

"Why not? Did something go wrong in production?"

Vivian began her litany as she opened the first bottle but the neck of the bottle broke in half, leaving little bits of champagne-covered glass scattered across the floor.

"This is why. It was supposed to be the vintage that put our winery on the map. However, Alexander, in his infinite wisdom, decided to cut costs and bought cheap bottles. They were only recalled by the manufacturer after the second fermentation had started, making it impossible to put this beautiful, sparkling concoction into a different bottle." Vivian grabbed a second bottle and was successful in opening it without any breakage. I watched as she filled the glasses with a beautiful golden liquid full of nearly microscopically tiny bubbles.

While I tasted the champagne, I knew Vivian was watching me. It tasted like carbonated honey and vanilla. I looked up at her and smiled. "This is truly exquisite. I've never tasted anything like it." And I meant every word of it. It was sweeter than any champagne I had ever tasted but not syrupy. Even empty the glass still smelled of freshly crushed grapes, and the bubbles danced around on my tongue long after I'd ingested the liquid.

Vivian and I spent the next two hours touring the main house. It was a beautiful home containing a maze of rooms enclosed in halls, staircases, and doors. Each room had its own history and Vivian knew it all by heart. As we walked through the house, we talked and drank, and before I knew it, it was four in the afternoon and the whole bottle of champagne was gone. We were just returning to the foyer when the remainder of the guests entered through the main entrance. They were also carrying empty bottles of wine with them as well. Everyone was in a cheerful mood. Edward and Sarah joined the group at some point and made their way in as well. It's a good thing the Bakers had a professional harvesting crew because the volunteers definitely played more than they worked.

Senior, who led the group in, raised his wine glass to the group, "Ladies and gentleman, thank you for all of your hard work today. You have a little less than two hours before dinner. Wine and appetizers are waiting for you in your rooms. We shall meet in the dining room at six."

I knew I needed a shower and that Edward wanted to spend some time with me before dinner. I also needed to drink about a gallon of water and sober up a little. I had always loved a nice glass of wine but had consumed way too much alcohol for one afternoon. I put my foot on the second stair when I felt a strong hand on my shoulder. I turned around to discover it was Alex.

"I'm on my way back to the production building. I was wondering if you'd like to join me."

Before I could answer, I felt a warm hand at my waist. I didn't need to turn around to know whose it was. I already knew what Edward's hands felt like. He had moved from wherever he was to just behind me the moment I turned to speak to Alex.

"Oh, I'm sorry Alex, but I've already made plans with Edward. I was just heading upstairs to freshen up before dinner."

Edward turned me around with the hand on my waist and pressed his warm, wine-coated lips against mine. It was a long passionate kiss on Edward's part and I stood nearly motionless, only lifting one hand to his shoulder. It was meant to make a point to Alex, that I belonged to him. I really wanted to be mad at Edward. I did not like being the center of a scene and had never dealt with two men vying for my attention at once, but his soft, wet lips felt heavenly against mine. It had been a long time since I had been kissed like that. After Edward pulled his mouth away from mine, I looked up at him. The corners of his lips were turned upward and the smile it created was too sexy for words. I was completely dumbfounded.

Alex pretended he had seen nothing important and as he turned to walk out the front door said, "Well if you change your mind, you know where to find me."

Edward had not moved at all and was still standing on the staircase with his hands on my waist. "I'm glad you turned him down. Alex can make a fine glass of wine, but he's nothing but trouble."

I was still rattled by the kiss and spoke slowly. "So I've been told. And besides, don't we have plans?"

"We do, but I need a shower first. I'll go get changed and meet you in your suite in a bit." He kissed my neck before walking away and I inhaled deeply, trying to regain some semblance of my sanity.

Chapter Six

"HELLO, HURRICANE CENTRAL." MY Uncle Fred had a strange sense of humor.

"Very funny. It's your wayward niece, calling to check on you."

"Hey Kiddo! Where in the world are you? You haven't called in over a month."

"I know, I'm sorry. I'm at a winery in Virginia. Seriously though, is everything okay in Florida?" As soon as Fred's cell phone rang, I took off my tennis shoes and socks, put the shoes in the bottom of the closet and threw the socks into my empty suitcase, with plans to use it as a laundry hamper until it was time to leave.

"We're fine. Molly's flower beds are totaled and we don't have any landline phones, cable or internet, but that's all. The caller ID on my cell said Thomas Hall. Are you really at Thomas Hall Winery?"

"Yeah, you know it?"

"I'm supposed to be there as we speak. Every year we try to come up for Crush but the last few years something has always come up. This year, it looks like the weather screwed up our plans. I went to college with one of the owner's sons." My uncle was the frat brother on Edward's cell phone. Simultaneously Fred and I both said, "Edward Baker." Fred laughed and I listened. He laughed just like my father did. Hearing him laugh reminded me how much I missed hearing my

Dad's crazy stories about their childhood. I grabbed a bottle of water from the bar and walked over to the bed, stretching out across it as I stared at the ceiling. When Fred was done laughing I felt compelled to say something to him.

"Fred," I said. "I think I might like Edward, a lot. And what's really weird is he just spent the last four months looking for me. You need to tell me, and be honest, is this a bad idea? Because if it is, now would be the time to say something."

"Wait a minute. You're the mystery girl? He was telling me about you last month, but he never mentioned a name."

"Apparently that's me."

"Hmm, interesting." My uncle paused and I could tell he was thinking about this. "You know Kiddo, he's got a serious thing for you."

"I got that impression. He actually hired someone to find me. How crazy is that?" I closed my eyes and took a deep breath.

"Maybe a little, but I think the two of you could be good for each other. You'd both bring things to the table that the other's lacking." I wondered what things he meant, but had a feeling that was more of a conversation than I had time for before dinner.

"Well, thanks for the stamp of approval. I'm still a little flabbergasted by this whole thing though."

"It's like I've always told you. Take your time and trust your feelings. You'll know if it's right." I sat up and unclasped the necklace Edward had put around my neck at lunch. I laid it on the bedside table and leaned back against the headboard. I opened the water bottle and took a sip.

"Why didn't I listen to you the first time?"

"Because you were a teenager. Kiddo, have you been drinking?" I could tell he felt stupid asking the question as he said the words because he knew I rarely drank.

"Yeah, a little. Okay, a lot. Why?"

"Because, you're never this relaxed when it comes to talking about men and relationships, and you're at a winery."

"I suppose a little wine does help. But, I've got to get a shower before dinner, so I'm gonna go. Give Molly my love."

"I will. Have fun and tell Edward that 'Clark' said he'll call him in a few days. I had forgotten that all of my uncle's college buddies called him Clark so as not to confuse him with another Fred who was part of their fraternity's pledge class.

While we said our goodbyes I downed the remainder of the water bottle in the lost cause of sobering up before dinner.

I tried to figure out what to wear for the evening and as soon as I looked in my closet I knew I was in trouble. I slipped across the hall to confer with Sarah. She always seemed to know just what to wear. Luckily, Michael was in the shower while I was there. I needed Sarah's help but didn't want to deal with him right now. I returned to my room five minutes later with a crisp white cotton blouse and a pair of earrings. Now that I had lost so much weight, I could actually borrow some of her clothes. I laid out the shirt and earrings on the bed along with a clean bra, undies, black slacks, and heels.

It would have been the perfect time for a nap, but I knew I didn't have that much time. I quickly stripped off my clothes, added them to the suitcase, and hopped into the shower. I had only worked half a day in the field but I felt hot, dirty, and achy. The shower felt so good I could have stayed in it for hours but I knew Edward would waste no time arriving at my door. I quickly washed my hair, scrubbed down, rinsed off, got out of the shower and wrapped myself in a towel. I began to open the bathroom door when I saw myself in the mirror. I put some moisturizer on my face and took a minute to dry my hair with the hair dryer that had been left on the counter for me. Make-up would have been useless with the sunburn I had, but I put on some lipstick and mascara so it would at least look like I made an effort.

As I stepped out of the bathroom, Edward walked into my suite. When he looked through the door from the sitting room, he caught a glimpse of me in nothing but a towel and gave me a look that screamed, 'God please let her drop that towel!' But instead said, "Sorry. I guess I should've knocked."

"It's okay. Just wait in the sitting room and I'll be out in a minute."

I closed the door to the bedroom and dressed as quickly as I could. I was still trying to hook the clasp on my necklace when I walked into the sitting room. Edward had put on some quiet music and was pouring two glasses of Chardonnay. I walked over to the bar and he put down the bottle of wine. Without saying a word, he took the necklace and helped me put it on while I held my hair up and out of his way. As he hooked the clasp, I could smell the shaving cream he had used before coming to my suite.

When he was done, he handed me a glass of wine. While I drank, I thought about the man in front of me. Why was Edward so determined to find me and why did he seem so enamored with me?

"You look like you're in deep thought."

"A little. I was thinking about you actually."

"That sounds promising."

"You never answered my question at lunchtime. Why was it so important for you to find me?" I took a seat on the sofa in the sitting room and he sat next to me before he replied.

"The night we met, it didn't take long for me to figure out you were smart, beautiful, well-read, a seasoned traveler, all the obvious stuff." A piece of my hair fell into my face as I looked down at my glass. I picked it up with the intention of pushing it behind my ear but found myself wrapping it around my finger. "But the longer we talked and the more you told me about your life and the death of your husband I realized something about you. You aren't jaded at all. After everything you've been through, there's still a certain sweetness and selflessness about you. But it's not fake, it's who you are. Do you have any idea how attractive of a quality that is?"

I didn't completely hear his last two sentences. It wasn't that I was bored. I just couldn't bring myself to listen to his praises any longer. I had become preoccupied with the strands of hair around my finger and continued to wrap them around. As I did I could feel the tension on the strands pull at my scalp.

"I've never met anyone quite like you, Cassandra. When I got on my next flight that night, I closed my eyes in hopes of getting some sleep, but all I could think about was you and how amazing you are. By the next day, I knew I had to see you again, but I had to find you first."

"Amazing? Are you sure you're talking to the right girl?"

"Yes, I definitely am. Speaking of amazing, you look amazing tonight. Of course, I thought you looked great in the jeans and t-shirt you had on earlier. And the towel, well—"

"I think we can skip that one." I could feel my face getting hotter and knew it had yet to stop turning red. I tried to dismiss my embarrassment and took a sip of my Chardonnay as I continued to wrap the strands of hair around my finger.

"You don't get how beautiful you are, do you? Come over here." He gently grabbed my hand, stood me up, and guided me over to the full length mirror in the sitting room. As he did I unwrapped the hair from the finger of my free hand. "Look."

I looked in the mirror to see myself and found that Edward was behind me with his hands holding me at the edge of my shoulders. There was something about his touch that I found both calming and exhilarating at the same time. Regardless though, I hated looking at myself in the mirror without any true purpose.

"Okay, I've looked. I'm done." I tried to walk away but he put his arms around me from behind and continued to speak.

"No, I want you to see what I see, what we all see. Like how your beautiful emerald eyes catch the light and sparkle, or how your thick raven hair sets off your soft, beautiful skin." He pushed my hair away from my neck and both his eyes and fingers followed along with his words. "You have the most irresistibly long, slender neck and the most gorgeous neckline." He was tracing the edge of my shirt with his fingers. Listening to his soft, sexy voice and feeling his fingers lightly grazing my chest caused my breathing to become extremely labored. I was really enjoying this but knew he was moving way too fast.

"You might want to watch those hands, Mr. Baker. I don't think I know you that well yet."

He quickly stopped, releasing me from his grasp altogether. He looked down at the floor and ran his fingers through his hair. I was beginning to realize he did this whenever he was flustered. I liked it though and smiled.

"I'm sorry. I guess I was a little out of line."

"Not so much out of line as maybe moving at warp speed."

"Yeah, I tend to do that with, well, everything."

"Well, not with me. I'm not a warp speed kind of girl."

I took a seat on the sofa and Edward continued to stand at the bar. We both took a minute to enjoy the wine and music before striking up a new point in our conversation.

"Cassandra, this is probably going to make me sound like a stalker, but you are a hard woman to catch up with."

"How so?"

"No home address, no cell phone, no e-mail or mailing address, and every time I thought I had found you, I'd missed you by a couple of days. I guess my question is: why?"

"Well, you know I'm a widow."

"Yeah."

"After Tony died, I took a long look at my life and realized I hadn't done anything I wanted to do. I know that sounds strange at my age, but Tony hadn't even turned thirty when his plane crashed. So I sat down and thought about if I died tomorrow, what would I wish I had done. I came up with two things. The first was travel. So I sold the house and the cars, took leave at the university, packed a bag and bought a plane ticket."

"I know we talked about it the night we met but I'm still surprised you'd get on a plane."

"I have no problem flying. Tony didn't have the experience he should have as a pilot to be flying a Cessna 152 in the weather he was in. I'd love to blame someone else for his death, but ultimately his own arrogance killed him."

"You don't sound overly upset," he said.

"I was devastated at first. But I found out some things about Tony after he died that put things into perspective. Time and distance helped a lot too." The longer we talked about Tony, the more depressed I felt and that was not what I wanted that night. "Nothing personal, but can we change the subject?"

I drank some more wine and slowly swirled the stem of the glass back and forth between my fingers.

"Okay, then. What was the second thing?"

I paused, not certain I wanted to tell him. However, before I could stop myself I found myself saying, "Have a lot of children."

"You know, I could see that." Edward took a seat on one of the bar stools, all the while smiling.

"That usually scares men off pretty fast."

"I don't scare that easily."

"Really? Then why aren't you married with a bunch of kids running around the vineyard?"

"I've haven't found the right mother for my children, at least not yet."

I tilted my head, raised one eyebrow, and gave him my 'okay, tell the truth' look. It was a look that always worked on my students when I taught college.

"Well, that and time. It just seemed to get away from me. I always figured I'd meet someone along the way, fall in love, get married, and have a family. I didn't realize fifty would creep up on me so fast."

"You know, fifty's not that old. Lots of things are older than fifty: rivers, rocks, the Declaration of Independence —"

"Very funny," Edward commented sarcastically and smiled while he stood up and poured us both more wine. "It's a good thing you're cute."

"Sorry, couldn't resist."

Edward's smile became a very serious expression. "Cassandra, I need to ask you a question and I need an honest answer."

I already knew what the question was going to be. I do not know if it was because I was comfortable with Edward or because I was feeling a little tipsy, but I saved him the awkwardness of asking.

"It's about the difference in our ages, isn't it?"

"Well, I am old enough to be your father. I imagine he wouldn't be too happy about the two of us seeing each other." I held up my free hand in a stop signal as my other hand held the glass of wine I was sipping. When I was done with the wine I went on to tell him about my parents.

"No, my mom and dad died in a car wreck when I was twelve." Edward seemed stunned at my casualness about my parents' death. After seeing so many people I loved die, I had worked hard to appear unemotional when talking about their deaths.

"Oh God, I remember you telling me about that. It's so stupid of me to forget something that important. I'm sorry."

"It's okay, really. I had a great childhood and my aunt and uncle did a wonderful job raising me once mom and dad were gone." I stood up to move closer to him, intending to tell him who my uncle was, when I nearly tripped over my own two feet. The water hadn't helped sober me up at all. Luckily, Edward caught me and slowly pulled me close to him.

"You really are adorable."

"Edward, how old *are* you anyway?"

"About twenty-two years older than you."

"Is that all?" I continued to smile as I spoke.

He returned the smile as he put the palm of his hand under my chin and lifted my face toward his.

"About the kiss on the stairs earlier, I think I owe you an apology. It might have been, well, inappropriate. But I wanted to make sure that Alex understands you're —."

"Taken?" If any other man had said this at any other time, I think I would have protested. After being married to Tony, I thought I'd never want to 'belong' to anyone again. But when Edward said it, I found myself liking the possibility of being spoken for by him.

He moved his mouth closer to mine. I closed my eyes and the moment his lips brushed against mine, the door opened. It was Sarah and Michael. They both looked like deer in the headlights of a car even though they had seen him kiss me less than an hour earlier. After a tense moment, the two realized that Edward had no intention of releasing me from his embrace.

"Sorry C.C. We didn't know you had company. We just figured you'd want to walk down to dinner with us," Sarah said.

When I looked at Michael I saw the disbelief on his face. I knew it was hard for him to see me in the arms of anyone but my late husband. Edward could tell something was amiss as well. He slowly relaxed his arms until they had fallen away from me and were back at his side. Then he spoke up and suggested we all go down to dinner together.

As we walked out of my room, Edward quietly reached over and took my hand. "Thank you" was all I had time to whisper as we reached the grand staircase.

When we reached the top of the staircase Michael and Sarah continued down, but I paused as everything appeared wobbly. As I tried to assess my situation, Edward looked at me and began to laugh out loud.

"You don't think you can make it down the stairs, do you?"

"How much wine did we have in my room?"

"A couple of glasses." I only remembered one.

"Plus the glass and a half I had at lunch and the bottle of champagne your mom and I split this afternoon. Yep, I'm drunk."

Edward began to laugh louder. "You and Mom split a whole bottle! Oh hell, this is going to be an interesting night." He thought for a moment. "I have an idea. Just close your eyes and trust me."

Trusting men was not something I had done willingly over the last few years, but with no other options, I closed my eyes and felt Edward pick me up and carry me down the stairs. When he scooped me up, I squealed. Not out of fear, but surprise. Most men would never consider me a good size for such a venture, but Edward didn't seem to think it problematic. I giggled all the way down the stairs and when we reached the bottom, he gently set me down and I opened my eyes. I really liked this guy and I had not met a man I liked since the night I was on a United Airlines flight between Seattle and Chicago.

We were about five minutes early for dinner but were the last couple to arrive downstairs for dinner. Everyone was mingling about, drinking wine, and making small talk. Edward took me by the hand and led me to the only two people in the room I had yet to meet, Darla, Henry's wife, and Phoebe, his sister.

The two women were physically a study in contrast. Darla was about five foot ten and very thin, with no bust, butt or hips. She had short, heavily sprayed hair, lots of makeup, and a sharp angular face. Darla had the kind of face that easily could have looked hard had she had not teased and sprayed her hair the way she did and worn the layers of makeup that were perfectly placed on her face. She wore a sleeveless, linen blouse and matching skirt, high heels, and way too much jewelry. She was the woman who had been arguing with Alex earlier in the day. I then understood why Vivian disliked Alex so much. He had been sleeping with Henry's wife.

Phoebe, on the other hand, was a curvier version of her mother with long flowing hair and a soft heart-shaped face. She only had minimal makeup on, but she had all the grace and natural beauty of her mother. She was dressed simply but looked very elegant in a boat-collared sweater and navy slacks. She looked much younger than she was and I was certain her height of barely five feet had something to do with her youthful appearance.

"Sis, Darla, I'd like you to meet Cassandra Martin. Cassandra this is my sister, Phoebe Foster, and Henry's wife, Darla." Edward leaned over and kissed his sister on the cheek.

Darla took a moment to size me up. For what reasons, I was not sure, but even drunk I could tell it was not a good thing.

"Darla, it's a pleasure to meet you. I hope you're feeling better."

"What?"

"Henry said you had a migraine this morning."

"Oh, yeah. All better. Thanks."

She hadn't had a migraine or even a headache. I was certain of that.

"Hold on, my brother has a date at the winery? The world really is coming to an end, isn't it?" Phoebe and I both burst into laughter.

"Hey!" I think Edward wanted to defend himself but was enjoying watching the two of us laugh too much to do so. "Where are my niece and nephew?"

I surprised them both by answering the question for Phoebe. "They are with their father, much to the dismay of your mother, I might add."

Phoebe looked at Edward and raised an eyebrow.

"She spent all afternoon with Mom, drinking champagne."

Phoebe began to laugh again. "And she's still here?" She turned and looked at me, "You're one brave woman."

"Why? I like your mom."

Darla was fuming. What little I had seen or knew about her led me to believe she liked to be the center of attention. The fact that Phoebe and Edward were hovering over me irritated her. I guess that's why she felt the need to inject herself into the conversation. "Vivian is an overbearing matriarch, that's why."

I was shocked by Darla's bluntness. "Really? I never got that impression. Curious? Definitely. Concerned for her children's welfare? Absolutely. But not overbearing."

Phoebe looked at Edward, smiling but serious. "I think she's a keeper."

Edward started to respond but Darla interrupted with another question. "So, how do you like Thomas Hall? I'm sure it's different from where ever it is you're used to living. Most people are intimidated by the way we live. Few people can handle the adjustment quite like I did. I'm sure you're finding Harvest weekend unnerving."

"Thomas Hall is a very relaxing place and everyone has made me feel so welcome. I can't remember the last time I enjoyed myself this much."

This was not the response Darla was looking for. She was attempting to make me uncomfortable. So, I changed the subject.

"Darla, what do you do?"

"Do?"

Oh no, I thought to myself. Please tell me Henry had not married a gold digger. "You know, career, family, hobbies?"

"Henry and I don't have any children, thank God. I guess shopping's my hobby. I do whatever I want, whenever I want. I don't work. I mean, why would I?" He had married a gold digger.

"Some people like the challenge."

"Do you work?" She choked on the word.

"I'm currently on sabbatical from Ohio State University." Actually, I had given my resignation letter to the Dean, but he refused to accept it and placed me on sabbatical until such time I wished to return. I seriously doubted I would ever return to teaching there, but for the moment, it was the truth.

Darla looked me up and down as though she were taking a physical inventory. "Smart, chubby, and nerdy, who would have thought you'd be Edward's type. I always figured Edward would end up with one of those skinny socialite bitches he's always seen with at charity events."

"You're kidding, right? I love girls with curves." I felt his warm hand come to rest on my hip. "Oh yeah, and brains too."

I could tell he was trying to stay out of the dog house with Phoebe as he looked at her while commenting on my intelligence. "There's a reason I never married any of those girls. They were all either too stupid or too boney."

What came out of Darla's mouth next shocked me. "Well, if you're smart, you'll enjoy all this while you can. Assuming Edward picked up the same bad habits his father had at his age, you won't be around for long." Then she walked away.

Edward turned to me and his eyes exposed his anger with Darla's treatment of me.

"Cassandra, would you excuse me for a moment?" He lightly kissed my cheek and followed Darla out to the terrace, where she headed to smoke a cigarette before dinner.

Phoebe, much like her mother, was a great hostess. She smiled and gently touched my arm.

"Don't worry about Darla. She's one of those bitchy people who will say anything to destroy your happiness. It's what she does."

"That's got to lead to some bad karma."

"You would think, but I haven't seen it yet."

"She reminds me of my late husband." I thought about what I had just said. "Oh, poor Henry."

"It's funny you should say that. Right before you and Eddie walked up, we were arguing about how she treats Henry."

"Eddie?" We both started giggling like a bunch of school girls. I wondered if it was completely obvious that I was drunk.

"Hey, I'm his baby sister. I'm allowed to call him that." I nodded in agreement.

"What was Darla talking about anyway?"

"About eight years ago, Dad got caught with his longtime mistress." Phoebe continued in an honest, matter-of-fact tone. "The press in D.C. got a hold of it and rumors started flying around about Dad being the father of her child. It got a little messy for a while."

Henry walked up behind his sister and gave her a big hug, lifting her a few inches off the floor in the process.

"Hey, Sis! Missed you today."

"Yeah, had to do the whole Mom thing. I am kind of glad now that the kids are at their dad's place this weekend. I'll get to know Cassandra a little better than I could if the kids were running around here."

Henry looked over at me. "Are you enjoying yourself?"

"A little too much, I'm afraid. I have no tolerance for alcohol and I think your mother tried to get me drunk this afternoon."

"And succeeded." Edward had walked up next to me and handed me a glass of Pinot Noir while I was talking to Henry and Phoebe. He was not in the best mood but was trying to shake it off. So I playfully gave him an appalled look and lightly smacked his shoulder, which seemed to pull him back to a better frame of mind.

I knew Henry was trying to interpret the body language between us, but he continued to speak as he did so. "Well, if you're drunk, Cassandra, you're doing a pretty good job of not letting it show."

"Did I just hear the words 'Cassandra' and 'drunk' in the same sentence?" Vivian had worked her way across the room to us.

"I'm afraid so. I don't think I realized how much we had to drink this afternoon until it was too late."

"Well, a little overindulging now and then never hurt anyone."

I could not figure out why Vivian was smiling the way she was until I realized Edward had moved behind me and wrapped his arms around my waist. He had placed his chin on my shoulder and was grinning like the Cheshire Cat from Alice in Wonderland. It seemed appropriate, though, since I felt like I had traveled through a rabbit hole and ended up in Wonderland.

"But Mom, how am I supposed to get her drunk and take advantage of her if she's already drunk?"

Vivian and I smiled and shook our heads, but Vivian was the first to respond.

"What are we going to do with him, Cassandra?"

Before I could respond, Victor entered the room and asked everyone to take their seats as dinner was about to be served.

Dinner that evening was an exquisite meal. It consisted of leek soup, a rack of lamb with mint sauce, asparagus sautéed in butter, and a chocolate torte layered with hazelnut cream. The lamb was so tender that I never figured out why they bothered putting knives at the place settings. The hazelnut cream in the dessert was so smooth and silky that my mouth watered for more between each bite.

The wine and champagne poured as freely as the conversation throughout the night. They were so numerous and simultaneous that it was necessary for one to pick and choose their discussions. I chose to listen rather than speak. I figured in my inebriated state; it was probably for the best. I found it unnerving that Michael, who sat to my left, refused to acknowledge my presence at the table. I'm not sure why it bothered me, though, as he behaved as he always had. However, Edward was as attentive as he possibly could be without ignoring the other guests. We talked about the meal, what his mom and I had done all afternoon, and how I had come to know Sarah and Michael.

As we finished our desserts, one conversation grew louder and more argumentative than the rest. It was Senior and Alex. Alex had returned from the production buildings just as the main course was being served and had been in constant discussions with Senior since his arrival.

"Senior, if we purchase the other winery's excess grape harvest, we could increase our final product count by eighty percent. It would be crazy not to do this!"

"Alex, we've been through this before. We can barely handle the grapes we harvest from here. I'm not purchasing outside grapes. There is no way to control quality and pesticide usage."

"The quality control issue can be handled. If we don't start producing more wine, the winery won't be able to pay its bills!" With each banter, the men's voices grew louder.

"Exactly! But we can't seem to handle what we have, and until we can, we shouldn't expand!"

"Old man, you will run this winery into the ground! You know that, don't you? This is my life's work and I won't let you screw it up with your closed-minded attitude!"

As the two men continued to argue, my head began to pound. The alcohol was wearing off fast and I wasn't sure how much longer I could bear the volume of their conversation. I hoped to quietly escape the dining room, but everyone turned and looked when I rose from my chair.

"If you would excuse me, I'm still slightly jet-lagged and should probably retire for the evening."

Edward was quick to stand up. "I'll walk you up if you'd like."

I wasn't certain if I wanted him to walk me to my room. I was tired and had a headache. In addition, I didn't trust myself alone with him. But I didn't want to be rude either.

"Thank you. That would be lovely." As we walked, my silence clued him in that he would need to talk if I were going to speak. So when we reached the bottom of the stairs, he turned to me, took both of my hands into his, and smiled. "Should I help you up the stairs the same way you came down them?"

I didn't really want to let myself do it, but I smiled anyway. I liked Edward, but I was not the type of girl to lead a man on or even intentionally flirt, for that matter. "No, I think I'm sober enough to manage the steps myself, thank you. I am going to have to be careful here at Thomas Hall, though."

We continued the conversation as we slowly climbed the stairs.

"Why is that, my love?"

As the words left his mouth, I felt my heart leap into my throat. So I pretended not to hear the words 'my love' and went on to answer his question. "I've been here for twenty-four hours and in that time, I've had more to drink than I have in the last, well, forever."

"Oh, come on, not even as a teenager?"

"I was way too young to drink in high school and didn't drink in college."

"Way too young in high school? Isn't that when most teenagers start drinking?"

I looked at him to see his response to what I was about to say. "I graduated from high school at fourteen."

"That's impressive." He didn't look as shocked as I thought he would. "What about college?"

"I got my Bachelor's at seventeen."

"And?" He seemed confident there was more.

"My Master's at nineteen. Well, almost twenty."

"Then?" Edward was smiling and I knew why.

"I finished my Ph.D. at twenty-two." I raised my eyebrows at him and smirked. "But you already knew that, didn't you?"

"Private investigators find out things when they're looking for people."

"I suppose." I wondered what else he knew about my past.

As we reached the top of the staircase, I looked at Edward for direction. The hallways were like mazes, and I was still unsure which direction to turn. He smiled and guided me to the right.

"You know, it must be amazing to have the discipline and clarity of purpose you had as a teenager. I didn't develop that until I was in my thirties. I'm not even certain I'm that disciplined now."

"Edward, the only thing I have ever been clear about in my life is that I don't trust myself alone with you. Why did I just say that? I feel like ever since I arrived at Thomas Hall, my inner monologue keeps spilling out of my mouth. It happened with your mom earlier."

"Really. What did you tell her?"

"Oh no. I'm not telling you that one and she's been sworn to secrecy."

"Maybe you'll tell me someday." He continued to smile as we talked. "The same thing has happened to me before. I think it has to do with feeling extremely comfortable with where you are. I'm sure everyone has a place like that, whether they know it or not."

"Where's your place, Edward?"

"Wherever you are."

"Nice line, but it still doesn't make me trust us alone. Argh! There it goes again!"

I looked down at the floor and bit my lower lip lightly. We were in front of the door to my suite now. He took his hand, lifted my head, and gently pulled me close to him. "Well then, my love, I'll just say goodnight to you here then."

I closed my eyes as he leaned over and kissed the side of my neck a couple of times. Each time his lips returned to my skin, I felt a rush of excitement pulse through my body. Then he lightly brushed his lips against mine and whispered, "Goodnight." When I opened my eyes, he was gone. And I was exhausted.

Chapter Seven

I had never woken up hungover before and quickly decided I would never do it again. The bright morning sun poured into my bedroom windows, making my head pound even harder. And to top it off, I could feel yesterday's sunburn kick in and wondered if I had slept with my face in a deep fryer. I got up and put some moisturizing cream with aloe on my face, which helped for all of about two minutes. I got dressed, brushed my teeth, put on a ton of sunscreen, and pulled my hair back away from my face. I remembered my thoughts yesterday but was too hungover to spend any extra energy pulling myself together. A ponytail and red v-neck t-shirt would have to do.

When I arrived downstairs, I realized the breakfast party was well underway, and I was the last person down. I was immediately greeted by a very cheerful Edward, who had been sitting next to his father. They had been talking about something that seemed to make them both happy. Edward walked over to me and kissed me on the cheek. Maybe I'm just paranoid, but I'd swear the entire party stopped to listen to our conversation.

"Good morning."

"It *is* morning, isn't it?"

Edward smiled. "Would you like a mimosa? It seems to be the drink of the day." He took my hand and led me across the room toward the table he had been sitting at with his father, only stopping to grab a couple of glasses of the orange juice and champagne mix from a member of the staff. He attempted to hand me one.

"Not even remotely funny. I think I'll pass for now." I can only imagine that the expression on my face would have been the same if he had offered me cyanide with my breakfast.

Edward laughed. "You know, you're even adorable hungover."

"I suppose this is the karmic price I paid for teasing you about your age last night."

Edward smiled and put his arm around me. I leaned into him and inhaled the fresh scent of laundry detergent and fabric softener. "No, I'm fairly certain you had done this to yourself long before then."

"Great. So I've still got to pay for that comment?"

"No, I think there's an escape clause on karma if you're drunk."

As I was quietly laughing at his comment, Victor walked up with a tray holding precisely what I had eaten for breakfast yesterday, Ginger peach tea, toast, and strawberry preserves. "Miss Martin, I took the liberty of fixing the same thing you requested yesterday. I also added something I thought you might find helpful."

On the tray was a glass of water and a package of Tylenol. It was official. I wanted to take him with me when I left. "Thank you, Victor."

"I'll put it next to Senior for you, Miss Martin."

Edward and I sat on each side of Senior. My elderly host made conversation while I ate.

"My dear, are you enjoying your stay with us?"

I took a moment to finish the toast in my mouth before speaking. "Very much so, sir. I've never spent any time at a winery and I'm finding it quite intriguing."

"Really, well, something tells me you're a quick study and will probably know more about wineries than I do in a very short time."

"I doubt that very much, but thank you for the compliment." I looked at Edward and could tell he was happy I had managed to accept a compliment, regardless of the nature.

"Speaking of studying, I understand you have not been completely honest with us, Dr. Martin."

Edward had told his father about my education. I could tell I was starting to blush but doubted anyone would notice due to the sunburn I was nursing.

"I prefer not to use the title 'doctor' unless I'm in an academic setting. It's just a little too pretentious for my taste." I opened the package of Tylenol and took two of the pills. I washed them down with the water on the tray. Not so much to get the pills down as to try to rehydrate myself.

"You are quite the sweetheart, aren't you? No wonder my son loves you so much."

I was certain I had heard Senior wrong. I knew he didn't just say love. I considered the option of standing up, walking out of the room, up the stairs, and getting straight back into bed. But I didn't want to be rude to Senior and his guests, so I opted to finish my breakfast instead.

When I was done, we headed back out to the vineyard. It was another beautiful autumn morning in the Northern Neck and a little warmer than the day before. Alex reminded us once again how to harvest the grapes and how sharp the pruning shears were.

Edward worked his way over and placed himself on the opposite side of the vines from me so we could talk. However, it wasn't long before Alex came over, stood next to me, and struck up a conversation. It was funny, but if I hadn't known better, I would have sworn he was related to the Bakers. He had narrower shoulders and appeared slightly less muscular than the Baker men, but he had the same blond hair and blue eyes that both Senior and Henry did.

"Good morning Cassandra. It's nice to see you again. Did you have a good evening?"

"It was rather interesting. I think I drank too much, though." I continued to cut grapes from the vines as we spoke and Alex found a spot next to me to work.

"It's an easy thing to do around here. I'll keep an eye on you tonight if you'd like." His hungry-looking smile made me think I should worry more about him than the alcohol.

I turned my head and looked at him when I responded. "Thanks, Alex, but I think I'll be fine."

Then I heard a man yell, "God damn it!"

It was Edward. His back was turned toward me and I could see a rip in his shirt. I was confused, but I knew something had just gone wrong. I dropped the shears and went to the end of the row of vines we were working, which wasn't far, maybe only ten or twelve feet. I turned around and headed down the side of the vines Edward had been standing on. By the time I reached Edward, Dr. Rice was walking up from the opposite direction.

"It looks like you cut yourself on something." Dr. Rice commented.

I looked at Edward and immediately knew what had happened. I had caught him on my pruning shears. And then I saw the thick, red drops of blood leaving a trail down the back of his shirt. I felt queasy and lightheaded as I assessed the damage I'd done. Edward and Dr. Rice must have realized something was amiss because they ran towards me as my knees gave out and everything began to swirl around my head before going dark.

While I insisted I was fine, Dr. Rice walked Edward and me back to the house. Senior and Vivian had gone ahead of us and Vivian was already waiting for our arrival and sat me in the recliner in the library with a glass of water and a cold compress. She went on to tell us that Senior had not slept well the night before and she convinced him to rest for a while. Edward looked at his mother with concern and she silently reassured him.

The library was a classic-looking room with several leather chairs and sofas, an oversized desk in the center of the room, and lots of lighting. Built-in bookcases covered every available inch of wall space. The books seemed neatly organized; however, the shelves appeared as though they might collapse from the weight they carried.

When Edward stripped off his shirt, I thought I was going to faint again, but for very different reasons this time. His body was chiseled as if he had spent all of his free time at the gym. It was obvious, even fully clothed, that he was in good shape. But I wasn't prepared to discover that his arms, abs, chest, and back were examples of the perfect male body. He looked even more like a Greek god than he had the day before. There couldn't have been an inch of fat anywhere on his body and for a fraction of a second, I was slightly jealous of that fact.

Dr. Rice came in and asked me a few questions. Once I told him that I had a tendency to faint at the sight of blood, he told me to rest for a bit and I'd be fine. He then took a closer look at Edward's wound and cleaned it well.

"Edward, it's stopped bleeding, but I think I should glue the cut back together to make sure you don't pull it open and bleed again. I have some surgical glue in my bag that will do the trick. But I just called my office, and it looks like you're overdue for a tetanus shot. We're going to have to go into town this morning and get that handled."

Dr. Rice left to collect his bag and Vivian followed him out of the room. I stood up and walked over to Edward.

"I am so sorry. Alex warned us about how sharp the shears were, and I took my eyes away from what I was doing for one second, and...." I was babbling and began to feel lightheaded again. Edward took me in his arms. His skin was warm and as I inhaled, I caught the faint scent of Irish Spring soap. He reached over and pushed away a fallen eyelash just below my left eye.

"Relax, Sweetie. You're hyperventilating. And besides, I'm fine."

After a few deep breaths, I unwrapped myself from his embrace and walked around to look at his back. The cut was no longer bleeding and it sat on his left shoulder blade. The curved incision was about an inch long. It wasn't the cut that interested me. He had a tattoo at the top of his left shoulder blade. It was two Greek letters encased in a diamond-shaped design. It was the same tattoo my uncle had on his left shoulder blade.

"Interesting."

"What?"

I thought about kissing his tattoo for a moment, but thought better of it and traced the letters with my right index finger and allowed my left hand to rest on his bicep. He turned to face me and ran his fingers through his hair.

"I suppose you mean the Kappa Sigma tattoo. I got it when I was in college. A group of guys from my fraternity went out and got them one night after a party."

"I like it. Luckily I missed hitting the Kappa by just a fraction of an inch. You know, my uncle has a tattoo just like it. I think you know him."

"Really? Did you ever get in touch with him?"

"I did." I walked over to the table, took a sip of the water Vivian left, and then continued. "He and Molly are fine. He told me to tell you that Clark says 'hey' and he'll call you in a couple of days." I smiled and watched him in anticipation of his reaction.

He leaned against the large oak desk in the center of the room and took a long look at me.

"Fred Clark is your uncle? He was the frat brother I was on the phone with yesterday. But Cassandra, your last name is Martin."

"Martin's my married name. I never bothered changing it back after Tony died. Besides, why do you think Sarah and Michael call me C.C.? Cassandra Clark."

Edward was quiet, too quiet. I was worried that he was beginning to think the difference in our ages would be a problem, but I wasn't about to bring it up. After all, he was old enough to be, well, my uncle.

"Edward, are you all right?" I could feel my stomach twist into a knot, and an outward expression of it must have shown on my face. While I constantly tried, I'd never been good at hiding certain emotions like nervousness or concern. He stood up and smiled.

"Don't worry. I'm fine. I'm just trying to figure out how we'd never met before we did. Between Sarah and Michael, Fred and Molly, you'd think we'd have met ages ago."

"You'd think so. Maybe it just wasn't the right time until now. If you believe in the whole philosophy of destiny, it would make perfect sense."

"Could be." He stared at me in silence for a moment longer, but I couldn't figure out where his thoughts were. "What else did Fred have to say?"

"Well, he told me that, no, never mind."

"What?" I realized that Fred's opinion was important to Edward and I wondered how he would respond to my uncle's comment. I took a deep breath and said the whole thing in one breath.

"Fred thought we'd be good for one another. Something to the effect that we both had qualities the other could benefit from."

"He's a smart guy." Edward walked over and held me in his arms once more, wrapping his arms low on my waist. "I've never gotten bad advice from him."

I leaned against his bare chest and his skin vibrated with the same electric energy that radiated from him whenever I was with him. It was so intense that I could feel it pulsate through my bloodstream. The realization that this was what made me so lightheaded struck me like a lightning bolt and my thoughts began to race. I could so fall in love with this man and it would be so easy. All I'd have to do is just close my eyes and fall. Sarah's words from a few days earlier began to rain down like a mid-summer storm: 'be open, maybe it's time, think about it, you're too young to be alone.'

He brushed a piece of hair from my face snapping me away from my racing thoughts. He softly smiled at me until I smiled too. The smiling part was hard though. The guilt of injuring Edward had already begun to hang like a dark cloud in my mind. He leaned over to kiss me and as I closed my eyes, the door to the library opened. Dr. Rice had returned along with Vivian. She scolded Edward for not allowing me to sit down and rest. Dr. Rice glued Edward's shoulder back together while I rested on one of the oversized leather sofas, with Vivian sitting beside me, but I didn't dare watch the doctor do his job.

Vivian insisted that I stay at the house for the remainder of the morning. I didn't really feel like going back out anyway, mostly from embarrassment, so I kindly adhered to her orders.

After Edward and the doctor headed to town, I excused myself to my suite to get cleaned up. I grabbed a long steamy shower, washed my hair, and put on khaki pants and a green polo shirt I 'borrowed' from Sarah's closet. I was beginning to understand why she brought so many clothes. I had just gotten dressed and was pulling my hair up into a bun when Vivian came in to check on me.

"Are you feeling better, my dear?" I could tell she was genuinely concerned about me but maintained all the grace and charm you would expect from a Southern matriarch. She took a few bobby pins and fixed some loose pieces of hair in the back that I couldn't reach. "Everyone will be returning for lunch soon."

"I'm feeling much better, thank you." It was weird. Every time I was with Vivian, I felt differently about her. Sometimes I felt completely comfortable around her and other times, her presence made me fidgety. But today, I felt like she was inspecting me as though I was a potential wife for her son, and it made me nervous. "If you don't mind, I think I'll just stay here. I'm really too embarrassed to be in public anymore today."

We both took a seat in the chairs of the sitting room of my suite while we talked.

"Nonsense. You can't hide up here all day. After lunch, the ladies are all going to the spa and the Harvest Formal is at the house this evening."

I felt a sudden wave of panic cross over me. "What? A formal? I didn't bring anything appropriate for a formal!"

As if on cue, Sarah poked her head through the door. "Don't worry. I packed a couple of extra dresses for you to choose from."

Vivian looked at each of us and seemed to understand the nature of our friendship. Sarah had taught me all I knew about hair, makeup, and clothing. She always seemed to know when I would be in over my head and would conveniently provide the appropriate life jacket, which in this case was a formal gown. Sarah walked in and stood beside me, arms rapidly gesturing while she spoke.

"We might need to find you some different shoes, though." She always thought of everything. "We can go in that little shop attached to the spa. I always find the cutest shoes in there. Well, I'm off to shower before lunch. C.C., you should go downstairs and have a glass of wine with Vivian. You'll feel better." She kissed me on the forehead and happily bounced off toward her room.

"She loves you very much, you know."

I took a moment to think about what Vivian had just said. "I'm very fortunate for it too. She was my roommate at The University of North Carolina. Not many nineteen-year-old girls would befriend their nerdy fourteen-year-old roommate who was completely clueless about anything not concerning academics. I don't think I would have survived life there without her. She's the closest thing I've ever had to a sister."

"Well then, let's respect her wishes and go have a glass of wine."

Victor brought us each a glass of champagne. If I was going to drink today, I wanted more of that wonderful concoction I had gotten drunk on the day before. I had just finished the first fantastic sip when everyone returned from the field for lunch, along with Dr. Rice and Edward in tow. Edward carried with him a large white box with a giant purple ribbon on it. He handed it to Victor, who took it and quickly left the room. I was about to greet Edward when I found myself surrounded by the other houseguests, who inquired about my health and expressed their concerns. I thanked them and assured them I was fine, just extremely embarrassed. Then we all sat down for lunch.

The meal was much heavier than yesterday's lunch. I assumed it was because it was meant to be the main meal of the day. It was three courses beginning with a Caesar's salad topped with lobster that was still warm from being freshly steamed. It was followed by poached Salmon in a very lemon-heavy sauce that was just sour enough to make my mouth pucker, then finished with fresh peaches and cream. I passed on the dessert as I was not only stuffed but not a big fan of peaches.

Edward and I sat across the table from each other at lunch. Every time I looked up, he was smiling at me. I was still upset with myself for slicing open his back with the pruning shears. It was all I had been able to think about since he and Dr. Rice had left to go to town. As much as I wanted to smile back at him, I just couldn't bring myself to do it. I still felt too guilty for filleting him, even if it was an accident.

At the conclusion of lunch, Vivian stood at the head of the table and commanded everyone's attention. "As you know, this evening is the Annual Harvest

Formal here at Thomas Hall. Gentlemen, I understand that Senior has made plans for you. Ladies, we will be departing in about ten minutes to go to the spa for the afternoon."

Everyone stood up and began to mull about while waiting for the ladies to leave. Edward walked up behind me and began to massage my shoulders. "You don't look happy. What is it? I'll fix it."

His demeanor made it clear he was the type of man who demanded perfection at work, and in doing so, handled any major problems personally. He was trying to make me happy by doing the same thing and while I had every reason not to like his approach, I found the idea of being taken care of by him somehow appealing.

"I'm just upset with myself for hurting you today. So, unless you can turn back time, you can't fix it."

Edward blew out a loud sigh and turned me around so that we were standing face to face. "Quit beating yourself up; it's really my fault. I shouldn't have turned my back to the vines. I've been doing this long enough to know better. Anyway, the shot Dr. Rice gave me hurt worse than the cut."

"Still, I slice you open and then faint. I'm not graceful, nor am I productive in the fields, and I don't handle emergencies well. I'm beginning to feel completely useless here."

"Oh, Sweetie, I don't ever want you to feel that way." I knew he was being serious. Then he paused and I saw that mischievous grin creep up the edge of his lips. "You'll never be useless as long as you look as beautiful as you do right now."

I wanted to say something, but I was again at a loss for words. Maybe it would have been more productive for me to have majored in English or Communications in school. I looked at my feet. Edward took my head in his hands and gently turned my face upward to his. He spoke softly and slowly but kept a serious tone in his voice.

"You really need to stop doing that. You're a beautiful woman, whether you believe it or not. I wish I could figure out how to convince you that it's okay not to be embarrassed when someone gives you a compliment."

His voice sounded different when he spoke to me than when he spoke to others. It softened, not only in volume but in language too. Everything he said to me seemed smoothed around the edges, like a pebble you'd find washed up along the seashore. And I found it mesmerizing.

While he spoke, I stared into those beautiful eyes of his. They reminded me of hot chocolate, warm and creamy. I wasn't quite sure what to say, but I felt as warm as his eyes looked. I was convinced a girl could get lost in those sweet pools of chocolate and never be heard from again.

Edward realized I wasn't listening to him, stopped speaking, and smiled at me as we locked eyes as I continued my journey into his beautiful eyes. I wanted to freeze that moment, but Sarah disturbed my trance when she walked up beside us and spoke with the same monotone voice she had used when talking about Edward at the vines the day before.

"Say goodbye, you two. It's time for the ladies to go." She paused before she continued. "And C.C., we need to have a talk."

The closest town to the winery was Willow Creek. It was a quaint old southern town that looked as if it had been created by Norman Rockwell himself. Willow Creek's 'business district' consisted of one street, Main Street. It had a bank, a post office, City Hall, and all the stores you would expect to see in any Small Town USA. As the limo pulled up to Zoe's Day Spa and Boutique, some of the women noticed a flock of photographers waiting outside the door. Darla was the first to comment on the paparazzi, smiling as she did so.

"The press only hangs out in this town when there's a scandal involving someone from D.C. or Richmond. I wonder what's going on. Who knows, maybe we'll get our pictures in the paper."

I stared at my hand as I chewed on one of my fingernails and felt the tension pour into my once calm body. Small towns like this loved scandal-ridden visitors and I certainly qualified. I remembered the press that went along with my husband's death and my stomach turned. It was a small, but significant group of reporters and for over a week, it had driven me to the point of near insanity.

The moment Vivian stepped out of the car, my fears became a reality. A barrage of cameras began to click away and reporters started yelling out questions and it made me clutch my churning stomach.

"We're hearing Edward is officially off the market. Is it true?" I was mortified by how quickly our involvement had spread. I wasn't even certain how involved we were.

"Mrs. Baker, is it true that he's become involved with a woman half his age?"

"I heard she's some kind of child genius, any comment?"

"We hear her parents died when she was young. Do you know anything about that?"

"There are rumors that she was responsible for their deaths."

"Will she be at the party? Is she staying at the house?"

"A reliable source says she's carrying Edward's child."

None of the questions bothered me until the pregnancy one. I was lighter than I had ever been in my adult life, but hearing the reporter ask the question made me feel like the fat kid I still saw when I looked in the mirror.

And nearly all at once they screamed, "Is she in the limo?"

I wished I wasn't. I closed my eyes and returned to the day I had spent on the black sand beaches of Santorini. For a split second, I found peace. But the moment I opened my eyes, it was gone.

Like the matriarch that Vivian was, she turned to the press and said, "My son, Edward, is currently dating a brilliant young lady who will be in attendance at this evening's festivities. Now, if you will excuse me, my guests and I have appointments to keep."

Vivian waved the driver to re-open the door. One by one, everyone stepped out until I was the only one left. I wasn't sure I could do this, but I really didn't have a choice at this point. I knew if I refused to leave the back of the limo, it would cause a scene and I didn't want to do anything to embarrass the Baker family. But my stomach ached so hard that I wasn't certain if I'd be able to make it from the car to the door without help. So I pulled every bit of strength I had inside me and stepped out of the limo and into a sea of cameras. I don't know how, but they immediately knew I was the one they wanted and began to yell questions at me simultaneously. The noise was so intense. It was as if a wall of sound tried to knock me over as my foot caught a piece of uneven pavement. Quickly, I shuffled my feet until I regained my balance. I forced a brief smile and scurried through the door of the spa. I felt like I had been thrown in front of a firing squad.

Once inside the sanctuary of the spa, I saw an exotic-looking woman with long, straight black hair and caramel-colored skin begin pulling the window shades to the spa closed. While she wasn't a tall woman, she had legs that were long and lanky, accentuating her perfectly slim figure. I shut the door behind me and leaned against it. I looked down at the black and white checkered tile, knowing if I made eye contact with anyone, the tears filling my eyes would begin to fall and I didn't want to look like a nervous, crying wreck. But I was.

As I stared at the tiles, I caught a glimpse of Darla's feet stomping off to the back of the spa, angry about something and pounding her high heels into the floor as she went.

Vivian and Sarah were instantaneously at my side. Sarah knew me well enough to know that an incident like this could make me want to leave the country before the band played their first note at this evening's event. Vivian had a good idea that the press exposure was a terrible thing in my opinion, and followed Sarah's lead.

"C.C., are you all right?"

"No." I wanted to yell at her for even asking, but I could not say no without wanting to burst into tears and it caused my voice to crack as I whispered my answer.

Sarah put her arms around me and whispered into my ear. "I'm so sorry. If I had known it was going to turn into all of this, I wouldn't have made you come this weekend."

I lifted my face toward the ceiling and took a deep breath, "You didn't make me come. I did that on my own."

Vivian put her hand on my back. "Cassandra dear, the press is, unfortunately, part of Edward's life. I would like to tell you this is not a normal event for the Bakers, but I'd be lying to you. I learned a long time ago that women tolerate things we would never imagine for the men in our lives."

I half-smiled because I was certain she knew what she was talking about. I turned to her and said, "I'll never understand how men can be so oblivious to it, though."

The attractive woman finished her work, walked over to me, and smiled. "Don't worry, Cassandra, one day you'll get used to men being oblivious."

"You know who I am?"

"Darlin', everybody in town knows who you are. But you don't know me," the woman pushed her long, straight hair away from her face and shook my hand. "I'm Zoe Marshall, and you look like you need a massage. Come with me."

A fleet of hairdressers, manicurists, and makeup artists took everyone in different directions. I walked back to the changing room, slipped off my clothes, and into a robe. I was guided back to the massage room only to find Darla on the first of the two tables in the room. I was half tempted to skip the massage in order to avoid Darla. I could tolerate her when I was drunk, but I was not so sure if I could do it sober.

"Hey Cassandra, the press get lots of good pictures?" Darla asked sarcastically.

"I hope their cameras fall into the Chesapeake Bay." I followed Darla's lead, untied my robe, and laid face down on the table but propped my head up with my hands while I waited for my turn.

"Well, they could've taken my picture. I never mind having it taken. You know, when you date someone like Edward, this kind of thing is par for the course."

Just then, Zoe waltzed in. "It shouldn't have been in this case. Someone tipped off the press. I just talked to one of the photographers. He told me they got an anonymous call from a woman who told them everything."

"I don't know whether to be relieved or cry. I don't like the idea of people following me around without my consenting first."

Zoe decided to change the subject in the hopes of making me feel better. She popped herself up and had a seat on the table she had been leaning against. "So tell me, Cassandra, how was the harvest today?"

"It was fun until I tried to kill Edward."

"What! How?"

"I accidentally pruned his back instead of the vines."

Zoe gasped, and Darla's head popped up. "You what? Now that would have been worth walking out there to see."

Zoe seemed confused when she turned to Darla. "You don't go out with the others? I assumed everyone at Thomas Hall went out to harvest the vines."

"No, I don't do grapes. I don't do grapes, production, or any of that. I just drink the final product." Darla laid her head back on the table, but the lady massaging Darla told her she was done. She got up and looked at the masseuse. "Don't massage Cassandra too hard. I'm not sure the table can handle that much weight."

Between Darla's comment and the reporter's pregnancy question, I was starting to feel very self-conscious. I knew my weight was at the upper end of the healthy range, but up until an hour before arriving at the spa, I felt pretty good about myself. Now I wanted to bury myself in chocolate chip cookie dough and disappear off the face of the earth.

Zoe gave her an evil glare and responded. "You better head off to the makeup room. It will take a while for them to help you." After she left, Zoe turned her attention to me. "Don't worry about her. She's a real bitch."

"Yeah, not my favorite member of the Baker family so far."

"You know, Cassandra, it wouldn't shock me if Darla was whom the press got the anonymous tip from."

"She's not really that evil, is she? And besides, what has she got against me?"

"You exist, and the Baker family likes you a lot. Things have been shaky with her and Henry for a while now, and the family's getting fed up. The last thing she wants is someone around to steal the spotlight and make her look as bad as she really is. It wouldn't surprise me if she were trying to run you off." I wondered how Zoe already knew so much and how she knew the Baker family's opinion of me. After a moment, I decided I probably didn't want to know.

"Regardless, something about her makes my skin crawl," I said.

"Well, the wine's being poured out front. It might help with that crawly feelin'. Want a glass?"

"No, I think I better wait until later. I'd love some water, though."

Zoe slipped out of the room and returned with a wine glass filled with water. "No one will notice it's not alcohol if it's in a wine glass."

I was still upset at this point but didn't want to ruin Sarah's time at the spa. I took the glass from Zoe. I don't know why, but I felt like she was someone I could trust and she could tell I still hadn't recovered from the photographic mob.

I took the glass from her. "Thanks. Can I tell you something kinda personal?"

"Of course, what's the matter?" She sat down next to me so that we could speak quietly as the masseuse worked on my shoulders.

"I don't know if I can do this. I don't handle public life very well. It's the kind of thing that could make me lose my mind. And while I might even be crazy about Edward, I'm not sure this, whatever this is with him, is a good idea."

Zoe smiled and spoke in a soft, calm voice. "You know, I went to school with Henry. I've known the Bakers for a long time. Edward's a really great guy. He's been like a big brother to me. He's definitely worth the craziness, at least in my opinion."

"Thanks, I needed to hear that. Between Darla and the press, I was beginning to think I should just jump on a plane and head back to Costa Rica."

"Well, don't go anywhere. I know Edward would be disappointed if you did. You're at a spa, so try to relax. When you're done with your massage, we'll get your hair and nails done. Then we'll get you made up. One of my makeup artists told me she can probably make that sunburn look better." She turned to leave when I called her back with a question.

"Zoe, I need shoes for tonight. Do you have anything in your shop in a size nine?"

"I'm sure I do. If not, I'll lend you a pair of mine. What color is your dress?" I hadn't really thought about it. How was I supposed to pick out shoes for a dress I hadn't seen yet?

"I don't know. I'm borrowing one from Sarah."

Zoe thought for a moment. "You might laugh, but I think I have just the thing. I'll put them on the counter. Looking for anything else?"

"Everything. I didn't know there was a formal this weekend until lunchtime today."

"I'll pull some things that might be useful and you can shop when you're done."

"Thanks."

"Now relax. You look like a bundle of nerves and massages are supposed to be good for that." She gave me a friendly smile and patted my shoulder as she turned and headed out of the room in the direction of the boutique, assumingly to handle my request.

I felt a little better after my massage and even better after the pedicure and manicure. By the time my makeup and hair were done, I was pretty sure I could handle whatever the evening offered. Zoe had somehow bumped me through the line so that everyone else was still at their last station when I was done, giving me time to explore her shop. Not only did she have everything I needed, but she had it in my size, color, and style as well.

I returned to the vineyard relaxed, refreshed, and with my hair, nails, and makeup done perfectly. I felt like I looked better than I had ever before in my life and retired to my suite. I laid out my purchases on the bed. The new shoes Zoe picked out for me were strappy sandals that had rhinestone-covered straps and clear glass slipper-like heels. Along with the two pairs of thigh-high silk stockings, a garter belt, a strapless bra, lace panties, and a silky nightgown and robe. I really did not need the robe or gown, but the thought of owning a jade green satin nightgown and robe made me feel as beautiful as Zoe's team had made me look. As for the stockings instead of pantyhose, well, I decided if I was going to do this whole sexy underwear thing, I was going to do it right.

I felt ready for the evening, but there was still the matter of a dress. I was heading toward the sitting room, with intentions of walking across the hall to Sarah, when there was a knock at the door. I assumed it was Sarah with the dresses. "Come in."

I was surprised when Victor, carrying the large white box Edward had brought in at lunchtime, opened the door. "Miss Martin, I was asked to deliver this to you." He walked into the sitting room where I met him and handed me the box. "Enjoy yourself this evening. You look lovely."

"Victor, I know you're very busy tonight, but could you have someone find out when Mass is at the Catholic Church tomorrow. I haven't been in a few weeks."

He smiled. "Mass is at ten. I usually attend Sunday mass myself, but I doubt I will tomorrow."

"Thank you. I think I'll decide in the morning."

"Very well then, Madam."

Victor turned and left the suite. I quickly opened the box. Inside laid the most beautiful full-length purple dress I had ever seen. It had an intricately beaded corset, a drop waist bodice, and matching purple tulle skirting. While the bodice was sufficiently boned to wear strapless, I was happy to find it had a silk halter tie attached. Straps on a dress of that nature always made me feel less self-conscious. Along with the dress was a handwritten note with perfect penmanship.

Cassandra, I saw this in town and thought of you. Only something this spectacular could ever do your beauty justice. Please wear it tonight and be my date. All My Love, Edward

I was overwhelmed to the point of near tears. I had never been treated by a man this way before and had no clue how to process it. I took a few deep breaths, took the note, and carefully placed it on the nightstand. I slipped off my clothes and changed into my new strapless bra, panties, stockings, and put on my new robe. I walked into the sitting room and caught a glance of myself in the mirror. It was the same mirror Edward had forced me to stand in front of the night before. My hair and makeup still looked good, but the lipstick was the wrong color for this dress. I went into the bathroom, took a different shade out of my bag, and put it on over the first color until it looked better. Then I walked over to the bed and looked at the dress again. I thought about the trouble he must have gone to in order to get this dress. I needed a drink. I had just opened a bottle of Chardonnay when Phoebe poked her head through the door.

"Cassandra, it's me. I've got Sarah's dresses."

"Come on in. I was just pouring some wine. Want some?"

"Sure." Phoebe was wearing a purple dress as well. It was a shade of lavender and was long and silky with spaghetti straps. It was an effortless dress but she carried herself in such a way that it looked very elegant. "Where do you want these?"

I took the dresses from Phoebe and handed her a glass of wine. "I'm not sure I'm going to need these after all. Go look on my bed."

Phoebe followed me back into the bedroom. I hung the dresses in the closet for the moment and had a few sips of my wine.

"Whoa! That's quite a dress. Where did you come up with that on such short notice?"

"I didn't. Your brother did. But I'm worried he might have miscalculated my size. I think we might need a stick of butter and a miracle to slide me into that."

"I don't know. I'm pretty sure he's closer than you think." She looked curiously at me. "So, what's the deal with you and my brother? It looks like he's pretty serious about you." She picked up the note, read it, and then laid it back down.

"Why do you say that?" I finished off my glass and debated pouring myself another one.

"Well, lots of reasons, but this dress in particular. Only the Baker women wear purple at Thomas Hall events. It's a tradition."

I took a minute to digest what Phoebe said.

'Only Baker women.'

I felt my chest tighten from nervousness as I tried to respond. "I know your brother is all 'love at first sight' kind of crazy about me, but this is happening way too fast. It's just too much. I wish I could slow things down, but I just don't know how."

Phoebe smiled as though she understood completely, although I am not sure she really did.

I poured myself another glass and did the same for Phoebe. I took a sip and looked at the clock. It was nearly seven and the party would be starting soon.

"Phoebe, can you help me see if I'm going to fit into this dress. I always seem to get tangled up trying to put on a formal gown."

"Sarah told me you would need help. Get your shoes on, and then we'll get you into this dress."

I put on the new shoes and slipped off my robe. One of the first things a girl learns about long dresses is to put her shoes on first because she'll never find your feet again in a long dress.

We managed to get the dress on, but had to lose the bra because it kept showing along the edges in the back. I was surprised that Phoebe managed to get it zipped with no extreme effort. However, there was no room for error either. She tied the straps. I turned around and looked in the full-length mirror.

I couldn't believe what I saw. The dress was intricately beaded and form fitting from the sweetheart neckline to the dropped waist. The beading at the top of the dress was in direct contrast to the light and full layers of the tulle and silk skirting that barely brushed the floor. I looked beautiful. I had never felt that way in my life.

Chapter Eight

There are moments in your life that are so surreal that you feel like you've stepped into a movie. The whole evening turned out to be a series of those moments, one immediately followed by another. Phoebe had walked down to the main floor ahead of me and I lingered for a moment to watch the partygoers arrive. I had always been one of those people who preferred watching parties from the edges and not get wrapped up in the middle of the chaos.

The house was so exquisite that it really didn't need much in the way of decorations. A few pieces of furniture had been moved to make more room for the partygoers, and fresh flowers had been well placed throughout the first floor. While I couldn't see them yet, I could hear a small band somewhere downstairs warming up and beginning their evening's performance.

Sarah and Michael were already downstairs, along with Dr. Rice and several dozen others. Waiters were walking through the crowd offering the guests a variety of drinks, food, and sweets. Although I hadn't tasted any of it yet, I knew it would be wonderful. I had yet to eat anything at Thomas Hall that wasn't absolutely delicious.

Senior and Vivian were standing at the bottom of the stairs near the entrance, greeting what seemed to be an endless stream of guests. Standing next to Senior and Vivian were Phoebe, Edward, and Henry. Henry turned around and saw me first, then nudged his brother with his elbow. Edward looked up, and when

I saw the expression on his face I knew he was in love with me. Regardless of how terrifying the prospect was to me, there was no stopping him from feeling the way he did. For a split second, I thought about hopping the first flight to Moscow, but the feeling soon passed. I knew this was where I was meant to be.

As I made my way down the stairs, Edward whispered something to his father, causing him to look at me and smile as well. By the time I reached the bottom step, every conversation in the room seemed to have dropped from a steady hum to a whisper and everyone looked at Edward and me as we came face to face. The attention of the other guests made me so nervous that as I descended the staircase, I could feel my face turning red, my hands shaking, and feared I would lose my footing and fall.

Edward appeared speechless. I could tell this was something he was not used to, but the look on his face said it all. He reached down and gently pulled my hand to his lips and kissed the top of my fingers, which rested gently in his hand. As I looked at him, I realized I had never been on a date before with a man who looked so sexy in all of my life.

"Oh, sweetheart, you look positively stunning."

I wondered if there would ever come a time I would truly feel comfortable accepting a compliment from a man. But I tried my best to look at Edward, smiled, and mumbled a quiet "thank you." It was the hardest thing I had done in a long time.

My efforts didn't go unnoticed. Edward smiled and tilted his head slightly to the side. "Now that's better. Come with me. There are some people I'd like you to meet."

Edward took me around the room and introduced me to what seemed like a million people, all of them wealthy and influential. I tried my best to be polite and make small talk with them, but I was intimidated. The guests he introduced me to were senators, CEOs, and diplomats. I found it odd that all of these people were interested in me and seemed to fall somewhere under Edward in order of importance. I knew he was a successful person in the biotech development world, but I obviously didn't have a clue as to how important he truly was.

As we mingled, the band played beautiful music. It was mostly romantic, big band music from the forties. We were talking to an elderly Congressman and his wife when Edward leaned into me and whispered in my ear, "It's time for us to dance."

I turned to him and gave him a definitive answer. "I don't dance."

"Oh yes, you do. You just don't know it yet."

I put my hands up in protest. "No. I'm sorry, but I'm not doing it."

"You don't get a choice." He smiled as he grabbed both of my hands and gently pulled me to the middle of the dance floor. As the band played, he led me around. I had always been a terrible dancer. If there was a foot within a two-yard radius, I was certain to step on it. But not when Edward led. He made it all so simple. He pressed his right hand firmly against the small of my back and placed my hand into his left hand. I leaned against him as he sang the words to the songs in my ear.

I closed my eyes, took a deep breath, and just let myself fall in love with him. I did not know if it would be a decision I'd later regret, but it seemed like the only thing left for me to do.

I couldn't remember a moment in my life where I had felt so overrun with joy. We danced through three or four more songs. I'm not sure how many. Occasionally he would comment on something or ask me a question. I don't think I ever stopped smiling and I'm certain he knew exactly why.

Then, in an instant, the moment was crushed as the flash of cameras started to go off. Somehow, two photographers that were at the spa had gotten into the house. Edward turned me, so my back was to the cameras and walked me straight into the study. Meanwhile, Henry, Victor, Michael, Dr. Rice, and a group of men were busy escorting the uninvited guests out of the building.

Edward wasn't happy with the situation and had to work to maintain his composure. "Wait here. I'll go handle this." Edward sat me in a chair, walked out of the room, and closed the door behind him. The door immediately reopened. It was Phoebe and Sarah, with Darla following behind them.

"I've been telling Mom for years that we need more security at these parties, but she never listens!" Phoebe was fuming and I could tell that she felt as though the whole family's privacy, in addition to mine, had been violated. "I swear to God, if a single one of those pictures ends up in print, I'll sue the media company that does it!"

Phoebe sat down in the chair beside me, trying to calm herself so that she might be of some use to me. Sarah, however, was still standing next to Darla and was more concerned with my immediate welfare.

"C.C., are you okay?"

I thought about it for a minute and then told her the truth. "Yes, I'm fine."

Sarah looked shocked. She expected me to be a basket case and with good reason. I had been known to fall apart over much less. But the way Edward handled me in those first seconds left me feeling safe and secure.

"Are you sure?"

"Yes, I'm sure. I just feel bad the party was interrupted." Sarah looked at me as though I were a complete stranger and put one hand on her hip.

"Cassandra Louise Clark-Martin," Sarah had never called me by my full name in the decade I had known her. "Less than eight hours ago, you were ready to have a nervous breakdown and flee the country over the press mob. And now you don't even blink when they rush in and crash a party just to get your picture? What's going on?"

"I don't know. It's just that with Edward here, I feel like...."

Sarah slid her hand off her hip and looked almost emotionless. "Oh, I see." I wasn't quite sure what to make of the tone in her voice.

"See what?"

"Never mind, you're a smart girl. You'll figure it out soon enough."

Darla took a moment to butt in with her two cents worth.

"I don't know, I thought the whole press thing made the party more exciting!" As she spoke, I noticed she wasn't wearing purple, but a skin-tight red, strapless dress that showed a little too much skin.

Phoebe threw a disgusted look at Darla. "I don't think so. What's with the tacky red dress anyway?"

"At least I won't look like a giant grape in the pictures. You know Cassandra, you'd be a real looker if you dropped some weight." She was looking at me as she spoke and while her words were meant to cut away at my joy, her eyes told the truth. She was jealous, though I couldn't figure out why. Regardless of the jealousy in her eyes, Phoebe took offense to Darla's weight comment.

"Don't you have to get back to the party? I'm sure there are at least five or six men here tonight that you haven't slept with since you married my brother."

"Bitch."

"Slut."

Sarah and I looked at each other clueless at what to say. We both knew how the two women felt about each other but were surprised they would say it to each other's faces.

Sarah looked at Darla, "Why don't we go see how things are going out there and we'll let Phoebe and C.C. know when it's safe to come back out to the party?"

"Sounds like a plan. I have people I want to make sure I see tonight. I'm done here anyway. Later!" The two of them turned and left the room, but not before Sarah turned back and made a funny face in reference to Darla, making Phoebe and I snicker. Phoebe turned in her chair to face me.

"Ignore Darla. She's just jealous because you look better than she does tonight."

"She isn't wearing purple."

"Trust me, it hasn't gone unnoticed. Nor has the fact that you are." Phoebe seemed calmer as she spoke. "Cassandra, are you sure you're okay?"

"Yes. Why does everyone keep asking me that?"

"You've had a rough day." She was right. While the evening had been surreal, parts of the day had been downright stressful.

"I've survived worse."

"Just don't let it influence how you feel about my brother. Okay?"

"Trust me, if anything, it's confirmed exactly how I feel about him," I said.

"Hopefully in a good way." Edward had re-entered the room and had dropped down on one knee next to me, smiling and holding my hand. I reached over and fixed a piece of his hair that had fallen out of place.

"You know, you look very handsome in that tux," I said as our eyes locked momentarily and I felt a smile creep across my face. I glanced in Phoebe's direction just in time to see her roll her eyes.

"Okay, you two, let's get back to the party."

The three of us quietly slipped out of the study and back into the party. About two steps out the door, the CEO of the company Edward was posturing to take over asked if he had a moment for him. When he looked at me, I knew he wanted to say no, but I interceded.

"Of course he has time for you. This merger is very important to him. Why don't the two of you step into the study and I'll go get you both a drink?"

Edward never stopped looking at me. I was certain he was undressing me with his eyes as he smiled. While I probably should have minded, I didn't.

Phoebe walked with me to get the guys their drinks and waited at the door while I took the glasses into the study. Edward looked up from a stack of papers and had put on a pair of glasses while I was gone. He looked even sexier than he had before. I forgot how to breathe for a moment. I handed the men their drinks and looked at Edward.

"Don't be too long Honey. The other guests are already asking about you." It was a lie, but I didn't want to share him with anyone tonight.

Edward smiled and understood. "Yes, Ma'am."

I turned and as I walked away I heard the short, plump CEO say, "You are one lucky man." And I swore to myself that as long as I lived, I'd never forget Edward's reply.

"I just pray to God my luck holds out."

Phoebe was waiting by the door and had heard the conversation as well. She looked at me and smiled. I wanted to say something to her about what we heard but I couldn't find words to match my feelings. I just smiled back. It was a long moment before I was able to find words to break our silence.

"Phoebe, tell me about some of these people. I have a feeling you know a lot more about them than your brother does."

She tucked her arm into mine, in a sisterly sort of way, and as she began to talk we walked over to the bar and picked up freshly poured glasses of Champagne.

"Let's see, that guy over there is Zachary O'Keefe. He's our family lawyer that handles our private matters. He may as well live here as much as dad has him out to change his will." I wondered what constituted a private matter and why Senior changed his will so much, but didn't want to interrupt her. "The heavy-set bleached blonde next to Alex is his mother. Her name is Jennifer White. I just met her tonight. It's the first time she's been out to the winery. The twins sitting next to her are my aunts, Virginia and Violet. Oh, and the tall, thin guy over there is Victor's son, Oliver Moore. He's an artist that lives in New York. I heard he makes pretty good money with his work, but the rumor mill in Richmond is saying he gambles most of it away."

"Wow, I was right when I said you probably knew more about these people than your brother."

Phoebe and I spotted her parents at the same time, looked at each other, and smiled. They were holding hands, and when they saw the two of us still arm in arm, they smiled and waved from across the room. I wondered if that was what Edward and I would look like at that age. I had never thought about spending the rest of my life with anyone but Tony, and after he was gone, the thought of a lifetime with one person terrified me. And yet, I found my mind was roaming in that direction. I had definitely gone completely nuts.

Phoebe was still focused on her parents. "I wonder if this will be Dad's last."

I turned and looked at Phoebe. "Last what?"

"Didn't anyone tell you? Dad's got terminal cancer. When he was diagnosed five years ago the doctors only gave him six months to live. Dad just keeps on going. But at his appointment last month, the oncologist discovered the cancer had spread even more. He's been a lot more tired lately. I'm worried he's running out of time."

"I didn't know. I'm so sorry. I wish there was something I could do to help."

"There is. You could marry my brother so Dad will quit worrying about him."

"I don't think that will save your dad."

"No, but it would be a good way to steer clear of the quartet of guys walking over here. They're frat buddies of Edward." She pointed in the direction of four guys, all in their mid to late forties, walking in our direction. I recognized one of the guys. His name was Marcus Weller. He had occasionally visited my uncle when I was living with him and my Aunt Molly.

"C.C., is that you? Turn around and let me get a better look at you." I did the obligatory model spin and Marcus nodded his head. "You look amazing! What are you doing here?"

Phoebe piped up proudly. "Haven't you heard? She's Edward's girlfriend."

I had heard it said earlier in the evening, but it was just starting to sink in, girlfriend. The only thought that ran through my mind was, "God help me."

"Oh." Marcus looked at me as if I had just broken some cardinal rule of the fraternity. I wondered if this was how everyone was going to react to us together. "That's, um, interesting. How's Clark feeling about this?"

Edward walked up next to me and slid both his arm around my waist and his voice into the conversation. "I called him this afternoon and he gave me his blessing to date his niece. Then Clark threatened to kill me if I broke her heart."

"That sounds like my uncle." The other three guys laughed. I assumed they all knew Fred. Marcus, however, wasn't listening to us. He had started putting his best moves on Phoebe. They were the same moves he had tried on me the fourth of July I was eighteen. It looked like it had been a while since Phoebe had the attention of any man over the age of ten, and she was definitely enjoying it.

Edward looked at the three remaining men and said, "Gentlemen, if you'll excuse us, I believe I owe this woman a dance."

He took my hand and led me back toward the dance floor. He decided we should pick up our evening right where we left off. We had only been dancing for a few moments when I wondered whether we'd be able to find our way back to that same feeling we had before the press had invaded the party. The end of the first song proved that we had.

The dance floor was more crowded now than when Edward and I had danced before. Darla, trying to draw attention to herself, was dancing with the wine master of Thomas Hall's biggest competition, St. Phillip's Winery. She had one leg wrapped around his and was shamelessly grinding up against him. I felt sorry for Henry, who had planted himself at the bar, looking forlorn. Out of respect for Henry and the Baker family, I pretended not to see her inappropriate behavior and focused on dancing with my very handsome date.

As we moved across the floor, I felt the heel of a woman's shoe land squarely on my left foot. When I looked down, there was a huge hole in my stockings surrounded by the shredded remains of silk that had previously held them together. When I looked back up, I saw Jennifer White, who was reluctantly dancing with Senior. Both Jennifer and I stopped dancing and the men followed suit.

"Oh my God, I am so sorry! Did I hurt your foot?" The middle-aged woman looked frantic. A few stray hairs had fallen from the bun that held her hair up and she had chewed all the lipstick off her bottom lip. I could tell this was not the first thing that had gone wrong for her this evening.

"No, I'm fine. It's just a torn stocking. I have another pair upstairs. I'll just go change them."

Jennifer shook her head. "I just can't seem to get anything right tonight."

"Really, it's okay. That's the nice thing about being a house guest this weekend. I can redo anything that needs fixing throughout the night. I'm surprised I haven't run them myself by now."

Senior took a moment to introduce us. "Cassandra, Edward, have you met Jennifer White? She's Alex's mother."

Edward reached out and shook her hand, and I did the same. "It's a pleasure to meet you. You have a very charming son."

"Don't let him fool you. He's a handful."

"Well, if the three of you will excuse me, I'm going to go change these stockings."

Edward walked me to the bottom of the staircase with every intention of following me up. I stopped and turned to him.

"You should wait down here while I go up."

"I'll wait in the sitting room of your suite," he said.

"I don't think that's a good idea. The whole town will be talking before the sun comes up."

"They already will be."

I hated being the fodder of town gossip and buried my head in one hand and shook it from side to side. "Edward, please."

"Okay, I'll meet you by the bar." He pulled me back and gave me a quick kiss before letting me go.

I moved up the stairs as gracefully as possible. I arrived in my suite and quickly stripped off the ripped stockings and opened the package the new pair was in. Before I putting them on, I made a quick trip to the bathroom, checked my hair, fixing one piece that didn't want to stay in place, and touched up my makeup. Putting on the stockings with the dress on was not as easy as taking them off, but after a short struggle, I managed to get them on straight. It took some effort to put my shoes on fully dressed as well, and after I did, I headed back down to the party.

As I reached the bottom of the stairs, I heard the sound of voices coming from the front sitting room. I thought one of them was Edward's, so instead of turning right and going back to the party, I turned left toward the sitting room. As I approached the door, I realized it wasn't Edward's voice but Senior's. I hadn't noticed that the two men had such similar voices. I had no intention of eavesdropping, but the conversation was too enticing not to stop and listen.

"Damn it, Senior!" Jennifer White? What connection did they have? "I only ever asked you to do one thing for Alex: stay out of his life! But you couldn't do it, could you? No, you had to build up the winery on your property and hire him. You had to offer him a house here at the winery. What are you going to do next?"

"I'd like to tell him the truth."

"No. Alex has no clue who his father is and I want to keep it that way."

"Oh my God! Alex is Senior's son." I whispered to myself. I wondered who else knew. I felt compelled to continue listening.

"Oh, come on, Jennifer. He should know."

"No! Not now, not ever! If you even think about telling him, I swear to God I'll kill you!"

I could hear her heels clicking as she walked across the floor. I turned and swiftly walked toward the bar.

A few things about Thomas Hall Winery had begun to make perfect sense.

The party was in full swing when Senior tapped the side of his wine glass with a fork and asked for everyone's attention. "Ladies and gentlemen, I would like to thank everyone for coming out to Thomas Hall this evening. It has been another glorious season for our grapes, as well as our family and friends. At this time, I would like to ask you all to join me on the terrace for our annual fireworks display."

As the bulk of the party-goers headed toward the main terrace doors, Edward, who was still holding my hand, led me in the other direction.

"Come with me. I know a better place to watch the fireworks."

We walked out the front door and turned right toward the vines we had harvested over the last two days. The sky was perfectly clear and the stars shone brightly along with the crescent-shaped moon. Just before reaching the vines, there was an old willow tree that sat at the edge of the main house's property. Beneath it, a blanket had been laid out along with little battery-powered paper lanterns. Champagne was already on ice and fluted glasses sat next to the bucket, along with a single long-stemmed red rose. I put my hands on my hips and playfully asked, "What is the meaning of all of this, Mr. Baker?"

Edward smiled and took my hand, assisting me to the ground next to him. "It really is the best place to watch the fireworks. And if I'm ever going to get a chance to be alone with you tonight, I figured I would have to make it happen and quit leaving it to chance. Because that just doesn't seem to be working."

I slipped my shoes off and set them on the corner of the blanket as Edward poured us both champagne. He leaned against the tree and I slid over and sat next to him. My sleeveless dress left me chilled, causing a shiver to run down my arms. Being attentive, he quietly slid his jacket off and wrapped it around me.

The sky suddenly lit up with the first sparks and he wrapped his arms around me and held me tight. I wasn't usually fond of being squeezed that tightly since in my past, it usually was the precursor to something violent. When Edward did it though, I felt safe and loved.

As the sky sparkled with an exciting display of pyrotechnics, we both sat in silence. You could hear the oohs and aahs of the crowd at the back at the main house, along with the accompanying music. The light and colors that illuminated the sky added a touch of magic to the evening. As we watched it all unfold, Edward and I drank champagne and he held me as though he were a chair for me to lean against. We had just finished our glasses when the grand finale of the fireworks came to an end.

"I guess we should get back." I must have frowned when I said it because Edward tried to convince me otherwise.

"There's no rush. It's crowded enough at the house where we won't be missed."

We looked at each other and smiled. He poured us each another glass to drink and I leaned against him and stared at the stars. I was in no hurry to return. I'd had more than enough to drink, way too much to eat, and hated having to be social in large crowds of strangers, especially when I was a focus of attention.

We sat and listened to the laughter and music coming from the main house. I was more than a little surprised when Edward asked me about Tony.

"Cassandra, what was your husband like?"

"You really want to know?" I knew he'd wished he hadn't asked the question by the time I was done.

"I wouldn't ask if I didn't."

"Before I tell you anything, I want you to promise that you won't repeat this conversation to Michael."

I detected a note of confusion in Edward's voice. "Okay, whatever you want."

"My late husband wasn't a very nice guy. He was a different person to the world than he was with me."

I heard Edward swallow hard. I think he knew the answer to his next question before he asked it. "In what way?"

I guzzled down the remainder of my glass. I thought it might be easier to talk about it if I were less sober. "Tony was controlling when we were dating. I think I mistook it for protectiveness because he could be so sweet and caring. More than once, he even came to my defense concerning my beliefs on pre-marital sex. After we married, though, he turned abusive and violent. He would criticize everything I did and when I didn't live up to his standards, he had no problem using force to get ..." I stopped there. I didn't want to continue this conversation.

I felt Edward pull me in even closer and hold me tighter as though he were trying to protect me from my own past. "And Michael doesn't know?"

"No, and there's no reason for him to know now. Michael was his best friend and there's no need to hurt him now by telling him the truth. What's the point in telling someone a dead man's secrets?"

"What about the guys before him? Were they the same way?"

"There were no other guys, just Tony."

He leaned down and whispered into my ear, "Cassandra, I promise that I will never, ever hurt you. I don't want you to think for a second that I would ever do that to you. I will always protect you, my love." He buried his face in my hair and inhaled deeply. I don't know why I cared, but I hoped that the hairdresser had used hairspray that smelled good.

"Always? That's a pretty long commitment," I said.

"Not soon enough to protect you from Tony though."

We silently stared at the stars a little longer. I knew Edward was trying to process everything I had laid out before him.

"So there was really no one else, huh?"

"Not unless you count the stuffed Pooh Bear I slept with until I was fourteen."

He laughed and responded. "Lucky bear! Where can I sign up for that job?"

We both laughed and I hoped we were done with that conversation when Edward asked me another question.

"Why did you stay?"

"I loved him and I was his wife. I'm a big believer in the 'until death do us part' section of wedding vows."

Edward gave me a little squeeze. "I'm fond of that part too."

"Is that why you never married?"

"Exactly why. Whenever I was involved with a woman, I would ask myself if I could see us together for the rest of our lives. The answer had always been no." I noticed he said 'had always been' but decided not to press him further for an explanation. The conversation was turning much more serious than I felt like being and thought it might be fun to tease Edward a little.

"Whenever sounds like a big number." I tried to sound as serious as I could.

"Well, I ... a ..."

I couldn't stand it any longer and burst into laughter. "You don't need to defend yourself, you know. I do realize that I'm kind of inept when it comes to relationships."

"I don't think inept is the right word. I think limited is probably better."

"Limited, I like that word better too." I found myself smiling at the possibility of broadening my limited horizons with Edward. Although I didn't know how or where that would happen. Or if it was even realistic.

Edward must have thought the same thing because he shifted the direction of the conversation. "Cassandra, where will you go when you leave here?"

"I don't know yet. I'm pretty sure I'll stay in the U.S. for a while. I'll go back to D.C. with Sarah and Michael and decide from there."

He split the remainder of the bottle between the two of us. We sat in silence drinking champagne. I was trying to come up with something to say when Edward leaned over and whispered in my ear. "What are you thinking about?"

"Tonight."

I knew he was smiling without turning to look at him. "Elaborate."

"As long as it's Saturday night, I'm here at Thomas Hall, but tomorrow when the sun comes up I'll be leaving with Sarah and Michael. It's hard to leave a place like this, especially after an evening like this one."

I could tell Edward wanted to say something but didn't know where to begin, so I turned the question back onto him. "What about you? What are you thinking about?"

"How to convince you not to leave Thomas Hall tomorrow." I tried to interrupt him, but before I could actually get a word out, he stopped me. "Just listen before you say anything, please. I want to take you on a real date. You know dinner, a movie, dancing, the opera, whatever you want. I want to get to know you better but if you keep jumping on planes to God knows where I can't make that happen. I have a major corporation to run and I'm about to close a huge deal. Stay here at Thomas Hall, at least for the week. I have to be in Chicago Monday morning, but I'll be back Thursday afternoon."

We both sat in complete awe of what we had said to one another. I did not want to leave and he wanted me to stay. I thought about it for a moment when I remembered what Fred had told me. Trust my heart. I closed my eyes. I knew what I wanted to do, but there were a couple of realities that needed addressing. I reopened my eyes and stared at the stars.

"Edward, I can't impose on your parents. They have been such good hosts, but I know your Dad's health isn't good and you know they would insist on entertaining me."

"So come to Chicago with me."

"I'm not certain that's a good idea. I barely trust myself alone with you. And besides, you'll be busy working. I'd just be in the way."

"You're right. Chicago's probably a bad idea. I wouldn't get any work done. So stay at my place here then. When I come back, I'll stay at the main house if you'd like."

"Then you understand that I'm not one to just jump into bed on a whim. I'm just not that kind of girl and I wouldn't want to give you any false hopes of a wild weekend in bed when you return."

He sat me up and turned me around to face him. "I know exactly what kind of girl you are, the perfect girl for me."

He guided my head closer to his and placed his lips against mine. It wasn't anything like the surprise kiss on the stairs or the light brush on the lips or kiss on the cheek we had exchanged all weekend. But the kind of kiss that makes your toes curl with excitement. I am not sure I understood the feelings of passion I had for him in that moment. I had never felt like that about any man, not even my late husband. I could barely restrain myself and Edward had no intention of discontinuing his advances.

After a while, I realized his kisses had drifted away from my lips and worked their way down my neck and onto my cleavage, at least as far as my dress would allow. At some point, Edward's jacket slipped off my shoulders and I leaned against the base of the tree, closed my eyes, and rested my head so my face was up, staring through the branches at the stars.

I had just begun to wonder what Edward would do next when he wrapped one arm around my waist, pulling me closer to him. He used his free hand to untie the silk straps his sister had tied into a bow earlier that evening. I found it amazing that he could do all of these things at once while continuing to kiss me at the same time. I knew he wanted me undressed, and I'm sure he thought it was the next logical thing.

"Edward ..."

"Please, love, just a little more ..." He continued to kiss the bare skin along the edge of my neckline.

I knew what he thought would happen when he untied the bow and was curious to see his reaction. When he let go of the straps, he stopped, leaned back a bit, and arched a single eyebrow.

"Hmm. That didn't do what I thought it would."

I couldn't help but laugh. "You mean fall off?"

"Well, yeah."

"I hate to break it to you, but you have no one to blame but yourself. It's the way the dress is made. And since you bought it ...."

"I guess next time, I'll have to be more specific with what I want when I buy clothes for you."

"The next time?"

Instead of responding, he began kissing me again, allowing his lips to move down my neck and onto my cleavage. This time I had to protest. I wasn't sure why, but I knew there was a fine line there, that if we crossed, I wouldn't be able to retreat from. I was treading dangerously close to that line and he was walking it like a tightrope. Edward, however, showed greater restraint upon my objection this time and simply worked his way back up my neck with his kisses and back to my lips.

I wanted to stay there forever, on that blanket, under that tree, wrapped in Edward's arms. All of the problems I had ever had seemed to disappear, along with time and space. But time and space did return when we began to see the headlights of cars leaving Thomas Hall.

If I were truly the Cinderella I felt like, I would have returned to the main house in rags, with a pumpkin in my hands, as it was well after midnight when we returned to the main house. Most of the party guests had departed, leaving only the houseguests. Many of those staying overnight had changed into more comfortable clothes and were seated in the library. Edward was holding my hand. I was wearing his tuxedo jacket and still holding the rose he had given me in the vineyard. When Senior saw the two of us together, he smiled.

"Go for a little roll in the fields, you two?" Darla laughed as she said it, knowing she would embarrass me.

"No, actually, I was trying to convince Miss Martin to stay on at Thomas Hall a while longer. She seems happy here and I'd like to spend more time with her after I close this deal I've been working on."

Darla looked disgusted. "Stay? Here at Thomas Hall?"

Senior stood up and walked toward us.

"Well, son, were you successful?"

"I don't know, was I?" Edward turned and looked at me with the same Cheshire Cat grin he had on his face the previous night just before dinner.

Everyone looked at me, and I suppose the radiant glow on my face said it all. I knew I was blushing and looked down at the floor. When I did, I caught a glimpse of Michael out of the corner of my eye. He looked drunk and irritated. I couldn't decide if he was upset with me or if something else had annoyed him, but I felt the need to say something to defuse the situation.

"I would like to stay a bit longer. I'd really like to learn more about the winemaking process. However, I don't want anyone to feel like I need to be entertained like a houseguest." I looked back over at Michael. Whatever I had said seemed to settle his nerves. He knew I was the academic type and I often used my educational curiosity as an excuse to ease the tension that simmered between the two of us.

"Cassandra's going to use my house. I'm never there and it will give her some space of her own. I can stay in my suite at the main house when I get back next weekend." Edward was trying to make it sound platonic, although everyone in the room knew how he felt about me.

Senior gave me a big hug. "This is very good. I know Vivian and I will enjoy having you here and we'll get to see our son two weekends in a row." It was only then that I realized Vivian was not in the room.

"Where is your lovely wife?"

"She wasn't feeling well. Exhaustion, I believe. She excused herself for the evening just before you walked in."

I could tell he wasn't telling the truth. Senior shifted his eyes away from mine as he lied, and I wondered what Edward and I missed while we were under the willow tree.

It was nearly two in the morning before I got back to my room. Sarah walked up with me, leaving the guys downstairs, smoking cigars and talking politics.

When I left, Edward whispered in my ear that he would come say goodnight before heading back to his place.

I walked over to the bar and opened the refrigerator. "Sarah, you want something to drink? I need some water."

"Thirsty or drunk?"

"All of the above."

"I'll take a bottle of water too."

"Can you unzip me? This dress is getting tight. I shouldn't have eaten so much tonight." I opened the bottle of water and guzzled half of it. Sarah walked behind me and unzipped the dress.

"Some evening, huh?"

"It was insane! I was so worried I was going to say or do something wrong, but everything seemed to fall into place. Even with the whole paparazzi thing." I was on cloud nine and the excitement still resonated in my voice. I changed into my new nightgown and robe while I listened to Sarah.

"Like you and Edward? I never thought I'd say this, but I might have to eat my words, at least where he's concerned. It looks like there could be something special between you two."

"We'll see." I already knew how I felt about him, but I wouldn't dare say it out loud, at least not yet.

Sarah took a look at my new nightgown and robe. "Expecting someone to keep you company later tonight?"

Sure, in my wildest, bravest dreams, I thought to myself. "No, I don't think so."

"It's just quite a departure from your normal t-shirt sleepwear."

"I'm just trying to dress appropriately for my surroundings. Someone I know used to hound me about that." We both laughed, knowing that she was the person who was always coaching me on appropriate dress. I debated whether or not to bring up Michael.

"What is it?" She could always read me like a book. I finished off the bottle of water, refilled it from the sink and walked across the room, and sat down in a particular chair I had become rather fond of.

"It's about Michael." Sarah started to interrupt me, but I kept talking. "I know he's not thrilled about me staying on at Thomas Hall. And I know that he hates the idea of me with anyone other than Tony, but you said it yourself, maybe it's time or at least time to be open to the possibilities. Sarah, I know you and Michael had a rough year, separating, reconciling, and all, but I need you to talk to Michael for me."

"Not a problem. Things are good between us now, I think. But you know, you could try talking to him yourself."

"He hates talking to me."

"No, he doesn't. He just never knows what to say." Sarah had changed earlier and looked just as glamorous in sky blue yoga pants and matching tunic as she had in her evening gown earlier. "You realize you have a bigger problem than Michael at the moment. It's your lack of wardrobe. The clothes you have are nice, but you're going to need a lot more for the lifestyle the Bakers lead."

"I know. I thought I'd try to get into town this week and go back to the boutique. I really like Zoe and she has a fabulous sense of fashion."

"That will work. I'll leave you whatever I think you can use. I'll have Victor bring over one of my suitcases with clothes when he has your things moved to Edward's house."

"Thanks. What would I do without you?"

"I still can't believe you're staying here, though. It seems, well, impulsive. I guess I just don't see you as that kind of girl."

"And selling my house and belongings to travel wasn't impulsive?"

"Okay. So maybe you are. Speaking of impulsive and unexpected, you missed an interesting moment tonight."

"Really, what happened?" I leaned over a little to ensure I was giving her my undivided attention.

"Well, to make a long story short, it turns out that Alex's mother, Jennifer, was Senior's long-time mistress. Vivian thought Senior had invited her at first and drug him into the library and read him the riot act. Phoebe said she had never seen her mom so angry. She calmed down a little when she found out Jennifer was Alex's mother, but she was not a happy camper."

"And she shouldn't have been. I overheard Senior and Jennifer talking in the sitting room before the fireworks and Alex is Senior's son."

"Oh my God! You're kidding me, right? So that's why Vivian 'retired' for the evening so early."

"I don't know if Vivian knows Alex is his son, but Alex doesn't."

Sarah said, "Well, I'm not telling either of them anything."

"Me either. Something tells me Vivian's a lot feistier than most people give her credit for and I wouldn't want to end up on her bad side."

"Hey, speaking of being on someone's bad side, I never got a chance to apologize for abandoning you Friday morning. The winery is having a serious financial issue and Michael and I were looking at the books."

"What kind of problem exactly?" I was the only one of the four of us who hadn't pursued a degree in accounting, but I spent so much time listening to them in study groups that I had developed a pretty good foundation.

"It's not important." Before she could even finish the sentence I knew what the problem was.

"Someone's embezzling money from them. It's the only financial thing you wouldn't want to talk about with me."

I knew why Sarah didn't want to tell me about the embezzlement. After Tony died, the company he worked for discovered that over a six-month time frame, my late husband had embezzled nearly five-hundred thousand dollars. I never did figure out why he had done it or find any trace of the money. The company determined that I wasn't legally obligated, but I used most of Tony's life insurance to pay them back. I didn't need the money, and it seemed like the right thing to do.

"That's a pretty serious allegation. Any idea who's doing it?" As we sat, I began to pull what seemed like a hundred bobby pins out of my hair. It had been pulled up in an elaborate fashion and while it still looked good, the pins had to come out before I could go to sleep.

"Not yet, but we're talking serious money."

"How much exactly?"

"A little over a million. I was hoping to find some answers this weekend, but it only left me with more questions. I'll figure it out eventually." I could tell Sarah had an agenda with the conversation that she hadn't gotten to yet. So I tried to move the conversation along.

"Sarah, after lunch, you said we needed to talk. What's up?"

"Edward can be very charming, but he's a very powerful man. Be careful."

"I don't understand."

"I figured as much." Sarah rubbed her eyes. "Guys like Edward aren't good at working on relationships. They think they can run them like a corporation. Just don't let him get controlling with you."

"I'm still not sure I completely get what would make him controlling. He just doesn't seem like the type."

"I'd think you would get it considering your first husband's behavior. But I'm exhausted. We'll talk more about this later. I'm going to call it a night."

Sarah looked tired. It had been a long day and an even longer night. She stood up to leave when there was a light tap on my door. Sarah opened the door for me. It was Edward. His bow tie was undone, the top button of his shirt was unbuttoned, and he was holding his jacket with one hand flung over his shoulder. He was smiling as he greeted Sarah.

"I thought I'd say goodnight."

Sarah walked around him and headed across the hall, and as she did, she said to Edward, "Behave yourself. She's like a sister to me."

Edward acknowledged her comment with a smile and nod and walked into the sitting room of my suite.

"Wow, this night just gets better and better." He took his free hand and put it around my waist.

"Why do you say that?" I asked.

"Cassandra, you look just as beautiful now as you did earlier, maybe even more." I struggled not to look away but still couldn't come up with anything to say. "Anyway, Sweetie, I just wanted to thank you for tonight. You were amazing."

Edward leaned over and gave me a long, lingering kiss. His lips tasted like scotch, which I found surprising. We had been drinking champagne all night, and it never occurred to me he would switch to something besides Thomas Hall wines or that such a thing was even in the house. While we were kissing, I could feel his hand slide down my body, all the while holding his jacket. The one hand stayed at my waist, but the other continued down my body until it came to rest on my bottom. I felt utterly helpless but all the while safe in his arms. Helplessness and safety were not a combination of feelings I had ever experienced. And it made me nervous when I thought about it.

Chapter Nine

I LIKE TO SLEEP in until nine at the latest, but it was eleven-thirty when I opened my eyes. I knew I had long missed Sunday Mass and I wondered if Sarah and Michael had headed back to Georgetown yet. I threw on my jeans and a clean t-shirt, brushed my hair and teeth, and tapped on the door across the hall. I was shocked to find that not only were Sarah and Michael still there, but Sarah was still asleep.

"Did I wake you?"

"No, but Sarah's still sleepin'."

Michael worked hard to control his southern drawl at the office, but I noticed that the moment he left the office, he slipped right back into that Carolina accent we had all picked up in college. Sarah's was completely gone as she seemed to have this unique ability to speak with no accent whatsoever. I'm not sure I had ever lost my accent so much as it had just melted in with all the other nuances of languages I had picked up throughout my travels. Michael, as usual, remained the rock of consistency. He had barely changed at all since college. The only difference was now he dressed better, and this particular morning was no exception. He was dressed in jeans and a polo shirt. In college, the jeans would have had holes in them, and the fake polo would have been stained and wrinkled. But now, the shirt was clean, freshly pressed, and the jeans looked new. Sarah had definitely reworked his wardrobe.

"Oh. Well, I'm going down to get something to eat." I paused, trying to decide what to say next. "You want to join me?" He seemed pleasantly surprised that I had offered.

"Yeah, gimme a second to leave Sarah a note. Besides, I wanna have a talk with you before we leave."

I really didn't want to talk with him about staying at Thomas Hall. I thought I knew the conversation that was coming and I was not looking forward to it. I was certain this would end with him yelling and screaming at me about my inappropriate behavior this weekend and how I wasn't behaving the way a grieving widow should.

"Let's go." We started walking and Michael continued. "First, Sarah doesn't know we're havin' this talk, and I'd like it to stay that way."

"Okay, I guess." I held more of their secrets than any one person should have to keep for a couple. I figured one more wouldn't kill me.

"I know you hate me and think I blame you for Tony's death which is completely ridiculous. It couldn't possibly be your fault that he's dead." He tried to continue, but I interrupted.

"I don't hate you. I always thought you hated me. From the time I started dating Tony, I always felt like you thought I was a bad choice for him."

Michael smiled. He wasn't exactly my type, but when he smiled, he was a decent enough-looking guy. "No, I was mad at you because I thought you could do better and that you were wastin' Tony's time. I figured eventually you'd meet someone else and drop Tony like a hot potato. And I got tired of hearin' him complain about the no sex before marriage thing. But, I must say, I was impressed you held firm on that one. After you and Tony married, I realized he had turned you into a doormat. I hated that you'd let that happen."

"Why didn't you say anything?"

"I couldn't. He was my best friend. I didn't want him to cut me off because he would have forbidden you to see Sarah. She would have been miserable and you were gonna need a place to go someday when things went bad between ya'll."

I wondered what Sarah had told him. "You make it sound like it was only a matter of time."

"We both know Tony had a temper on him. It was just a matter of time before he turned violent, don't ya think?" I already knew the answer to his hypothetical question.

We had reached the dining room only to find a beautiful brunch buffet set out. We seemed to be the first ones to arrive. So we helped ourselves to the food and took a seat. From there, I reinstated the conversation.

"Then why have you looked so angry all weekend? Whenever Edward and I are together, you look like you're about to blow a gasket." I picked up a slice of toast off my plate and took a bite.

"Yeah, I know, and I'm sorry. It's just a shock to see ya'll together. I mean, I've only ever seen you with Tony."

"I get it. It took me a lot of frequent flier miles to get beyond that myself."

Michael finished the first bite of his waffles before he asked, "You like Edward, don't you?"

"Yeah, I really do."

"Don't you think he might be a little old for you?"

"He and I talked about that. I think it will be okay. We seem to be at similar places in our lives. It seems like I've taken the fast track of life, and he's been so career-focused he kinda forgot to get a life for a while."

"Then you should stay. But if you change your mind, you know Sarah and I are just a phone call away."

"Thanks." I felt like the conversation had been a turning point for the two of us. I had always wanted us to have this relationship when Tony was alive, but it took Tony dying and me moving on for Michael and me to enjoy each other's company.

Sarah walked into the room looking tired but happy.

"What are the two of you talking about?" Michael and I looked at each other and smiled. I decided to have a little fun with this newfound friendship.

"Well, Michael has decided to keep a harem and I was negotiating my place as wife number two."

I hadn't seen Edward who had entered the room from the other side as I was seated with my back to the door he entered through. "Oh God, I hope not." He kissed me on the top of my head. "I have plans for you that won't work if you're married to the Sultan here."

Sarah jumped in and said, "Like what? Nothing scandalous I hope."

We all laughed and enjoyed the moment. While Sarah and Edward fixed their plates I thought about how long it had been since I had laughed so much in one weekend. And it felt good.

The day seemed to fly by. The other houseguests slowly departed, and it was after lunch before Senior and Vivian made their first appearance. Senior looked tired and frail but was as cheerful and entertaining as ever. He sat and told us great stories about his childhood and college years until well into the afternoon. Michael and Sarah headed home to Georgetown around five and after we said our goodbyes to them, Edward and I moved my small bag and one of Sarah's suitcases over to Edward's place.

Edward's house was a beautiful two-bedroom Mediterranean-style villa. The outside was similar to Henry and Phoebe's homes, but it was obvious the floor plans were different for each house. The interior was much like the exterior as it was decorated in a beautiful, yet masculine, fashion. The only difference was that the interior seemed to have a more Old-World Tuscany feel to it. There were lots of windows that provided a light, airy feeling and the walls were painted in rich shades of vanilla and chocolate. Edward explained that his mother had been insistent on building the home for him, and while he appreciated it, he would just as soon stay at the main house. As he gave me the tour, I began to realize how little time he truly spent there. While Vivian had an interior decorator handle the furnishings, the walls and shelves were void of the pictures, books, and mementos most people have in their homes. As we got to the bedrooms, Edward stopped at the first door.

"You'll be sleeping in here. It's the master bedroom."

The master bedroom was something out of an Italian fairy tale. White shutters allowed light to pour into the room, emphasizing the range of colors on the parchment-painted walls. The solid glass doors to the patio were framed by heavy chocolate-colored drapes that hung on a wrought-iron rod and matched the other iron accents in the room. Two oversized chairs sat facing the foot of the beautiful king-sized bed and flanked the fireplace on the wall opposite the bed. Fresh flowers were in a vase on the nightstand. No detail had been overlooked.

"I had Victor move my things to the guest room for now." He took a step closer to me.

"For now?" I was curious as to what he'd say next.

"Until I get what I need moved up to the main house."

"Oh."

"Disappointed?" It was then that I realized he was holding me loosely, smiling with his head tilted slightly back to get a better view of me. When I looked at him, I just wanted him to kiss me again like he had last night.

"I'm not sure." It was the only attempt at flirting I had ever made and I wasn't sure of the reaction I'd get.

"Well, maybe this will help you decide, because it's all I've been able to think about today." He leaned into me, pressed his hand into the small of my back, rested my body against the door frame, and kissed me. First softly, but then with such passion, I wasn't sure I would be able to stop him or if I even wanted him to. His free hand worked its way up my body, making a blind effort to find bare skin whenever possible by pushing my shirt along with the direction of his hand. I felt like the bones in my body had melted away from the heat that radiated from him. I could barely stand upright. Finally, I found the strength to pull my lips away from his. I could scarcely speak, and even then, the words only came out breathlessly.

"Edward, Honey."

He continued to kiss me, saying each word between the kisses. "What. My. Love."

At this point, my heart was palpitating so fast that I thought it would simply leap right out of my body. "I forget."

He silently went back to kissing me, slower this time, and started at the edge of my v-necked t-shirt. I found this completely intoxicating and knew I could be in big trouble. His fingers from one hand pulled along the edge of my shirt giving him even more skin to kiss. The other hand slid up my body and softly cupped my left breast. After a moment, I took my hand and removed his from my breast.

"We should stop." I was breathing so hard, it was as if I had just run the fifty-yard dash.

"Why?" Edward continued his mission to kiss every piece of bare skin he could find.

"I'm not sure either of us has this much self-control. And we're supposed to be at the main house for dinner soon."

He moved his lips back up to my ear but never stopped kissing my skin.

"How soon?" His lips found mine and it was a few minutes before I found the willpower to pull them away.

"Probably not soon enough."

Edward pulled his head back and looked into my eyes. My breathing was still labored, so I leaned my head back and closed my eyes. I was confident he knew at that moment he could have me if he wanted me and his actions, along with certain body parts that had been pressed against me, made it clear he did. I couldn't even imagine how else he could make me feel if he could do that to me with nothing more than his lips.

I found myself wishing I were many things, like someone who could not care less about the Catholic ideals my faith instilled in me. That I was someone who could put it all aside and follow my desires, but it was just too soon for me. I knew I would regret it afterward and Edward knew it too.

He slowly slid his hands back to my waist and let out a quiet low growl with a primal sound. He pushed a stray hair from my face and said, "Damn, this is going to be harder than I thought."

Monday morning I went into the kitchen to make some tea. I found a lime green cell phone on the kitchen counter with a note from Edward:

My Sweet Cassandra, Call my cell when you wake up. My numbers are programmed in the Contacts. All my love, Edward

I picked up the phone and examined it. It had been over a year since I had owned a cell phone but knew the company that made this phone was supposed to be one of the best. It took me a minute to figure out how to find the saved numbers and get the phone to call the right one.

"Good morning."

"Good morning, Beautiful. Hold on a second." I could hear him tell people he needed to take this call and asked them to clear the room. "Did you sleep well?"

"I did. What are you doing?" I walked over to the sofa in the living room and took a seat while waiting for the water to boil.

"I'm meeting with the board of directors of a company I'm buying this week. Have you had breakfast yet?"

"No, but shouldn't you be working?"

"I'm good. Do you like the phone?"

"Yes. It's cute, and I can actually use it, unlike yours."

Edward laughed. "Well, there's no phone at my house at Thomas Hall and I wanted you to be able to reach me anytime you wanted. I remembered you struggling with my phone, so I thought you'd like that one better. Use it to call anyone, anytime. It's yours."

"Thank you. It's very thoughtful of you."

"Anything for you, my love."

"Shouldn't you get back to being the boss and buying big companies?"

"I guess. I wish you were here."

"No, you don't. You wouldn't get any work done."

"You're right. Plus, the sooner I get done, the sooner I get back to you."

"Then you should go."

"Okay, I'll call you tonight." Then he said it. "I love you."

I was pretty sure I knew how I felt about him, but I wasn't ready to say it out loud. Thank God he realized it too.

"And Sweetie, I know you love me too."

It was quiet, too quiet after the excitement of the weekend. By two o'clock that afternoon I was about to lose my mind. I was at a remote winery, living in a guy's house that I hardly knew, waiting for him to return at the end of the week.

I began to question my actions. I swore after Tony died that I would never allow my life to revolve around a man again. Yet I was doing precisely that. I picked up the phone and called Sarah.

"Hi, it's Cassandra."

"Well, I guess Michael wins. I said you'd panic before ten, but he said you'd make it until about three."

"You two were placing bets on how long it would take me to lose my mind? Gee, thanks."

"So, what's wrong?"

"I'm scared," I said.

"Of who? Is Edward already turning into a damn control freak? I swear to God I'll –"

"Sarah, what do you mean Edward being a control freak? He's far from it. My problem isn't who; it's what."

"Nothing. Forget I said it." Sarah was acting odd where Edward was concerned. I just didn't know why. "Wait a minute. You're afraid of falling in love? You know that's funny since you were always the hopeless romantic of the group."

"He told me he loved me."

Sarah's reply sprang from her mouth. "What did you say?"

"Nothing."

"How do you feel about it?"

"Like this relationship is sitting on the fast forward button of its own remote control. I mean, this isn't the way people fall in love. They're supposed to meet through people they know, hang out, get to know each other, date for a long time, and *then* fall in love. People just don't meet on airplanes and then spend the week in each other's homes." With each sentence, my voice became louder and more panicked.

"Just because you fall in love one way the first time doesn't mean that's the way it's going to happen every time. Do you want me to come get you?"

"Not yet. Maybe I'm just overreacting," I said as I exhaled.

"Well, give it the rest of the day. If you feel the same way tomorrow, I'll come get you. Okay?"

"Okay. And tell Michael thanks for believing I'd make it past lunch."

Senior and Vivian had invited me to dinner Monday night and while I tried to convince them they didn't need to entertain me, Vivian assured me it wasn't a big deal for me to have dinner at the main house. Upon my arrival, I was surprised to find that Darla and Henry were also in attendance. I could immediately tell something was wrong between the two of them. Henry, however, was gracious as always.

"Cassandra, what a pleasant surprise. I didn't know you'd be here for dinner this evening. It's good to see you again." He walked over and gave me a hug.

Darla watched the scene unfold as she slumped in the chair, glaring at us as if she were trying to prove we were lovers covering up an affair.

"Cassandra."

"Hi, Darla." I joined the others who were about to sit down at the table.

"I'm surprised you're still here. Edward must have thought you were damn good in bed to keep a girl like you around."

Vivian was quick to scold her. "Darla, that is completely inappropriate!"

"It's okay, Vivian. I have to admit this seems to be happening very fast. I could see where it would be easy to assume that we were lovers."

Henry, being his father's child, spoke up to defend my honor. "Well, I seriously doubt the two of you are sleeping together. If you were, Edward definitely wouldn't want to stay at the main house this upcoming weekend and I did overhear him ask Victor to make sure his room was ready for him."

Senior and Vivian looked at me and then at each other. Vivian raised a single eyebrow and Darla glared at me for a moment before she began her tirade on Henry.

"You're defending her! That's it, Henry. I've had it. You threatened to divorce me today and now you're defending this mousy little slut! I don't need this shit. I don't need you either, but I will take you for every penny you own! Do you understand me? Every penny!" Darla was still screaming as she stomped out of the house, her heels clicking against the floor. I found it odd that even in jeans she wore high heels.

"Henry, I'm so sorry. I didn't mean –"

"No, Cassandra, don't apologize. I should be apologizing to you. Darla's behavior is just out of control." Henry took a deep breath. "You may as well know, too. We came tonight to tell everyone that I've asked Darla to move out. Zachary O'Keefe is drawing up divorce papers. I just can't keep doing this. We should have never gotten married."

Vivian walked over and hugged her son. "Don't worry, dear, it'll be fine."

"I think I'm going to go. I've lost my appetite."

I was shocked that Senior didn't look more worried about his son.

"Why don't you stay at the main house tonight? I'll have Victor bring you up a plate later."

"Thanks, Dad." Henry stood and said goodnight to everyone before he headed upstairs. As soon as he was out of sight, Senior turned to Vivian.

"You think he means it this time?" She asked as she returned to her seat.

"Only if we're lucky."

I was surprised to hear this coming from the two of them.

"You mean this isn't the first time this has happened?" I asked.

Senior laughed. "Dear, it's not even the first time this month. I'm sorry she drug you into it though."

"Not a problem. I was just an easy scapegoat."

"Well, my dear, you are far too kind. I'm sure Senior will agree."

"Absolutely, but all this drama has made me hungry. Let's eat, shall we?"

Victor brought in wonderful plates of veal parmesan and grilled vegetables. I love Italian food, and the chef who cooked this meal knew what he was doing. After the main course, Victor brought each of us a bowl of fresh berries with cream.

We had just finished eating when Alex came into the dining room.

"Cassandra, I thought you left with the others yesterday." I had forgotten he wasn't in the study when Edward and I returned from the fireworks after the party.

"No, I decided to stay on a bit longer and try to learn some more about Virginia's wine industry."

"Well then, when you get moving tomorrow, head over to the production building and I'll tell you everything I know." Alex gave me a look that made me question his intentions, but I ignored it as my interest in him romantically was non-existent.

"That would be lovely, thanks. It looks like you've got business to handle though, so I think I'll head back to Edward's for the evening."

As I stood to leave, Senior cleared his throat. "Cassandra."

"Yes sir?"

"Will you join us for dinner tomorrow night dear? I would like to talk with you again."

"Then I'll be here around six."

I walked over and kissed him on the cheek. Vivian just smiled and shook her head. We both knew Senior would not live too much longer and if having dinner with him brought him joy, I was happy to oblige.

Victor led me to the door and when he opened it I turned and faced him.

"Victor, is Senior getting worse or was he putting on an act this past weekend?"

"You're observant. He's getting worse." I let out a sad sigh and he shook his head in agreement. "You know, in this day and age, it's barbaric for a man to have to suffer like this. Society dictates that if a dog or cat is suffering that you should put it down, but still the highest order of the animal kingdom is forced to endure lingering pain. A quick, planned death would be so much better for everyone, if you ask me."

I was shocked by his statement. Not knowing how to respond, I just said goodnight.

As I walked down the path to Edward's house, thinking about what Victor said to me, my cell phone rang. It took me a minute to figure out how to answer it. I was going to have to read the manual at some point.

"Hello?"

"Hi, Beautiful. What are you doing?"

"Walking back from having dinner with your parents. They were quite insistent I join them this evening."

"Mom told me she planned to have you up tonight."

"Your dad invited me back tomorrow night. Edward, his health's deteriorating fast, isn't it?"

I could hear Edward clear his throat. "How did you know he was that ill?"

"Phoebe told me."

"I don't think he'll make it to Christmas."

"I'm so sorry."

"Me too." He paused for a moment and I knew he wanted to change the subject so I didn't respond and let him lead the conversation. "Tell me about your day."

"Let's see, I talked to you, read, had a moment of panic, talked to Sarah, went for a walk, and read some more. Then I watched Darla and Henry fight, had dinner with your parents, and now I'm talking to you. The day seems to have come full circle, hasn't it?"

"A moment of panic?" After I said it, I had hoped he hadn't heard that part. It was probably just as well. He needed to know where I was coming from.

"Yeah. Can you believe Michael and Sarah were actually placing bets as to how long I'd last before losing my mind here?"

"Would you believe Kelly, my assistant, won the office's pool?"

I couldn't help but to laugh. "Honey, did I really need to know that?"

"I guess not. I just wanted to hear you laugh. And I like it when you call me Honey."

Chapter Ten

Tuesday morning I headed over to the production building. As I was walking in Henry raced up beside me.

"Good morning."

"Hey Henry, what's up?"

"Running late. Listen, I'm sorry about last night. Darla was being, well, Darla."

"Don't worry about it. Is that why you're late? Patching things up with her?"

"No, we made up late last night. I overslept. Then I had to go by the bank for the winery."

"You've been to Willow Creek and back already this morning?" Something didn't sit right with him going to the bank for the winery, but I'd have to think about why.

"I ran a few other errands too. I guess that's the nice thing about being the owner's son. No one will fire me if I'm late."

Henry and I were both laughing when Alex came up to greet us.

"Henry, what do you think it would take to get Senior to hire Cassandra to work here?"

Henry and I responded in unison. "And do what?"

"I don't know. A sales rep, tour guide, eye candy. She's bound to be smart enough to do something."

I fell into laughter as Henry explained what he knew of my education to Alex and the poor guy was more embarrassed with each passing word. I felt bad for him. I knew how much I hated to embarrass myself, so I regained my composure and tried my best to make him feel better.

"Today, though, it seems you're the professor and I am the student," I said.

"Guys, I'll see you later. I've got some paperwork to do." Henry headed off to his office and Alex and I moved toward the same machinery Vivian showed me Friday. As we walked, Alex struck up a conversation.

"The winemaking process is really quite simple," he said.

"If it's so simple, why doesn't everybody make it themselves, like they make iced tea?"

"Okay, the making of it is simple; the supplies are a little pricy." He smiled and continued. "You know how the grapes are harvested. Then they're brought here to the production rooms."

"What kind of time frame do you have before the grapes are compromised in any way?"

"Well, it depends on a lot of factors. Temperature, storms, mostly weather-related stuff. I like to see the grapes in here within the hour. That's why we use such small bins to move them. The harvesters, at least the professional ones, work fast so that the harvest comes in at a rate that doesn't alter the sugar content. Once they're here, they go straight to the conveyor belts that lead to the destemmer & crusher machine."

Alex showed me how the destemmer/crusher worked. The one they had, while small, was state of the art. It was programmed electronically to either dispose of the skins and seeds for white wine or allow them to remain in order to make red wine.

"I've been trying to convince Senior to buy another one of these. It would balance out our equipment ratios better and utilize the rest of the supplies at Thomas Hall more efficiently."

"Allowing for Thomas Hall to use not only all of your own grapes but other vineyards grapes, upping your total output."

"Exactly."

"Why does Senior have a problem with that?"

"He's always coming up with one excuse or another," Alex said. "I think the winery's got some money troubles, but he won't tell me about them."

"What makes you think that?"

"I'm sure you've heard about the bottle fiasco."

"Yeah, it's too bad too. The final product's beautiful."

"Thanks. I took the fall for those bottles, but it was Senior who approved and ordered them. He was worried about the bottom line our first year out with a champagne and thought it would be best to order cheap bottles. He needed to save face in the local wine community, and since I'm young and people think I'm inexperienced, I told him I'd take the blame."

"Weren't you worried about your reputation? Your career?"

"Not really, Senior promised me I'd have a job here as long as I wanted. Anyway, back to the tour. From the destemmer/crusher, it's off to the steel tanks."

We walked toward the tanks as he continued his winemaking for the house-guests' tour. I was bored. He was telling me things I already knew. I wanted more: more substance, more information, more hands-on, but I wasn't getting it. Alex sensed my dissatisfaction with his explanation and stopped as we arrived at the towering stainless steel vats.

"Cassandra, why did you come here today? You know everything I'm telling you already."

"I told you, I wanted to learn more about how the winery works, but in more detail."

"I don't think so. It sounds good in theory, but—" Alex leaned into me until my back was pressed against the cold, metallic cylinder of the first settling vat. He leaned against the vat with one hand and pressed both his body and his lips against mine. It took a second for me to process Alex's advances, but when I did, I pushed him away. While it wouldn't have taken much force, I used all my strength and he tumbled back for a few steps.

"Alex, I think you've misunderstood my intentions! I am only interested in learning about winemaking. I'm sorry if I gave you the wrong impression."

He straightened his shirt and looked at me. "I'm sorry, you're right, I obviously misunderstood. But you just look like you're so infatuated with, oh wait, I should have known. This is about Edward, isn't it?"

I bit my bottom lip and looked at my feet. "Is it that obvious?"

"Does the sunrise in the East?" He pushed his hand against my chin until I was staring him in the face. What is it with these Virginia men and eye contact?

I could feel my face heating up. "Great. So basically all I have to do is wake up now?"

"Yeah, I just hope for your sake, some conceded ladies man doesn't assume it's all about him." His self-deprecating humor was his saving grace. I laughed at his statement and patted him on the back.

"It's okay, really."

"Do me a favor though, don't tell Edward. I'm certain I'd be a dead man."

"Under one condition, teach me about how to make wine."

Alex was true to his word. He taught me so much about the business of winemaking that I thought my brain would overload. Of course, he still took every opportunity possible to make friendly passes at me. His interest in me originally was more sexual than educational but he turned out to be a fine teacher.

Throughout the day, I found myself seeing or hearing things that would remind me of Edward, which was weird since we never were in the production building together. I'm not the type of person to mentally drift, so I was shocked to find myself pining over him and not paying attention to what Alex was trying to teach me.

It was about nine-thirty in the morning when I met up with Alex and the next time I looked at my watch in was ten minutes before six. There was no time to shower and change before dinner.

I loved showering at Edward's place. The smell of the Irish Spring soap in the bathroom reminded me of him. The day before I had spent so long in the shower, daydreaming about Edward, that I actually ran out of hot water.

I used the bathroom at the warehouse to wash my hands and face and redo my hair. I thanked Alex for a wonderful day, grabbed a golf cart and headed to the main house.

While I had no intentions of being treated like a houseguest, I enjoyed having dinner with Vivian and Senior on what appeared to be turning into a daily basis. Not necessarily for the food, although it was delicious, but for the conversation.

Vivian told me about the nosy ladies in her bridge club who, first thing that morning, pumped her for information about me. Apparently there were several ladies at the country club who were worried I might be a gold digger and Edward was foolish enough to fall for my act. Thank goodness neither Vivian nor Senior believed that for a moment. She also told me about her weekly lunches with her crazy sisters and was certain I should join them sometime soon.

Senior and I talked about the winery. I asked him more about annual fluctuations in production levels, distribution of product, and sales factors. I could tell he was enjoying our conversation, but physically he was weaker than he was the day before. I had never seen anyone battle a terminal disease and appreciated the fact that my parents had died relatively quick deaths instead of the long suffering Senior was enduring.

At about eight, I excused myself to head toward Edward's house. This evening it was Vivian who stopped me.

"In a hurry, dear? You aren't going back to the production building with Alex, are you?" I knew she wasn't a fan of his and I think she was worried Alex could sweep me off my feet and steal me away from Edward.

"Oh no, I'm exhausted. It's just that I haven't heard from Edward all day and I'm hoping he'll call me sometime in the next half hour like he did last night." And like magic, my phone started ringing. Vivian smiled.

"Say goodnight to my son for me dear."

"I will. Goodnight Miss Vivian." I answered the phone. "Hi Honey."

"Thanks, but I don't think I'm the *Honey* you were expecting." It was Sarah.

"I was expecting Edward."

"I figured as much, but Honey? Gross! Anyway, I'm actually trying to track him down. Have you talked to him today?"

"No, but I will. What's up?"

"Remember the problem with the winery's books?"

"Yeah and I think I know what's going on too." I had thought about it off and on throughout the day. "The problem isn't with the checks is it? It's the physical withdrawals."

"Okay, C.C.," Sarah was agitated that I already knew independently of her. "How did you figure that out?"

"Henry was late at the warehouse today because he had to go to the bank on winery business. If a firm like yours is handling the books, no one from the winery should ever need to go to the bank. Henry's skimming, isn't he?" I asked.

"You're good. I just confirmed everything you said with the bank a few hours ago. I just don't know what to do now. I know I should call Senior, but—."

"Don't. Talk to Edward instead. Senior's not doing well. But tell me this, Sarah, why would a Baker embezzle from a Baker?"

"That's what I want to talk to Edward about."

"We've been talking a couple of times a day so I should hear from him soon."

"A couple of times a day?" She asked.

"Yes."

"Can I ask you something?"

"You've never asked my permission before."

"I know I joked around last week about Edward being 'Mr. Right' but you don't think he could be the one, do you?" I was fed up with Sarah's attitude where he was concerned and wanted some answers.

"Why don't you like Edward?"

"I do. Really. I'm just worried he's going to break your heart."

"What do you know that I don't?"

Sarah paused and I knew she had something to say that I wouldn't like. "Damn it, C.C. I don't know. He's just so different." She was stalling, wanting to say something more, but wouldn't.

"What do you mean, different?"

"So serious."

He was serious. It was one of the many things I liked about him. "And smart, and sweet, and funny, and caring, and sexy, and —"

"And rich. Wait a minute! Did you just say sexy?" Sarah asked.

"Maybe."

"Okay, don't get mad, but I've got to ask. Did you sleep with him?"

"No."

"But …"

"I've been thinking about it, a lot."

"Holy shit!" I could hear Sarah exhale on the other end of the line. "C.C., you need to have the talk with him."

"The no sex before marriage talk? We already –"

"No, the when was your last HIV test and birth control discussion."

I could feel my face getting hot. "Sarah, seriously?"

"Yeah, seriously," she said.

"How do you even start that conversation?"

The call-waiting on my cell phone beeped in. "Hey, that's probably Edward on the other line. I'll have him call you." I disconnected Sarah before she could say anything else.

"Hi, Beautiful."

"I missed you today," I said.

"That's promising. What did you do?"

I arrived at the house just as he said 'hi'. I kicked my shoes off by the door, walked into the master bedroom and sprawled across the bed while we were talking.

"Learned what makes Thomas Hall wines so wonderful."

"Spent the day with Alex, huh?" Edward didn't sound excited.

"Yeah. I had done some reading on the subject but I was still surprised how much chemistry is involved in the making of wine and how many possible combinations of variations there are in the process. I think I like geography better. You draw a line, call it a road, and it's a road. Cartography is definitely a more concrete field."

"My dad says that's what makes wine an art. Interpretation combined with science." I could tell by the tone of his voice he was happy with the interest I was taking in his father's business and the fact I didn't say Alex's name once seemed to make it clear I had no interest in him whatsoever.

"Speaking of the winery, Sarah needs to talk to you about the books."

"Did she tell you what's going on?" As he was speaking I thought about the conversation Sarah told me I needed to have with Edward and lost track of our current discussion. "Cassandra, are you there?"

"Hmm? Yeah, I'm sorry. She told me the night of the party and we both figured it out today. I don't think she should talk with your dad about it though, so call her."

"I will. Something's distracting you. What is it, my love?"

"Just a weird conversation I had with Sarah earlier."

"What did she say?"

"You really want to know?" I was really hoping he didn't care.

"Yes. She's your best friend and now you've got me worried."

"She said we needed to have a talk about blood tests and birth control. And please don't ask how it came up in conversation. My face is already redder than a stoplight."

Edward burst into laughter at the other end. "She's right. We should have that conversation. But Sweetie, you are the only person I know who can actually blush over the phone."

He was still laughing as he continued. "I tell you what, I'll start. My last blood test came back clean in June. The company offers them twice a year to their employees for free and I try to set a good example."

"Mine was the December after Tony died."

"That wasn't so bad now, was it? I still find it amazing though that you haven't been with anyone since he died. Anyway, next topic: birth control."

"Edward, I'm Catholic. As in the Church doesn't believe in birth control Catholic."

"So there really is no discussion about that then." I could tell he was smiling as he spoke. "See, you didn't even die of embarrassment."

"I'm really lousy at this relationship thing, aren't I?"

"No, you're just learning."

"Thanks." He knew exactly what to say to make me feel better. "You sound tired tonight."

"It was a long, boring day and my mind kept wandering," he said.

"Wandering where?"

"You have to ask? My mind's been wandering to wherever you are for the last four months."

I made arrangements the night before with Victor to have someone drive me into town Wednesday morning for Mass but was pleasantly surprised to find he was the driver. Apparently, Vivian was concerned that if the press got wind that I was out and about, the potential of a media circus could ensue and I might need help.

About halfway into town, Victor's cell phone rang. I could only hear his half of the conversation but I could tell someone he cared about needed money and Victor was trying to reassure the person on the other end of the phone that he would do what he could.

After he hung up I thought I'd see if there was anything I could do to help.

"Victor, I don't mean to pry, but is everything all right?"

"Thank you for asking Cassandra." I could tell the phone call had left him shaken. "It seems my son is having some financial issues. I'm hoping the bank can help. I have an appointment with a loan officer this morning after Mass."

"Victor, if you need money, I have a little you could borrow."

He took a quick moment to look over at me while he drove. "That's sweet, but unless 'a little' is in the upper six figures, I'm afraid it won't do."

I was taken aback by the large sum of cash he needed. I wondered exactly what kind of trouble his son had gotten into. "I'm afraid I can't help you with quite that much."

He was the type of man who would never ask anyone for a loan, let alone go to Senior and Vivian. Plus, I was pretty sure he knew about the winery's financial issue. Not much got past Victor.

"Thank you anyway. You know, you're quite a remarkable woman. You barely know me and yet you were willing to give me anything within your means. Who taught you that?"

I had never really thought about it. Offering him the money seemed like the right thing to do. "I guess my Mom and Dad. They were very generous with their time and money when they were alive, especially where I was concerned."

"Parents will do anything for the sake of their children. Even if they know it's not the smart thing to do." I could tell Victor really didn't want to take out the loan he was about to ask for from the bank but knew it had to be done.

"Are your parents the reason for your religious conviction as well? I know Edward asked me to prepare his room at the main house for the weekend. I thought it was an odd request at first, but I think I'm starting to understand."

"It seems most of the Baker Family were surprised by that. But to answer your original question, my strong religious ties started after my parents died."

Mary Magdalene Catholic Church was a small brick building with a chapel, six classrooms, a central office, and an office for the presiding priest. However, the area's small Catholic population did not come close to fully utilizing its capacity.

Victor and I made up a third of the weekday morning's congregation. I have always enjoyed Mass, but this one was special. It had been a long time since I had attended a mass in a language I understood and the small space gave it an intimate feel that drew me closer to God.

After mass, Victor gave me his cell phone number and told me to stay in town as long as I wanted since he had enough to do to keep busy until after two in the afternoon. He offered to drive me to wherever I wanted to go in town on his way to the bank. It was a beautiful morning though, so I chose to walk and sent him on his way.

I left the church and walked the two blocks to Main Street and stepped into the town's only coffee shop. A young guy behind the counter greeted me and asked for my order.

"I'd like a chai tea latte. Can I get that iced?"

"Sure. What size?" He said.

"Large, please. Oh, do you have non-fat milk for that?"

"Sure." The guy taking my order kept staring at me. "Um, this is kinda embarrassin' to ask, but ya wouldn't happen to be Cassandra Martin?"

"Yes. Do I know you?" I handed him a five to cover the bill, and he handed it back to me.

"Mr. Baker, Jr. asked me to charge your bill on his tab, Ma'am. I'm afraid I can't take your money."

I wondered how he knew I would come here. I put the five in the tip jar and thanked the young lady who handed me my drink and continued on my way.

I stopped at the drug store for a few essentials including deodorant, razor blades, and a new toothbrush. Edward had set up an account for me there as well. I was a little unnerved by the thought that he could have called every store in town and made these arrangements.

When I left the drug store I decided to head to Zoe's Boutique in hopes of getting some answers and having a nice visit with the owner. As I walked the four blocks, I became aware that I was not alone. The more I walked, the more people joined my pace. About a block in, I realized that it was the same reporters and photographers from the day of the Harvest Ball. The further I walked, the worse things got, and I picked up my pace. I reached Zoe's just as she was unlocking the door to open the shop. She let me in, left the closed sign up, and locked the door behind me.

"Zoe, you're always providing a safe haven for me. What would I do without you?"

"Get your picture taken a lot more often?" Zoe smiled. She had an amazing smile that could light up a room.

"Very funny. I came to do some shopping, but I should probably go. I'm sure this is only hurting your business."

"Are you kidding me? The last time you were here my business doubled the next day. I expect it will again tomorrow."

"Does the whole town feel that way?" I asked.

Zoe's smile changed and it gave me my answer before she spoke. "No, not really. The hotel and restaurant owners are enjoying the extra business, but most of the retailers think the press is annoying and obtrusive."

Zoe kept the shop closed for me and called Victor while I roamed about the shop, picking up several things to round out my wardrobe, including a few more of the nightgowns that Edward found so appealing the night of the party. When I was done, Zoe bagged my new clothes. I waited for her to write out the ticket and give me the total. Zoe looked at me, perplexed.

"Didn't Edward tell you? He set up an –"

"Oh no. Not here too." Most women would have loved this gesture and gone crazy shopping, which would have been easy to do at Zoe's. However, I'd never liked the idea of others spending money on me. I wasn't wealthy by any means but always seemed to have enough to cover my own needs. And I enjoyed that independence. I pulled out my cell phone and dialed Edward.

"Hey, Beautiful."

"Don't you 'beautiful' me. Why isn't it possible for me to spend any of my own money in Willow Creek?"

I could hear Edward trying to hide his amusement. "I didn't want you to worry about anything this week."

"I can buy my own clothes, Edward."

"You're at Zoe's?"

"Yes, and so is the paparazzi," I replied with disgust.

"Oh Cassandra, I'm sorry." He was no longer laughing and I could tell he sincerely meant his apology. "I know how you feel about that. I could probably get a restraining order to keep them away if you'd like. We'll simply claim they're stalking you."

"No, it would just make them even crazier. And quit changing the subject. If I had known you'd set up an account here, I wouldn't have spent so much money."

"Don't worry, I've got it covered."

I could tell this wasn't a big deal to him and it had been a thoughtful gesture. So I conceded. "You're not going to let me argue with you about this money thing, are you?"

"Nope, but I've got to go. I love you, Sweetie and I'll call you later."

I hung up the phone and shook my head. Zoe smiled.

"He can more than afford it, you know."

"Are you sure?"

Zoe laughed as she responded. "Cassandra, he's a very wealthy man. Didn't you know that?"

"You're not the first person who's made that comment."

As I was speaking, we were interrupted by a knock at the door. Zoe walked over while I stayed back at the register and lifted the shade before opening the door. In the two seconds the door was open, it seemed a thousand flashes from cameras went off. When the door closed, Victor was sandwiched between two huge men.

Victor introduced the two men as Brick and Bubba. Brick held out a business card and I took it. B&B Personal Security Experts, Thaddeus "Brick" Jones. Both men were giants. Brick was the shorter of the two, standing at about six foot four. Collectively the two men had to weigh around six hundred pounds, but it was hard to tell if the weight was muscle or fat due to the way they were dressed. They wore dark suits, white dress shirts, black ties, and dark shades.

Edward had called them after we hung up and hired the guys to handle security the rest of the day. I would have protested, but I knew at his advanced age, Victor was in no position to be of any help to me. I realized he should have been at the bank and not standing in front of me.

"Victor, aren't you supposed to be at an appointment?"

"I was just finishing up when Zoe called." The look on his face indicated that things had not gone well. "I do have some other business to attend to though, so I'll leave you in the hands of B&B." He gave me a small smile, then turned and walked out into the sea of cameras.

I was done in town by one and the B&B boys drove me back to Thomas Hall. I thanked them both for everything and told them they could go. But they were insistent on checking Edward's house before leaving.

The entire place had been turned upside down. The furniture was turned over, dishes pulled out of the cabinets, and tables and drawers cleared with their contents all over the floor. Surprisingly though, nothing was missing. It looked like a robbery, minus actual theft. On the bathroom mirror, the words *Leave Now Bitch* were written in lipstick; and not in any shade I owned.

I called the main house and Vivian answered the phone. I explained to her what happened and that Brick and Bubba were insistent on my calling the police. It was Edward's house, though and while I didn't know what to do, I didn't want to worry Edward. A few minutes later, Vivian arrived at Edward's villa with a cleaning crew and thanked Bubba and Brick for their help, and dismissed them, telling them she would deal with the issue of the police.

Vivian had me return to the main house for the afternoon and stay for dinner before retiring to Edward's for the evening. She and I were both confident that the destroyed house was nothing more than an angry shopkeeper who felt the media's presence was hurting their business. There wasn't anyone else around I could think of who would want me gone, and nothing was taken or broken, minus a couple of light bulbs. I agreed with Senior and Vivian that calling the police would stir the press even more and that was the last thing I needed. By the time we finished dinner, Edward's house was not only put back together but cleaner than it had been when I left that morning for Mass.

Chapter Eleven

I woke up Thursday morning to the smell of coffee and soft jazz playing on the radio in the kitchen. Why was there coffee brewing? I didn't drink coffee. Edward! I looked at the clock. It was nine. He was early, about eight hours early. I quickly brushed my hair and teeth and slipped on my jade robe over the coral-colored nightgown I had slept in. I felt the excitement of the day begin to build inside me. The day was ours, just ours. No groups of people to entertain, no parties to attend. It was the time Edward had asked for and the day I had thought about all week with longing.

"Good morning Sweetie."

"You're early. What a nice surprise."

He walked over and held me tight, buried his head into my hair, and took a deep breath. Then he slowly began dancing with me to the music on the radio. As the song finished, the whistle on the tea kettle began to blow.

"Why don't you have a seat and I'll make your tea. I do try to pay attention to details like that."

The kitchen table was set for breakfast and in the center was a vase with two-dozen long-stemmed red roses. I leaned in and inhaled the scent of the freshly cut flowers, sat at the table, and smiled.

"Really, then were you paying attention last night when I was upset that you didn't return my call? I hate talking to voicemail."

"Yeah, about that, I'm sorry. I didn't see the voicemail notice on my phone until almost midnight and I don't like to call after ten."

A couldn't believe he thought I was serious and started to giggle. "You know, I'm just teasing you. I know you won't always be available to me. The roses are beautiful. Thank you."

"You're quite welcome, but I wish I could be available to you twenty-four seven. I'm sorry about the craziness yesterday. Why didn't you call me about the incident here at the house? I didn't like hearing it from Bubba."

"Sorry. I didn't want to worry you." It hadn't occurred to me that Bubba would call him with a report.

"I figured as much. I just wish I had been here to protect you."

"I was fine. And you did protect me. You sent Brick and Bubba. Besides waking up to you here, makes it worth the trouble." He sat my tea on the table and leaned over to kiss me as I heard the toaster pop.

I worked hard to restrain my thoughts of dragging him straight to the bedroom. His lips seemed to have that effect on me. While I had made a conscious decision not to have sex outside of marriage, the thought had definitely crossed my mind more than once since I had met Edward. I pulled myself away from the thoughts that seemed to be delivered with each of his kisses.

"So what should we do today? After all, today is the reason you asked me to stay."

"What do you like to do on a date?"

"Good question. I don't know. I haven't been on a date since before Tony and I were married."

Edward returned to the kitchen and was spreading the jam across my toast. "You mean to tell me you haven't even been on a single date in –"

I cut him off in order to avoid actually having to figure out how long it had been. "A long time? No."

He walked over and gently placed the toast in front of me. "Would you like me to fix you some eggs or something to go with the toast?"

I smiled and looked at him, "No, this is perfect. Thank you. But where's your breakfast?"

"Oh, I ate a couple of hours ago." I assumed he grabbed something at the airport. He sat down next to me and continued our date discussion. "Well, let's see. We could fly to Paris for dinner, catch a show in New York, spend a day on the beach in St. Thomas, anything you want."

Edward's suggestions weren't dates, they were vacations. While they all sounded amazing, it was a bit extreme for a first date.

"I was thinking something more local, at least for a first date."

"You're the only woman in the world I know who'd turn down those options for a night in Willow Creek." He smiled and shook his head. "I guess we could go to dinner and see a movie. I haven't been to a movie in ages. I wonder what's playing at the theaters. There's more than one. The one behind City Hall on Elm Street does all the first-run movies and the old Egyptian Theater on Main Street does a dinner and movie thing. They show older movies and sometimes do movie marathons."

"The latter sounds good to me if there's something decent playing. The lower the profile we can keep in Willow Creek, the better."

While we were talking Edward opened the local paper. It only came out once a week, on Thursdays, and he had the latest edition in his hand. He held the paper arms length away and squinted in order to see without his glasses.

"Looking at the front page of the Lifestyles section, I think you're right."

He handed me the paper and I took a look. 'Jr.'s New Lover & Her Tragic Past'. If the title wasn't bad enough, the picture was one of Edward and me under the willow tree at the moment he untied the strap on my dress.

I could feel my face turning red but I wasn't blushing. I was angry and upset. I buried my head in my hands and shook it back and forth. "I can't do this, Edward. Maybe you're used to this kind of public life, but I'm not. My life is way too full of scandal and tragedy for the kind of press exposure you seem to attract. I think that I should just pack my things and go."

I stood and Edward jumped up to stop me from moving.

"Oh no, you're not. I haven't spent the last four months looking for you to let you disappear now." He had grabbed both of my wrists in a gentle but commanding way. Most people wouldn't have thought twice about it. But when I froze with fear, he knew he had done something wrong. He softened his voice.

"Cassandra? What just happened?"

I tried to speak, but nothing came out of my mouth.

"Sweetie, talk to me. Did I do something to scare you? You look terrified."

"Please. Let go of, of my, wrists." I closed my eyes and tried to breathe.

He looked down at his hands, not even aware of the fact he had been holding me by them. He immediately moved his hands away from mine, wrapping them around my waist, and pulled me in closer to him.

Edward had grabbed my wrists the same way Tony always held my arms, just before he would hit me. I wasn't prepared for the effect it would have on me.

"Oh God, Sweetie. I'm so sorry. I didn't realize that it would … Oh hell, I'm such an idiot."

"No, you're not. I didn't know it would bother me either. It's okay. I'm better now." But I really wasn't. I took a deep breath and tried to push the memory of Tony out of my head and plastered on my best fake smile. "What were we talking about?"

"The newspaper. Look, don't worry about it. In a week, this will all blow over."

"No, it won't. It never does." The smile on my face melted away and I fought off the urge to burst into tears as my anger with the press seemed to want to manifest itself that way. I buried my head in Edward's chest.

"Trust me. The paper's not as bad as it looks. It's really a nice picture of you."

I turned my head and looked at the picture again. "Edward, it makes me look like, well, a—."

"A beautiful woman in love?"

I was so frustrated with the article and the picture that I found myself sounding like a nine year-old girl who wasn't getting her way. I stomped my right foot and said, "I hate you."

Edward smiled. "No, you don't. You love me, and you know it."

I paused, took a deep breath and blew it out. "You're right. I don't hate you. I'm just so frustrated with the whole press thing. Can't you just buy the newspaper and shut it down?" I knew my request was ridiculous, but his answer surprised me.

"Unfortunately, no. We've tried to buy the local paper before, but the family who owns it will have no part in selling it."

He pulled me even closer and kissed me like he had the first time he brought me to his house. I could feel my heart beating faster and the heat generated between us made my temperature quickly rise. When the two of us reached the point of stop now or losing all control, Edward looked at me.

"So, what are we going to do today?"

"Not that," I said half-heartedly as I tried to catch my breath.

Edward curled his lips up into one of those sexy little grins of his. "You can't blame a guy for trying." He let go of me, picked up the paper, and opened it to the movie listings. "The dinner and movie theater is doing an Agatha Christie Marathon starting tonight."

"I love Agatha Christie, but maybe we should just stay at the winery today." I took a bite of my toast, attacking it as if it were the press.

"No. If you want to go to the movies, we'll go and have a great time. If you're worried about the press or the town gossips, I'll rent out the whole theater for us."

I could tell Edward was serious. This relationship was becoming far too complicated for me. I turned and walked back to the bedroom. Every fiber of my being was yelling, 'Run. Run now.' But my heart was saying, 'Stay.' I opened the closet and looked at the clothes. Do I pack them or wear them? Do I listen to my heart or my head?

Edward had followed me back to the bedroom and leaned against the door frame with his arms folded. He could tell I was contemplating whether to stay or go.

"Sweetie, please tell me you're just trying to figure out what to wear today."

"Sure, of course." I think he believed it about as much as I did. "You know, New Zealand's really nice this time of year. It's springtime there." Edward walked past me and took the white shirt I had worn to dinner the first night at

Thomas Hall and laid it on the bed. Next, he went through and pulled out an above-the-knee forest green skirt that Zoe had talked me into the day before.

"I'll dress you myself if I have to. You promised me a date, remember?" I thought about letting him for a brief moment. I knew if he attempted to dress me that I would end up spending the rest of the day naked and would never want to leave this house again. But I wasn't ready to share a bed with him, at least not yet.

"Fine, I'll get dressed. Then we'll have lunch with your parents before we head into town. They're expecting me in a little bit and I'm sure they'll be happy to see you."

"They were happy to see me when I got in at midnight."

I turned and looked at him as I pouted. I was surprised to find I was upset he had arrived last night and I didn't know.

"And you didn't come to see me then?" I had been awake until at least two-thirty and I know I had the lights on because I was reading Janet Evanovich's latest book.

"Cassandra, if I had come down here last night, I wouldn't have been able to control myself. I stayed away for your well-being, not mine."

Edward pushed the robe off my shoulders, letting it cascade to the floor. He leaned down and kissed my shoulder, wrapping a finger around the thin strap of my nightgown. He slid it off until it draped over my upper arm. And he kissed his way across my collar bone to the other shoulder. I leaned my head back and closed my eyes. His lips pressed against my skin was exactly what I wanted, what I needed.

He started to slide the second strap to the edge of my shoulder but then stopped and put it back. My body released waves of both disappointment and desire that caused me to hold my breath for a moment.

"Why did you stop?"

"Because you told me we weren't doing that today."

I had convinced Edward not to rent out the whole theater but had conceded to letting him hire Brick to be our driver for the evening, just in case there was a problem. The first movie didn't start until four-thirty, so after Edward bought our tickets and made arrangements for a private balcony table, we went for a walk in town, with Brick always close by.

While the press and paparazzi were visible, they kept their distance on this occasion. They had no problems attacking when I was alone, but the combination of Brick and Edward seemed to be what it took to keep from being mobbed.

I poked my head into Zoe's boutique and said hi. She was busy helping teenage girls pick out Homecoming dresses. When the girls saw me, they all stopped and looked at one another. They had obviously seen the picture in the newspaper. Zoe gave me a hug and waved outside to Edward, who smiled and waved in return. He had remained outside to talk to an elderly man who had retired from Thomas Hall a few years earlier. They were catching up on family, friends, and town gossip. I didn't stay to visit with Zoe as she was busy but told her I'd call her later.

Then we walked past the jewelry store. Edward smiled and tried to lead me in, but I stood in the doorway and shook my head from side to side in protest.

"Honey, that's really not necessary."

"I know, but it'll make me happy, so indulge me, okay?"

"You know, I've never let a man buy me jewelry before."

"Never?" I knew what he was asking. Tony had never bought me jewelry. Not even a wedding band.

"Never."

Edward took my hand and held the door with the other as he led me inside. "Then, Sweetie, you're way overdue."

It was around ten-thirty when we returned to Edward's house from the movies, and I was still wearing the diamond earrings he bought me earlier that day when I went into the kitchen to pour us each a glass of wine. I couldn't help but play with them while we watched *Murder on the Orient Express* and *Ten Little Indians*. Every time I looked at Edward that evening, I would find him staring at me and smiling. He may not have been to the movies in ages, but I am certain he didn't see a moment of either feature. I know I missed a few scenes myself as I found myself making out with him, as if we were a couple of high school kids hiding out in the dark theater balcony. His kisses were always so inviting and intoxicating that I couldn't resist. There were still two more movies scheduled to play that evening, but I could tell Edward was tired, so I convinced him we should call it a night.

When I opened the refrigerator, the only wine in there was a half-empty bottle of Pinot Noir and I was in the mood for something lighter.

"Honey, do you think your mom and dad would mind if I popped over to the main house and grabbed a few bottles of wine for your place?"

Edward smiled, "You know they won't mind. Why don't I walk with you?"

We strolled down the rocky path to the main house. It wasn't a far walk but the way the trees and houses were positioned, it was impossible to see the main house from Edward's cottage.

It was a beautiful evening. A light breeze caused the leaves on the vines to flutter as the half-moon shone bright enough to guide us along the path. I loved walking the path on nights like this. Every star in the universe seemed visible in the sky. My star-gazing was interrupted by Edward.

"Sweetie, do you like it here?"

"At Thomas Hall? How could I not?"

"Good, because I was hoping you'd stay a little longer."

I knew he would ask this question before the weekend was out. I had thought about it a lot. I hated the press and all the attention that went with it. Edward was so used to it that I don't think he realized the stress it caused me. But as aggravated as I was with the press, I was just as infatuated with him, and I was completely in love with the winery. Besides, there was nowhere else I had to be.

It was the beauty of the life I had chosen to live for the last year. It gave me the freedom to keep exploring, whether it was a city or country I had never seen or the potential of finding someone to share my life with, although I had never allowed myself to explore that option before now.

Somehow we were already standing inside the foyer of the main house. It seemed like a much longer trip when I walked it by myself. The floors of the foyer were solid marble and so well cared for that when the chandelier was on, the light reflecting off the floor lit the hall like it was the middle of the day. The only light this evening was the moonlight and it gave the room a soft, romantic glow.

I was just about to address his request to stay when his cell phone rang.

"God, I hate this thing." He answered the phone in a way that made it obvious he was annoyed. "Hold on." He looked at me and smiled, "Why don't you go down to the cellar and get the wine and I'll work this out with Kelly." We both knew his assistant wouldn't be calling him here, at this time of night, unless something crucial needed attending to.

I walked toward the kitchen and found the door to the wine cellar. I flipped the light switch only to remember it hadn't worked for Vivian the weekend before. I carefully walked down the spiral, wrought-iron staircase in the dark. I flipped on the switch at the bottom of the stairs and it turned on the dim lights at the base of the cellar.

I took two steps and nearly slipped on the wet floor. As I regained my footing I saw Senior lying face down in the middle of a huge puddle. His arms were down beside his body and he was holding a crumpled piece of paper in his left hand.

I knelt down, rolled Senior over, and tried to check for a pulse. Instead, I found a gash in the side of his neck so cavernous that my two fingers slid into his neck. Then I realized the puddle on the floor was blood. We were both covered in it and I knew I was about to faint again. However, the horrible pain in the back of my head that followed was completely unexpected. When I turned to see who was attacking me, everything went dark.

Chapter Twelve

MY TIME AWAKE IN the Emergency Room that night had been brief. I drifted off thinking about how I had gotten to this point and the next time I opened my eyes I was in a different room. I could only discern that I had been moved from the ER to a regular room. There was no other bed and I was certain Edward had been insistent on a private room. He was spending way too much money on me.

Sarah and Michael were sitting next to me. I had never heard Michael sound so concerned about anyone. Sarah was trying to convince Michael not to call my uncle yet and he was certain that Fred should have been called hours ago.

"Someone literally tried to beat her to death with a wine bottle and she nearly bled out! Fred needs to know." As Michael spoke all I could think about was Senior lying on the floor in a pool of blood.

"I know, I know. But I know C.C. too. She hates for him to worry and she's going to be fine. Let's wait a couple of more hours then maybe C.C. can call him herself, okay?"

"Sarah." I tried to speak normally, but I couldn't let out more than a whisper without the feeling of sharp stabbing pain in my chest. I wasn't sure if Sarah or Michael would hear me over the sounds of the equipment running in the room and the automatic alert system in the hallway announcing a code of some nature.

"Hey, you're awake." I could hear Michael let out a sigh of relief while Sarah was talking to me.

"Where's Senior?" Michael and Sarah looked at each other then back at me. I was afraid I already knew the answer.

Edward raced into the room. I didn't have the strength to turn my head, but I heard the pace of his footsteps as he entered the room.

"You're awake. Thank God." He sat down beside the bed and held my hand. He didn't look much better than he had the night before. He was unshaven, sleep-deprived, stressed, and red-eyed. But at least he had changed his shirt.

Michael walked over to Edward. "We're gonna go get some coffee and give you two a minute alone. You want somethin' to drink?"

"No, I'm good right now. Thanks."

Michael leaned over me and stroked my hair. "We'll be back soon."

Sarah lightly kissed my cheek and when they left the room I realized I still hadn't gotten an answer to my question. "Edward, where's Senior?"

He hesitated before he spoke.

"He's dead Cassandra." It sounded like it was the first time he had verbally acknowledged his father's death and he choked a little getting the words out. "What happened down in the cellar?"

I closed my eyes and tried to remember what had happened. I randomly spoke as I recalled the night's events.

"We were walking. Your cell phone rang. I went down to the cellar and turned on the light. I saw Senior on the floor. I flipped him over and then ..."

"Yes, love."

"And then, nothing. It was dark. Then I was here."

"You didn't see anyone else in the cellar?"

"No, I turned to look but I was hit in the head before I saw anyone. I'm so sorry. I ..., I ..." I could feel tears begin to roll down my face.

"Shhh." He leaned over me and whispered into my ear. "It's okay. You need to try to stay calm." He smiled and caressed my face and neck with his hands. "I'm just so glad you're alive. The thought of losing you last night nearly killed me. I swear I will never leave you alone again."

I did my best to push back the tears. "It's okay. Really, I'll be fine."

"Marry me."

"What?" I knew I didn't hear what I thought I just had.

"I can't risk losing you again. Until I met you all I ever did was live for my work and now I see what I've been missing. When I saw you lying unconscious in that pool of blood, I thought I was going to lose my mind. I need you to marry me. You have to marry me."

"But, I've never even told you that I love you." As I spoke, I felt as if my head were in some strange fog that blurred my senses.

"It doesn't matter. I know you love me. You don't have to say it."

"Edward, your father just died and I'm pumped full of painkillers. Maybe you could ask me another time?"

"Okay. But I will ask you again. And it will be soon."

The remainder of Friday morning was a blur of falling in and out of consciousness. Every time I woke someone was sitting next to me. It was usually Edward or Sarah, but Michael, Phoebe, Alex, Zoe, and Henry were there at different times as well.

I was still in terrible pain and by lunch time the nurses had gotten approval from my doctors to hook up a morphine drip along with a second unit of blood. Apparently, I had been given one unit Thursday night. The nurses checked on me constantly while I was receiving it, as there were some concerns about allergic reactions. The red-headed nurse thought it was funny that Edward covered up the bag with part of the newspaper because he knew it would make me feel faint if I saw it.

At some point, I managed to stay awake for more than a few minutes at once. When I woke up Henry was sitting with me, feet propped up on the edge of the bed, reading a Dr. Phil book on relationships and repairing them.

"Something need fixing?"

Henry looked over the top of his book and smiled. He tried to put his feet down but I shook my head and he left them in place. He looked so much like his father. While I had only known him for a short time, I knew I was going to miss Senior.

"You're up."

"You didn't answer the question," I said as I scratched an itchy spot on my left arm, just above the location where my IV line had been inserted.

"My marriage, but what's new?" Henry closed the book and gave me his full attention. "I just don't know what to do with Darla?"

"What do you mean?" I used the controls to adjust the bed so I was sitting up, albeit at an exaggerated angle to insure I wouldn't be in pain.

"Cassandra, I don't think you need to be worrying about me. You nearly died last night."

"I know, but I'm not going anywhere. So talk to me." I rubbed the back of my right hand. It itched too.

"She just isn't a family person. I thought if she were part of my family, she'd change. I know she had it rough growing up but I was raised to think that family is—"

"Everything. It is Henry. But you can't change people. I learned both the hard way. What happened this time?"

"Mom asked us if we would come sit with you for a while. She was hoping if we did, maybe Edward would go home and get some rest. And Darla looked her straight in the face and told her she'd step foot in this hospital when hell froze over."

"Well, Darla doesn't exactly like me."

"She thinks I'm in love with you."

"But you love her, I can tell. You wouldn't put up with so much if you didn't."

"I just don't know how much more I can put up with."

"You want my two cents worth?" My face itched along with my arm and hand. I fought the urge to scratch my cheeks, but failed miserably.

"Sure, why not, I've gotten everyone else's."

"Do what's going to make you happy. Life's too short."

"That's the best advice I think I've ever gotten on the subject. I think I owe you." Henry smiled. "Itchy?"

"Yes, like I'm allergic to something." I scratched at the back of my neck.

"It's a side effect of the morphine." He buzzed the nurse and told her over the intercom of my itchy state and she brought me a couple of Benadryl.

"Since you're in my debt, Henry, you can fill me in on what's been going on."

"I don't think so. Edward has threatened anyone who says anything to upset you. And as his little brother, I know for a fact he means it when he threatens someone."

"Henry," I used the sweetest voice I could come up with. "I'll deal with him, I just need to know. Please?" I even attempted the whole batting the eyelashes thing.

"Okay. What do you want to know?" I couldn't believe he caved so easily.

"How about a timeline? Start with me being found in the cellar." I found myself scratching the top of my head. I wondered which was worse, the pain I had been in or the itching.

"Okay. When you didn't answer Edward when he called down to you in the cellar, he went to investigate. So you couldn't have been down there very long. The ambulance hauled you here at lightning speed and Dad was declared dead at the scene. I don't know all the facts but Alex was arrested and charged with Dad's murder, your attempted murder, and battery at some point overnight."

"Alex, really? Who would've thought?"

"Thought what?" It was Edward. I hadn't seen him come in as the back of my head was to the door.

I turned and answered Edward. "That Alex could possibly be responsible for Senior's death."

Edward looked at his brother and I could tell he was not a happy man. "Henry, what part of 'don't tell her anything' did you not understand?"

"But brother, she sweet-talked me."

Edward laughed at Henry and then looked down at me. "So basically you didn't stand a chance, did you?"

"Nope, but I think I'm going to take a chance with the cafeteria food. Need anything?"

"Yeah, bring me a Coke, would you?"

The itching finally began to subside and I was really high from all the pain medicine I had been given. I knew it wouldn't last so I figured I better have fun with it. "Hey Henry, I'd like a Big Mac, large fry, a chocolate shake, and two apple pies."

"I'll see what I can do!" Henry was still laughing as he left the room.

Edward sat on the edge of the bed. He didn't look nearly as good as I felt. I must have been staring at him for a long time because he finally commented on it.

"Are you staring at me because you love me or are you just that stoned?"

"Both, I think. You should get some of what they're giving me. You don't look so great." Edward smiled while I giggled.

"That's funny because you look gorgeous." When he leaned over to kiss me I closed my eyes. I don't think I opened them again for a long time.

Saturday morning, I woke to find Detective Hayes sitting beside me and reading the Washington Post. When I turned my head the other way, Edward was standing outside the door talking to a police officer who was guarding the door. The guard hadn't been there yesterday.

Something happened.

My voice was still weak but I managed to get the detective's attention. "Good morning, detective."

"Well, good mornin'. I'm sorry to bother you, but I need some information."

"I don't think I can tell you much, but I'll try."

The detective informed me that Edward told him about everything that had transpired on Wednesday and Thursday night. But what he needed to know was if I had seen anyone in my room last night. Apparently, someone had come into my room, cut the IV and oxygen lines in the room, and left a note.

"What did the note say?" I reached up to push my hair behind my ears. My earrings were gone.

"That's not important, what is important is that it was the same handwriting as the note Mr. Baker, Sr. was holding when the two of you were found."

"He was holding a note?" I closed my eyes and tried to remember everything I saw the night of the murder. Was there a note?

"Ms. Martin? Are you okay?"

I held up my left hand in such a way to let him know I was fine and just thinking. I felt a bracelet on my wrist. Not one of the plastic ones they use as an ID in the hospital, they were on my right wrist. I opened my eyes and looked down at it. It was an elegant, gold, engraved medical alert bracelet. I didn't even have to ask who was responsible. It had Edward's sense of taking care of everything written all over it.

"Detective, please tell me, what did it say?"

"Mr. Baker asked me not to tell you unless it was absolutely necessary. What I need to know is did you see anyone comin' or goin' last night?"

"I'll deal with him later. Oh, and the earrings I had on yesterday are gone."

"I remember those from the night you came into the emergency room. Those were some serious rocks. Were they real?"

"Yes, they were. I don't remember anyone outside the Bakers or the Abbotts being here."

"Your uncle was here." Edward was off the phone and was standing next to me. "He detoured through D.C. on his way to Vegas on business. I think I scared him when I called him."

"Is he still here?" I really wanted to see him.

"No, love. He told me to tell you he'd see you in a couple of days." I could feel the tears start to form in my eyes. I had always done a pretty good job of boxing up my emotions, minus nervousness and embarrassment, but the walls that held it all together were rapidly falling apart. I had never been one to cry, but it seemed like I fought the urge to do so a lot recently.

"Was I awake when he was here? Because I don't remember seeing him."

Edward knew I was about to lose it. He reached over and brushed his hand along my cheek. "No, you were sleeping. He was only here about an hour."

He looked at Detective Hayes, "Brian, I think we're done for now." I was surprised he called the detective by his first name. The detective patted the edge of my bed, then Edward's back on the way out the door.

"You're a lucky guy Edward." I'm not sure if he heard the detective's comment as he was giving me his undivided attention.

"Edward, whoever was in here stole my earrings."

"It's okay. I'll get you another pair."

"I don't need another pair. I just wanted you to know why I wasn't wearing them. I really did like them."

"God, you're sweet. You're lying in a hospital, beaten to a pulp, and you're worried about my feelings. You know I'd do anything for you."

"Good, then tell me what the note said?"

"No, not now."

"Yes, now." I wanted to be angry with him but I felt too sleepy. Edward had hit the release button on the self-directed morphine drip. "You can't drug me forever, you know."

"I know, but sleep well for now."

The most unexpected visitor of my hospital stay was Vivian, who was sitting in the chair next to my bed when I woke from a nap Sunday afternoon.

"Vivian," I said. "Why are you here? Senior's dead."

"That's why I'm here. Sitting with him wouldn't be nearly as exciting." She smiled and gave me a little wink. I liked her sense of humor.

"I'm so sorry. I wish I could remember more."

"Oh Cassandra dear, it's all right. We were all prepared for him to die. We've been preparing for Senior's passing for the last five years, not quite in this manner, but preparing nevertheless. But if I had to sit at the house a minute longer and listen to people who stopped by to check on me and make their condolences, I was going to scream. So I came here and relieved Edward. It's the first time he's been home since Thursday."

"Really?"

"The rest of the time, he's been here with you. Trying to handle business by phone, finishing up the funeral arrangements, or on the phone with the jewelers."

"Jewelers?" I looked at my wrist. "Oh yeah, the bracelet."

"Not just the bracelet but the earrings and ring too." I reached up and touched my ears. He had bought me a new pair of studs, identical to the pair that had been stolen. Then I realized Vivian had said something about a ring.

"Ring?"

"He told me he asked you to marry him."

Had he? I closed my eyes and thought. Then I remembered the conversation.

"What makes him think I'll say yes?"

"Because you love him. You know it, I know it, and he knows it. It doesn't matter whether you've ever said it aloud or not. It's obvious."

"How did you know I've never told him?"

"I didn't dear," she said.

"But –"

"Cassandra, you remind me a lot of my mother. She was a wonderful woman with a big heart. She rarely ever said the words out loud, but the people in her life always knew they were loved."

"Was Senior that way?"

Oh, no. He said it all the time." She looked thoughtfully and smiled. "Did you know that the night of the Harvest Formal, when you were walking down the staircase, Edward told his father that he was going to marry you someday very soon?"

"Really?"

"Senior liked that idea. He told me last week that he felt like you were meant to be part of the winery and the family. He was quite fond of you dear."

The pain of knowing that Senior was dead welled up inside of me and I feared the dam holding it back would burst at any moment. What happened in that cellar and why did whoever did this to Senior try to kill me? I had to find out. Then I remembered the conversation with Detective Hayes about the note. Vivian took a tissue from the box and dried away the tears that had begun to fall.

"Oh darling, I didn't mean to upset you. I just wanted you to know how Senior felt about you."

"I know. It's not that. Vivian, someone came in here Friday night and left a note. What did it say?"

"Edward asked me not to tell you. You know how men are. Anyway, the note basically said that if you were smart, you'd tell the police you saw nothing, mind your own business, and leave Thomas Hall for good. The language was a little less polite though."

"When is Senior's funeral?"

"Tomorrow afternoon, but you won't be going. The doctors said the earliest they'd consider releasing you would be tomorrow morning. I think that would be too much for you, don't you?"

"It might, but I need to go. My guess is whoever tried to kill me will be there and I want them to know I'm alive and well."

"Edward won't like this idea."

"He doesn't have to."

Chapter Thirteen

MONDAY MORNING STARTED WITH a series of fights. I fought Sarah to bring appropriate clothes for a funeral to the hospital. She didn't want to do it, claiming I wasn't well enough to go. But I threatened to tell everyone all the secrets I knew about her, so she conceded. When she arrived, she made it quite clear that she was not happy about being blackmailed and used a few obscenities to express those feelings. She understood why I wanted to go to the funeral but thought it was a terrible idea, and made certain that I understood that in no uncertain terms as well.

I fought the doctors to release me from the hospital. It was strange. Each doctor used the exact same words when they came in to examine me. They would walk into the room, look at my chart, and say "One more day would be a good idea," then leave. There was something odd about it. Dealing with them was a little easier though. I just signed an AMA Release form, basically stating that I chose to leave the hospital against medical advice.

I fought my own lack of energy to get a shower and dress myself. The two units of blood had helped speed my recovery, but my energy level was still not at the point I was used to functioning at.

By the time Edward arrived, I was exhausted, but I knew my biggest battle of the day was about to come.

"You are *not* going to the funeral and that's final!"

"I don't need your permission to go."

"You're too weak. And besides, I thought the doctors were keeping you here until tomorrow."

"How did you know that? Did you talk them into that decision?"

"Maybe. Anyway, it's not safe for you to go."

"You are impossible. Does everybody just do whatever you tell them? I seriously doubt the person who attacked me is going to make another attempt in broad daylight at Senior's funeral. So I am going and *that's* final." It was the first time I had ever stood up to a man before and I wasn't sure how long I could keep this sense of certainty up before I caved, especially in my current physical condition.

"Why? Why are you putting yourself through this? It isn't necessary!" He was yelling at me, but it wasn't out of anger. It was from frustration. I tried to calm my voice and looked into his eyes.

"Edward, it is necessary. Whoever killed your father will be at the funeral. I don't know why, but I'm certain of it. I want the person to know that I'm fine and I'm not scared."

"You sound like you're planning on hunting down Dad's killer. That's Brian's job, let him do it."

"He's not the one who almost died Thursday night. I'll do whatever I need to stop this, all of this."

"I think Detective Hayes is more qualified to handle this than you are."

"It may be his job, but it's my life and I am going to the funeral."

Edward closed his eyes, tilted his head back, and pulled on his hair with both hands. He took a deep breath and opened his eyes. I was sitting on the edge of the bed and he sat down beside me. "Okay, but we do this my way."

"What's your way?"

"You go in a wheelchair with a bodyguard and a nurse."

"Nope."

"What do you mean nope?"

"No bodyguard, no nurse, no wheelchair. But I will promise to keep Sarah and Michael with me the whole time."

"You know what? I'm not impossible, you are! There is no way you can walk the distance you'll need to walk at the cemetery." Edward looked astounded. "And you're right, no one says no to me."

"Well, get used to it. I'll probably say no a lot."

"Look. I'm just trying to take care of you. Will you please at least let me try?"

I hated the fact he was so upset. I knew he had just lost his father and I remembered how difficult the day of my parents' funeral was.

"Maybe we can compromise. I'll go with no wheelchair to the church, but I'll use one at the cemetery."

"That's not a compromise Cassandra."

"It's all you're going to get from me."

"Argh! Why are you fighting me on this? I don't want you to go at all!"

The red-headed nurse from the first night poked her head through the door. "Is she arguing with you, Mr. Baker? You know, that's a good sign she's getting better."

Edward shook his head and tried to smile. "Can't you drug her or something, Yolanda? And quit calling me Mr. Baker."

"She won't let us anymore. She was insistent on no IV pain medication from the time she woke up this morning but we've given her some pills to take home with her. I've got to go change another patient's dressing but Miss Martin finished her discharge papers before you got here so you can go whenever you're ready." She smiled and left the room. I could hear her humming as she headed down the hall.

"You know her?" I asked.

"Didn't anyone tell you? That's Darla's mom."

By the time the limo arrived at the hospital to take us to the church I was exhausted. Edward and Vivian were right. I was in no shape to do this. Just getting out of the wheelchair at the hospital and into the limo was painful. I still felt as if every move I made was like a knife jabbing into my torso. I wasn't sure I could even climb the stairs into the church. I reached into my purse and grabbed the bottle of medicine I had been given at the hospital and popped one of the little round, white Percocet pills into my mouth. Edward looked shocked that I could pop a pill so easily without water, but I think he was a little relieved that I wasn't a complete masochist.

"You sure you want to do this?"

We both knew what he meant and it had nothing to do with Senior or the killer. It was about everyone else I had lost. The death of an immediate family member is traumatic in its own right and I had lost four in a dozen years. I could feel the tears welling up in my eyes. I didn't want to cry, but I wasn't sure I could avoid it.

"Really, I'm good."

He put his hand at the base of my neck and softly kissed my forehead. When he was done he buried my head into his chest. Neither of us spoke the remainder of the trip, nor did we move. We sat in peaceful silence as we made the short trip to the church.

St. Paul's Anglican Church was the largest church in Willow Creek and it was packed beyond capacity with people spilling outside onto the streets. Along with the mourners, the press, which had doubled in size since my last media encounter, lined the sidewalk that circled the block on which the church rested.

The moment the limo door opened, the sound of camera clicks started. I knew I looked like death warmed over, but I didn't really care. As gracefully as I could, I stepped out of the limo and carefully walked up the stairs to the church, using Edward's arm for support. The reporters were all yelling questions from different directions so that you couldn't understand one question coherently. Not that I had any intention of answering a single question from the press; not now, not ever. But as I walked, I looked at every face, hoping something: eyes, a nose, birthmark, something, anything would help me remember if I saw anyone the night of the murder.

I was seated on the aisle of a crowded pew and when I looked to my right, I was sitting next to my Uncle Fred. He leaned over and hugged me tightly, a little too tightly, and I groaned.

"Sorry."

"Fred, I'm so glad you're here. I wish you didn't have to be though."

"I know Kiddo, I know. Actually, I'm surprised you came."

"I need to be here."

"For Edward?"

"Yes, but more importantly, for me. I'm sorry I missed you at the hospital."

"I wish I could have stayed longer. You seemed fine, well drugged, but fine. Edward, on the other hand, was a wreck. He's really crazy about you, you know."

"I'm glad the two of you are good friends." I paused for a moment. "Fred, he proposed to me."

I waited for a response. I waited for him to ask if Edward had lost his mind, if I had lost mine. I waited for him to say we didn't even know each other. When he responded, his answer left me stunned.

"He would make you very happy, you know. He thinks the sun rises and sets with you. I've never seen him like he's been since he met you. The question is do you love him enough to want to spend the rest of your life with him?"

"Would it be wrong for me to say I'm afraid to answer that question?"

Fred put his arm around me and hugged me again. This time more gently. "I think you just answered it Kiddo."

The church service was exhausting but it didn't last long. I'd heard it said that funerals were for the living because the dead didn't care. If that were true, I wondered why funerals left me feeling like the life had been sucked out of me and not them.

All three of Senior's children gave eulogies and each one touched on a different side of the cheerful old man who just over a week ago had welcomed me to Thomas Hall. Edward talked about how his father had always reminded him that there was more to life than work. After twenty years of listening to him, Senior had been thrilled to find Edward had finally listened to his father.

Henry talked about his father and the winery. Senior had never really enjoyed the corporate world, but had done his time in order to please Vivian's family. When the opportunity arose for him to get out of the biotech industry and follow his dreams, he focused on the winery and never looked back. Henry talked about following in his father's footsteps and was glad that his father's legacy would live on with the winery.

Phoebe was the last to speak. She spoke about growing up with Senior as their father. He had insisted on the best of everything for them but wanted them to know the simple pleasures in life. In their youth, Senior and Vivian had taken them camping, fishing, hiking, biking, and rafting. She spoke of the joy he carried with him, even in his final days, and hoped that everyone would remember him for the joy he brought to others.

As the service concluded, I realized a pit had formed in the bottom of my stomach and my neck muscles were so tight I could barely turn my head. I honestly thought attending the funeral of a non-family member would be less stressful, but I found no comfort in the knowledge that Senior was not related to me.

It had been cloudy when we arrived at the church and by the time we left, it was getting colder and darker. The weather had deteriorated so quickly that by the time we arrived at the cemetery, it was pouring rain. It was as if Mother Nature was adding insult to injury. I hated funerals. I hated the rain. I hated how they both made me feel. And I was in pain.

There was no way a wheelchair was going to get through the soft, muddy soil of the cemetery. The limo pulled up as close as it could to the gravesite and let us out. I took two steps, stopped and took a deep breath, and doubled over. Edward, who had ridden from the church with Vivian and his family, saw me bend over, and raced to help.

He helped me back into an upright position and then asked, "What happened to the wheelchair?"

Michael interceded on my behalf. "It's too muddy out here for anything with wheels."

Without a word Edward gently scooped me up and carried me to the seats under the tent at the gravesite. He sat me down in the second row, just behind his mother and took the seat next to me. Fred took the seat on the other side of me and Sarah and Michael sat behind us.

"You were right, you know. I shouldn't be doing this." I said to Edward.

"Actually, I'm impressed. You're a lot tougher than I thought. No one ever stands up to me. It will probably drive me crazy at some point, but I think I need a good dose of being told no every now and then."

"Even when you're right?"

I leaned my head on his shoulder while we waited for the graveside service to begin. As the minister began the first prayer, I looked around knowing my attacker was probably close by and most likely someone I knew from Thomas Hall.

As the graveside service continued, my thoughts traveled back in time. It seemed like yesterday I had attended my late husband's funeral. Life had been simple until Tony entered my life. After the dust settled, my life had been serene since his death too. At least for the most part. Romantic relationships made my life crazy. I looked at Edward. Did I really know anything about him? No. Did I love him? Yes. Did I want to repeat the same mistakes I had made with Tony? No. But did I really want to play my life so safe that I would always be alone?

The gravesite service was short and by the time we arrived back at Thomas Hall the rain was coming down in sheets. Vivian was having everyone to the main house for a reception afterwards. I couldn't do it though. The pain pill had long worn off and I knew if I took another one now I would fall asleep. But the pain was bad enough that I needed medication regardless of its effect. Edward had the limo drop us off at his house and sent Fred, Michael, and Sarah on to the main house.

I hadn't seen my uncle in about nine months and wanted to spend more time with him, but I needed to rest. The limo would be taking Fred to the airport in about an hour anyway. He needed to be back in Florida first thing in the morning. We promised we would see each other again before the year was out and said our goodbyes in the car.

The house had been cleaned and Victor had left a note on how to warm the dinner plates that were in the refrigerator. Edward put them in the microwave while I went in to change. But I couldn't. I hurt too much. I sat on the edge of the bed and took the long overdue Percocet, hoping it would relieve my pain.

"Edward, I need help."

He quietly walked in and looked at me. He knelt over my feet and gently took off my shoes. Then one leg at a time he rolled down my stockings, stopping only to kiss any bruise he stumbled upon. I stood up and turned around. He silently unzipped my dress and slipped it off my body. Then he unhooked my bra. I took my nightgown off the bed and slipped it over my head, pulling it down until I was covered. When I turned around he was holding my robe but I took it and laid it on the dresser. I slowly climbed onto the bed and when I looked at the clock, it said five fifteen. There was so much I wanted to say to Edward, but it would have to wait until another night.

Chapter Fourteen

I always thought it was bizarre to wake up next to someone you didn't fall asleep next to. I never got used to it when I was married. If you fall asleep alone, it makes sense you should wake up that way. Just the same, the next time I opened my eyes, I was nose to nose with Edward. The only reason I knew it was him was because the early morning light was creeping through the window and it backlit his face. Minus the tie, jacket, belt, and shoes, he was still in the suit he had worn to the funeral the day before. I thought about how handsome he was and what beautiful children we could make.

"What am I thinking? This is crazy," I whispered to myself.

He opened his eyes and smiled at me. "What's crazy?"

"I don't know. I was just talking to myself. Did I wake you?"

"No, I just woke up from a really great dream."

"I wish I could remember what I dreamt about when I sleep."

"You don't remember them at all?" He asked.

"Never, well almost never." I snuggled in closer to him. "So, tell me about your dream."

"No, I don't think so. You'll think I'm moving way too fast." He leaned down to kiss me and I playfully pushed his face away.

"No telling, no kissing."

"You're cruel." He grinned as he said it, and then looked deep into my eyes. "Okay, but you've got to promise not to freak out."

"Trust me, I won't."

"I dreamt about what our kids would be like. I wasn't even sure I wanted kids of my own until I met you and now the thought keeps popping up. Weird, huh?"

"No, what's weird is that I was just lying here wide awake wondering the same thing."

"Seriously?" Edward sat up and leaned against the headboard.

"Yeah, seriously."

"Cassandra, marry me. Just marry me, please. You know I love you. You'll never want for anything again. I can give you the world, but I need to know you're mine."

I knew the sigh I let out had been audible. I reached up as I shifted positions and pushed his hair out of his face.

"Edward, I'm scared to death of marriage. I thought I knew my late husband when we got married only to find out that I didn't know a thing. I don't really know you at all. But I don't want to be without you either." I felt torn, but Edward knew exactly what to say.

"What about a long engagement?"

This appealed to my intellectual side and I smiled. "How long?"

"I don't care. I just want to know I'm never going to lose you again. Right now I'm worried that I might show up at Thomas Hall one day only to discover that you've hopped on a plane again and left. After all that's happened here, no one would blame you, but I think it would kill me." I did not realize he was still worried about that. I knew I was not going to leave. After all, if nothing else, this whirlwind romance had taught me that life without love is a lonely existence.

"As long as you want me here, I'm not going anywhere. I promise." Then I kissed him. He had always kissed me, but it was my turn now. I took my time and enjoyed the softness of his warm, sweet lips. "But I need some time to think about this. I'll try to have an answer for you soon."

He silently stood up and walked out of the room. I sat up and dangled my feet over the edge of the bed wondering what he was up to. He came back in with a little blue box and got on one knee. "Marry me, Cassandra."

"I didn't mean this soon Edward!"

"Maybe this will help you make your decision." He opened the box to reveal a huge emerald-cut diamond set in platinum with smaller diamonds surrounding it. The center stone had to be at least five carats. I could feel a wave of shock flow through me as I looked at the ring. He was serious about marrying me.

"Edward, can you really afford this? It must have cost a fortune."

The corners of Edward's lips turned upward at the word 'afford' and broke into a full smile at 'fortune'. "Yes my love, I can more than afford this. You have no clue how much I'm worth, do you?"

"No. Should I?"

Edward began to laugh and scratched his head. "I think it's somewhere around four billion."

"Excuse me? Did you say billion?" I tried to take a deep breath and let it all sink in. But when I did breathe in, the pain was so horrible I had to lie down.

"Cassandra, are you okay?"

"It's just my ribs. I'll be fine in a second."

Edward laid down beside me, propping his head up with his hand.

"Good, I was afraid you were going to faint again."

"As long as there's no blood, I'm good."

"Cassandra?"

I knew what he was asking for, an answer. But before I could even consider everything that being married to Edward would mean, I heard the words spilling out of my mouth. "Eventually. I think. In due time."

"That's close enough to a 'yes' for me." He smiled as he took the ring out of the box and slipped it onto my finger. It was a perfect fit.

He kissed my fingers, then my hand. He meandered his way to the crook of my elbow with his lips and moved up my arm toward my collarbone and was kissing his way up my neck when his phone rang. He mumbled a few obscenities and looked at the caller ID. It was the main house.

"Hello. Hey, Henry. What was I doing? Trying to seduce my fiancée, why? Yes, that's what I said. What time? Cassandra too? Okay. Later."

Edward turned and looked at me.

"It was my brother. You and I have to be at the main house at one for the reading of the will and Mom wants us up for lunch at eleven if you feel up to it."

"Why do I need to be at the will reading?"

"Apparently Dad changed his will last week and left you something in it."

"Oh, okay," I remember Phoebe telling me at the party that her father was constantly changing his will. I looked at the clock. It was nearly eight and I was starving. Edward began kissing me where he left off on my neck. I decided I wasn't as hungry as I thought. I tried to relax and enjoy the moment, but every time I took a deep breath I was in pain. This wasn't going to work.

"Edward, can I take a rain check on this seduction when I don't feel like I've been run over by a tank?"

He looked up at me, still grinning from ear to ear. "At least you're asking for a rain check. Why don't I make you something to eat and get something for the pain? Then I'll help you get ready for the day."

Edward fixed my usual tea and toast. And some eggs, and bacon, and sliced up some cantaloupe. It was delicious and I ate it all. I hadn't really eaten anything the day before and hadn't had much of an appetite since being admitted into the hospital. As it turned out, Edward was a really good cook. I took a Percocet so it could start working before I had to shower and change. While I ate, Edward grabbed a quick shower, shaved, and put on some clean clothes. When he was done he ate a little breakfast and then followed me into the bedroom to help me get ready.

While I was in the shower, Edward went into the closet and pulled out my black slacks and a thin purple sweater I had borrowed from Sarah. He pulled out the drawers of the dresser until he found a matching pair of lace panties and bra. I know this because every drawer was still open the next time I walked into the room. I hated open cabinets and dresser drawers when I was a kid and it was still a pet peeve of mine.

When I stepped out of the shower, the Percocet had started to work and I moved a little more freely. I dried myself off and took a look in the mirror. I knew I was in bad shape but it was the first time I had seen all the damage at once. It was a frightening proposition. The bruises on my body had already started to fade but they were still visible and completely covered the right side of my torso. There was one spot where a plastic surgeon had removed the stitches the morning I left the hospital. I turned toward the mirror to get a better look at the right side of my back. I had been told a large piece of glass had ripped through my skin but I wasn't prepared for the scar I was about to see. It was a scar slightly rounder than a crescent about three inches in diameter. It was thicker in one spot which I assumed was where the cut was deepest. I took a second look at it. I really had been beaten with the bottom of a broken wine bottle. My self-examination was interrupted by the sound of Edward's voice on the other side of the door.

"Sweetie, are you all right in there?"

"Yeah, I'm just doing a little damage assessment."

"It's not that bad and the bruises will fade. You want me to come in and kiss it better?"

I wrapped myself in an oversized towel and opened the door and smiled at him. "You are a troublemaker, aren't you?!"

Edward grinned at me like a kid caught with his hand in the cookie jar. He walked with me over to the bed where I carefully sat as to keep the towel from falling off of me.

"Where would you like me to begin helping?" His smile told me exactly where he'd like to begin.

"You want to know where to begin? Go put on your shoes."

It wasn't the answer Edward expected. "My shoes?"

"Exactly. Then you can go up to the main house and drive a golf cart back for me."

"That wasn't what I had in mind." He got down on his knees and kissed me along the bottom edge of the towel, holding my hips as he worked his way across the top of my leg. As he reached the inward curve of my thigh, he slowed to bury his head between my legs, kissing one thigh, then the other. I wasn't certain where he planned to go next. I closed my eyes, leaned my head up toward the ceiling, and let out a moan of desire. I never figured out how he evoked that response from me with something as simple as a kiss. He worked his way back up my thigh and across the top of my other leg. I knew if we continued on like this we would never make it to the main house today. I exhaled, not even aware that I had been holding my breath.

"Honey, I don't think this is the best time for that." I wasn't sure if I meant because we weren't married yet or because we had to be at lunch soon so I was glad he didn't ask.

Edward laughed, knowing that I was right. He stood up as I smiled at him. He just stared at me, grinning uncontrollably.

"God you make me happy." He leaned over and nibbled on my neck. "Mmm, yummy. I'll be back soon."

After Edward left, I sat on the bed and dressed myself. When I finished dressing, I laid back and closed my eyes. It seemed like I had only been there for a second when I opened my eyes and found Edward sitting next to me. "Cassandra, Sweetie, it's nearly eleven."

When we arrived at the foyer of the main house, Vivian greeted us at the door while the other guests mingled close by. She looked tired today and understandably so. I'll never know how she managed the poise to have a houseful of people for lunch the day after burying her husband. I hadn't been anywhere close to being so composed the days and weeks after Tony's funeral.

Vivian reached out to greet me and looked at the engagement ring when she cupped her tiny hands around mine. She pulled it closer to her face to get a better look.

"Edward, dear, when I said make sure it's a nice one, I didn't mean you had to buy her the Hope Diamond."

"I wanted to give her the best ring I could get my hands on, Mom. I think Cassandra likes it, though."

Vivian turned her attention to me, smiling as she spoke but then looking more serious.

"Cassandra dear, you're not smiling. Aren't you happy?"

I wasn't aware that I had looked so serious, but I had not really thought about the fact we would be telling people we were getting married. And, well, I still wasn't one hundred percent on board with the concept. I loved Edward, but the idea of marriage scared me to no end. I managed what must have been a convincing smile and tried to address her concerns.

"Oh, Vivian, of course I'm happy. I just woke up from a nap and between that and the Percocet, I feel a little muddled."

"Well, I like the idea of having you as my daughter-in-law."

"Did I hear the words 'in-law'?" Phoebe was moving toward me with Darla following her at a break-neck pace.

"Yes, Sis, I told you I was going to marry her."

"It's one thing to say it big brother, but a whole different thing to talk her into it. Oh my God, I am so happy for you." Phoebe gave us both a hug and as she did, Darla grabbed my hand and took a good look at the ring. You could see the jealousy building in her eyes. Darla straightened her spine and looked me square in the eyes with the smuggest look she could make.

"I'm surprised, Cassandra. I really didn't think you'd marry him. I guess this means your first husband won't be the last one you bury. Maybe you can get a group rate at the funeral home for your husbands."

Vivian's response flew out of her mouth like a snake spitting venom. "Darla Baker, you should be ashamed of yourself! That has to be the most evil thing I've ever heard you say to anyone! And I've heard you say a lot of mean things to a lot of people!"

"Well, Edward is more than twenty years her senior." Darla continued to defend her comment. "What are the odds he'll outlive Cassandra?"

Before Vivian and Darla could continue, Victor announced that the first course of a three-course lunch was being served. If there had not been so many guests for lunch, I believe Vivian would have continued her scolding of Darla.

While I'm sure it was delicious, I couldn't tell you what was served. Darla's comment caused me to lose my appetite. I politely pushed the lettuce from my salad around the plate while I thought about what she said.

She was right. Minus an accident or some unexpected illness, I would most certainly outlive Edward. I had already buried three men that meant so much to me and I knew Fred wouldn't live forever either. How many more men could I bury that I loved? I had drifted off into deep thought when I realized Edward was kneeling beside me, worried, and everyone in the room was staring at me.

"Cassandra?" He was speaking to me as though I were in a trance. "Cassandra, what's wrong?"

"What? Oh, yes. Of course. I'm fine."

"Are you sure because you –"

I snapped my answer back at him. "Edward, I said I was fine."

But we both knew it was a lie. The whole table was watching my every move and the attention made me feel nauseous. I excused myself and went to the study. I used the powder room that was adjacent to it and splashed some cold water on my face before lying down on the large leather sofa in the corner of the room.

In just over a week, I had come to find that I couldn't imagine my life without Edward. But if I wanted to share my life with him I would have to deal with the fact that someday I'd have to let him go. He was nearly fifty. How long did Edward and I really have together anyway? Fifteen years? Twenty years? Thirty if we were lucky.

My thoughtful state was disturbed by a knock at the door to the study.

"Sweetie, can I come in?" Edward had already opened the door and stuck his head through the opening.

"Please." I sat up, smiled, and patted down the stray hairs that were trying to wiggle out the French twist that my hair was pulled back into. Edward walked across the room and sat down next to me.

"I'm sorry about Darla. She can –"

"She's right you know," I said.

His look and tone of voice had been serious when he entered the room, but his expression rapidly turned to that of despair.

"Ask me to marry you again, now," I said anxiously.

"You've changed your mind, haven't you?"

"Just do it. This morning I gave you a floundering, half-hearted answer and I want to make this crystal clear. So ask me again. Now."

Edward looked no more reassured than before but conceded to my request. "Okay, okay. Don't be so bossy." He let out a short sigh and said, "Marry me."

"Yes. Absolutely. I think you know that I'm crazy about you. And I know I'll probably outlive you. But I can't imagine my life without you in it and I want to spend every single second we have left on this planet together with you, and nobody else."

He was even more speechless than he was the night of the Harvest Ball. However, I knew he was happy with what I said as the smile that had been missing from his face returned.

The reading of Senior's will turned out to be a long and arduous process. There were nearly fifty people to whom he had bequeathed belongings or money. Some items were coins, old books, and items of sentimental value to old friends. People he had intentionally left out were given letters of explanation. Once those items had been handled and the people they were given to had been dismissed, the legal staff, headed by Zachary O'Keefe, continued the proceedings. I was surprised that I was still in the room.

Next in the reading, came smaller monetary inheritances. Cash distributions went to charities, people Senior had met in his life whom he deemed worthy, and four of his former mistresses, including Jennifer White.

Jennifer sat, almost in a trance, as though she had not completely accepted what was happening. Alex, who had been sitting beside her, looked distraught as well. He had been completely unaware that her mother had even known Senior, much less had once been his mistress. In addition, he was out on bail for murdering the same man.

Vivian didn't seem shocked that Senior had provided for Jennifer or any of the other women. I suppose she had known about them all along. I don't think I could have been as graceful and composed as Vivian had been about the whole thing. But I was not her and had not led her life. I knew from firsthand experience the things people did to hold their marriages together.

Once those bequeathed money had been dismissed the only people still in the room were Senior's immediate family, Alex, Victor, and me. Why was I still in the room? Mr. O'Keefe stood up from the desk chair and walked across the room.

"The following is in written form to which everyone here will receive a copy. However, Senior made a DVD to explain the remainder of the will himself."

When he pushed the play button, Senior's smiling face popped up on the screen.

"Hello everybody! If you're watching this then, well, I'm dead. Try not to be sad. Death is just a natural part of life. Anyway, I guess I should get down to the good stuff, huh? First, my dear man, Victor."

Victor just shook his head and smiled.

"I leave you, in addition to your retirement fund, a lump sum of two million dollars. Vivian and I spoke about this and we'd also like you to reside here at Thomas Hall for as long as it is owned by the Baker Family. In addition to which your health insurance will be paid for the remainder of your life. Enjoy your retirement, my good man." I knew Victor was relieved. The money would be more than enough to help his son through his financial crisis.

"Next, I leave Phoebe, Henry, and Alex each five million dollars and fifteen percent of the winery. I love the three of you dearly and I've always been proud to be your father. That includes you Alex, I'm just sorry your mom would never let me tell you."

Alex looked up at Mr. O'Keefe. His disbelief and shock were visible on his face. "Can you rewind that part once more?"

"Better yet, I've made you all a DVD. It's in the envelopes with the written copies."

Alex looked as though the weight of the world had been lifted from his shoulders. It must have been a terrible burden to grow up not knowing who your father was.

The DVD continued to play and Senior continued to speak to us. "My sweet Vivian, my one regret is that I leave you behind. A lifetime is not nearly enough time my love. I know how much you love Thomas Hall. It and the winery are the only things of real substance I own. So I leave you the property on which Thomas Hall stands, the buildings, and fifteen percent of the winery. In addition, any funds remaining after the distribution of the will shall revert back to you. I will miss you and love you always."

I looked over at Vivian. It was the first time I had seen her look truly sad. She reminded me of a young war bride sending her soldier to meet his fate. It was sad and sweet, all at the same time. I think it was seeing him again that did it to her. She wasn't looking at a dead man in a casket, but the happy, smiling man she had loved her whole life.

"Moving on to my oldest child, Edward. You've told me a million times there is nothing on this planet you need. We both know that's a bunch of bull. If you're as smart as you think you are, she's sitting next to you, wrapped up in your arms as we speak."

Everyone in the room turned and looked at the two of us and Edward kissed the top of my head and slid closer to me, gently wrapping me in his arms.

"While you don't need anything, I leave you all the remaining shares of stock I have left as well as ten percent of the winery. Just in case you're not as smart as we all think, I'm leaving you something else. You'll figure out what it is in a moment."

I couldn't figure out why I was in the room. Something seemed off with the percentages of the winery that Senior had left people but I didn't have time to crunch the numbers in my still foggy head before the DVD continued.

"Now last, but certainly not least, Cassandra Martin. If all is going as I hope it will, you're sitting next to my namesake wondering why the hell you're here. I want to make certain that the winery is well taken care of once I'm gone. After all, besides my children, Thomas Hall is my only legacy. Unfortunately, I've never been able to make it turn a profit. I honestly believe that if there is anyone who can turn this little slice of heaven into a successful winery, it's you. So I'm leaving you a thirty percent share of the winery. Good Luck."

"What?" I wasn't sure if I said it aloud or just thought it, so I repeated myself, "What?"

"Well kids, that's all I've got. There are some technical things that the lawyers will handle. Take care and I'll see you on the other side." Then the screen went blank.

I turned to Edward. "I don't understand? Why did he leave the shares to me? Did I miss something?"

"I guess Dad thought you would do whatever it takes to protect the winery. He may have appeared to be a crazy old man, but he was no idiot. He knew who was stealing money from the winery long before either of us. He was worried Henry would sell it off bit by bit to fund Darla's whims. And he was certain that Alex's youth and ambition would drive the place into bankruptcy."

"What about Phoebe?"

"He knew she loved this place, but she made it clear years ago that she had no interest in the winery business."

"So, why not you?"

"He knew I loved this place too. But he also knew I'd never have the time or energy needed to devote to making it successful."

"Oh," I sat, still stunned by everything that had just happened. "Edward, what was the other thing you're dad left you?"

He leaned his head back onto the sofa and grinned. "Sweetie, by leaving you in charge of the winery, he gave me the opportunity to keep you close to me."

"So, are you telling me that effectively he left you *me*?"

"I think it was his plan to get us married. Just in case I couldn't get my act together." He said with a wink.

It took a minute for everything to sink in. In less than eight hours I'd become the head of Thomas Hall Winery and engaged to Edward. Actually, it took longer than a minute.

Chapter Fifteen

I WALKED OVER TO where the lawyers had converged and waited for a break in their discussion. "Mr. O'Keefe, do you have a moment?"

"Only if you start calling me Zachary."

"Can I get you to come out next week and meet with us about how this business structure is designed to work? I have a feeling we'll all have a ton of questions by then."

"I'll call you later with my availability, but what it boils down to is you're the one calling the shots."

I shook my head, still in disbelief as Henry walked up next to me. "Taking charge already?"

"Just trying to avoid complete chaos at the winery."

"Dad was right, you're a smart businesswoman." Senior had obviously talked about this decision with Henry.

"I don't know anything about running a business, but I've seen the greed that follows death. Rule number one is to keep a lid on any potential explosions."

"Sounds like you've ridden this roller coaster more than once."

"Yeah, too many times I'm afraid." I paused for a moment trying to decide if it was the right time to talk to him but knew the sooner I had this conversation the better. "Henry, I need to talk to you about the money."

"What money?"

"The money you've been skimming from the winery. You could get in big trouble and I don't want to see that happen."

He closed his eyes and ran his fingers through his hair. I smiled, realizing it was a habit all the Baker men shared.

"I should have known you'd figure it out. I needed the money to hold on to Darla. I didn't go the corporate route like my brother and I just can't afford her taste. Tell me what you want me to do."

I thought about it for a minute and came up with a plan. "As soon as the money's dispersed, take some of your inheritance and put it back into the winery's account. As the chief shareholder, I'll declare that it was a loan and just look the other way on the fact that you didn't ask first."

Henry looked at me with total shock. "Is it really that simple?"

"I just made it that simple. Call Sarah Abbott and get the exact amount from her. But from now on, I sign off on all the financials."

"Wow, I don't know what to say? I guess, thank you."

"Don't do it again. And Henry, if you need money, for any reason, come talk to me. I'm sure we can work something out."

As we finished our conversation, Henry and I sat down on the leather sofa. Detective Hayes had just arrived and joined us there. Henry greeted him first, hoping for some definitive answers.

"Anything new on Dad's murder?"

"A lot I'm afraid. First, we're dropping the charges against Alex."

The detective went on to explain that not only were Alex's fingerprints not on the murder weapon, but the handwriting sample he provided didn't match either note. In addition, his alibi, a young woman named Jessie Jenkins, had checked out. Apparently, they met at Lucky Shots, the bar in town, earlier that evening and spent the night dancing and drinking before going back to her place at closing time.

Henry was quick to ask my next question for me and it was becoming more and more obvious that we thought a lot alike. "If his prints weren't on the weapon, whose were?"

"Several people's prints showed up: Edward's, Vivian's, Senior's, Ms. Martin's, Dr. Rice's, Darla's, Sarah and Michael Abbott's, and yours. The problem is Edward's blood is also on the weapon. But according to Ms. Martin, Edward was upstairs during the attack."

We all sat in silence for a moment. Then it dawned on me why Edward's blood would be on the weapon.

"That must be the same pair of shears I caught on Edward's back the morning of the Harvest Ball. Dr. Rice glued the cut back together and gave him a tetanus shot that morning. I'm sure he has a record of it somewhere."

"Good, I'll look into that. Any other thoughts?"

"Detective, there is one thing. The night of the party, I overheard an argument where someone threatened to kill Senior."

"Yes, I know. Vivian told me about their fight."

"Not Vivian. It was a fight Senior had with Jennifer White, Alex's mother."

I had Henry and Detective Hayes' full attention now.

"Tell me everything you remember."

I went on to tell them both about returning from my suite to the sound of voices raised in the sitting room. That I stopped and listened to the conversation and heard Jennifer's threat.

"I don't know if it was serious though. People say things like that all the time when they argue."

"No, it's worth looking into, considering the circumstances. I'll follow up on it."

"You said first Detective. Is there a second?" I asked.

"I'm not sure I can talk with you about that one." The detective looked at Henry.

"It's okay Brian, looks like she's going to be part of the family."

"It's about Senior's autopsy. He was a very sick man. According to the report he had tumors everywhere."

"We know. He was close to the end."

"You can say that again, Ms. Martin. The report I read concluded he would have died within a couple of weeks."

"You mean to tell me if the killer had been patient –"

"Mother Nature would have taken care of this for them." Detective Hayes looked like this case was causing him a lot of stress.

"Something's missing, isn't it Detective?"

"Yes, and please call me Brian. I don't have murders in this county often, but I'm damn good at piecing things together and it just isn't adding up. Everything I string together never quite fits. Maybe the answer is with Jennifer White. My instincts say probably not, but I'll go talk to her before she heads home to Maryland. There's a clue missing, whether I know what it is and don't realize it or if it's just not there yet. Anyway, I'll call you when I know anything new."

"I'd appreciate that," I said.

"Don't worry, I'll find out who did this. I don't want anyone who could do this kind of damage to you or Senior walking around the streets of Willow Creek."

The detective started to walk away, then turned back to me and said, "Congratulations on your engagement."

"What?" I realized he had noticed the ring. "Oh, thanks."

Brian left and Henry turned back to me. "So you're really going to marry my brother?"

"It does look that way, doesn't it?"

"You don't sound certain. Second thoughts already?"

"No, it's just complicated." I paused, trying to figure out how to explain myself to Henry. "I want to marry your brother, but I'm nervous about wading into that quagmire again."

"I understand. Marriage isn't easy, it's messy and it's complicated, but you already know that. Just remember, my brother doesn't."

"Thanks, Henry. I needed to hear someone say that. You're gonna make a pretty good brother-in-law you know."

"And you're gonna make a pretty good boss too, Sis." It seemed like eons since anyone had called me Sis and I was glad Henry had done so. Darla waved Henry over to where she was talking with Alex. As I sat there alone, I knew what I needed to do next.

I had not been in the wine cellar since the night of the murder and it was not a prospect I looked forward to. But I knew I needed to go down there if I was ever going to figure out who tried to kill me.

I stood at the top of the staircase and flipped the light switch. It had been repaired and the lights seemed much brighter than the night Senior's killer sent me to the hospital.

Each step into the cellar turned out to be much more painful than I had expected. Not from the physical sense, although my ribs ached with every drop to the next step down, but in the sense of emotional anguish. As the view of the wine cellar became clearer, so did the details of that night. While Senior's body and blood were gone, the faint line from where the police had outlined his body and the stain left on the cement floor by the blood remained. I walked over and knelt down to the spot where I had tried to check Senior's pulse. I closed my eyes and desperately tried to remember what I had seen. A piece of paper in Senior's hand, gardening shears, blood, shoes. Shoes? Not mine or Senior's, but red leather stilettos. I hadn't remembered them before that moment, but whose were they?

A thin, cold hand pressed against my shoulder and I nearly jumped out of my skin. Darla stood over me with a look of panicked concern that I had yet to see on her face.

"Cassandra, are you all right?"

I took her hand and she helped me to my feet. "Yes, thank you. I was trying to remember something, anything about the night Senior died."

"Any luck?" The tone of her voice changed slightly. It seemed odd, but I wasn't sure why.

"No, just bits and pieces." The concern on her face disappeared and was replaced with something I couldn't quite read.

"Listen, about what I said at lunch. I think I might have crossed a line."

It was obvious someone had forced her to make this apology. She did not look at me when she spoke and the words I'm sorry never left her mouth.

"It's okay. You did bring up some valid points."

Darla smiled. "Yeah, he's way too old for you."

"No, I mean Edward and I don't have any time to waste."

The smile melted from her face into a sour frown. "Oh, I see."

"See what?" I didn't understand.

Darla moved very close to me until we were face to face, leaving me feeling as if my personal space had been violated. I could feel my breath becoming labored from my nervousness. She had made my skin crawl from the start, but this was different. Different in a way that caused me to tremble in fear.

We both heard the footsteps of someone racing down the stairs and Darla took two steps back from me. It was Edward, looking panicked and breathless. He stopped at the bottom step and took a deep breath.

"Why in the hell are you down here Cassandra? You don't need to ever be in this cellar again. As a matter of fact, I forbid you to be down here."

"Excuse me? You forbid me to what?" I didn't like the idea that in less than a day after agreeing to marry him he was trying to dictate what I could and could not do.

"I'm staying out of this one," Darla said. She patted my shoulder and headed up the spiraling staircase leaving the two of us alone.

"Edward," I took a deep breath and tried to compose myself so I wouldn't start screaming at him. "I just inherited part of this winery. I'm going to have to be in the wine cellar on a regular basis, whether either of us like it or not. I understand your reasons for not wanting me down here, but you've got to calm down."

"If you understand, then why are you down here?"

"I wanted to take a look –"

"Cassandra, I asked you not to go snooping around."

"I wasn't. I was just trying to see if I could remember something, anything that might, well, help Brian."

"You're lying."

"Of course I am. Someone tried to kill me Edward. I can't just sit around waiting for it to happen again."

"I wish you wouldn't do this. It's just, I looked up and you were gone. Then we couldn't find you and I freaked out. I just have a bad feeling that this nightmare isn't over yet."

Edward was upset. The stress of the death of his father, my injuries, and the deal he still had hanging in limbo back at work were all taking a toll on him. I was fairly certain he was not trying to be controlling. He was just worried. And I understood the bad feeling he had because it tormented me too.

I couldn't come up with any better ideas, so I decided to try to lighten the mood. "So marrying me is a nightmare? You sound like an old married man already."

He laughed and draped his arm around my shoulders allowing himself to relax. "Come on Sweetie, let's go back to our house."

Chapter Sixteen

It was nearly six when we arrived back at Edward's house. I decided to take another pain pill, although I felt one-hundred percent better than I had the evening before. I didn't want to be in any pain if my plans for the evening came to pass. As I poured myself a glass of iced tea from the pitcher Victor had left for us, Edward walked up from behind and kissed the back of my neck.

"Edward, have we lost our minds?"

"Why do you ask, Sweetie?"

"We've known each other for twelve days and we're engaged to be married. I mean, I'm a smart girl. I try to look at things rationally, but I lose all sense of reason when I'm with you. And you, how often do you go around giving girls diamond rings the size of one of the Great Pyramids anyway? We should probably both be institutionalized."

"First of all, it's the only engagement ring I've ever bought and I have to say that it was a nerve-racking experience. There were way too many decisions to make." He wrapped his arms around me.

"Well, it's perfect."

"I'm glad you like it. Now, I want you to close your eyes." I complied, and he continued. "Good. Now tell me, can you picture spending the rest of your life with me?"

I smiled as I replied. "Easily."

"Okay, are you happy in that picture?"

"Very. Lots of children too."

"Really, how many?"

"I don't know. Three, four, five? Is that a problem?" I opened my eyes and turned to face Edward. "I know we touched on the subject of birth control before, but if children are going to be an issue, now would be a really good time for us to talk about it."

"Let's see; you want to marry me and have a bunch of my children." Edward's voice radiated happiness as each word left his lips. "No, no problem here. I just think it's odd that you never had any kids with Tony."

"We weren't married that long and ..." I could feel the blood rush to my cheeks and warm my face as I let my voice fade out and not finish my sentence.

"And?"

"Well, Tony wasn't exactly the most sexual person, at least where I was concerned."

Edward laughed. "You've got to be kidding me."

"I wish I was." I hesitated, debating whether or not to continue, but thought he should probably know. "In the two years we were married, we had sex maybe five times."

"And you shared the same bed?"

"When he bothered to come home."

"That's insane. I've slept next to you one night, and I spent half of it lying awake staring at you, wondering what it would be like to, well, oh hell. I love you, but I look at you and go crazy. Whenever we're alone like this, all I can think about is ripping off all your clothes and ..."

Edward pressed his lips against mine. I could feel his passion pulsing through my own veins. He pulled himself away from me and I tried to stop him, to no avail. "Sweetie, I think I better stay up at the main house tonight."

"Why?"

"You have to ask? Don't get me wrong, I'll wait until we're married if that's what you want, but I won't get any sleep lying next to you."

I put on my best pouty expression and looked up at Edward. "So I guess my raincheck expired already, huh?"

"Rain check?"

"The one from this morning, I thought I might want to cash it in tonight."

He was obviously debating whether to ask questions or just whisk me off to bed. "What about your whole 'no sex before marriage' philosophy?"

"Did you forget? I've already been married."

"Don't tease me, Cassandra."

I reached over, grabbed the back of his neck, pulled his head down to me, and kissed him. It wasn't a sweet, caring kiss either. It was more of a 'take me to bed or lose me forever' kiss. I didn't even realize I had the ability to kiss a man like that. Whether I understood it completely or not, I wanted him. No, I needed him. He pulled his head back from my lips and stared into my eyes.

"My God, you're serious, aren't you?"

"You didn't get it when I told you earlier that I wanted to spend every second of every day we have left on this planet with you, did you?" I took his hand and led him into the bedroom.

The sun had set and the bedroom was only dimly lit from the light left on in the kitchen. The sheets had been turned down for the night and the scent of fresh-cut flowers filled the room as there were several small vases around that had been filled since we left just before lunch.

I paused when I crossed the threshold to the bedroom. While I didn't understand it, I wanted him with an unyielding passion that could have easily consumed me. The impulsive, brave, confident me was screaming, "go for it." But the old, academic, mousy me wanted to stop and think about this. It was such a potent mix of emotions that I couldn't focus on any one thing. Edward continued, led me to the edge of the bed, sat me down, and knelt in front of me.

"You're having second thoughts, aren't you?"

"No, just trying not to think so much."

While he spoke, he stripped his shirt off. I had never been easily distracted by a man's looks, but I'd be lying if I said I hadn't thought about those abs at least twice a day since the first time I saw him shirtless.

Edward reached behind my head and my hair. "Then relax." He leaned onto the bed and kissed me with just enough force to lay me back against the sheets. His skin was hot, and I could feel his temperature continue to rise even through my clothes. I was already breathless when he pinned his hands against mine, our fingers entwined and clasping the other's hands. His lips were silky and wet and I knew they wouldn't stay in one place for long. He moved his mouth away from mine and worked their way down my neck and across my bust. His strong arms wrapped around me and he pulled my sweater over my head.

"God, you're beautiful." I wanted to say something, but Edward stopped me. "No, no arguing. I've seen you naked."

I smiled at him. "I'm not completely naked yet, you know?"

"Yeah, I'm going to have to fix that."

"Oh really, I—"

Edward stopped me from continuing. I thought the first night he kissed me at his house was the most passionate kiss I would ever receive in my life. I was so wrong. When his lips pressed against mine, I became completely intoxicated. I felt the palm of one of his hands slide up my leg and cross over to my thigh while the other hand gently cupped my breast over my bra.

It was only then that it occurred to me that I wasn't wearing any pants. I knew I had them on when I walked into the room and wondered how he'd managed to undress me without my knowledge. In the split second it took to realize this, he had undressed us both completely.

"Cassie?" He whispered to me while he laid a trail of kisses along my stomach, slowly working his way down my body.

I wasn't certain anything coherent would come out of my mouth, but I managed a "Hmm?" in response.

"I won't ask again, but are you sure about this?"

"Honey."

Edward stopped where he was and looked up at me, resting his chin on top of my belly button. "Yes?"

"Shut up and make love to me."

"Yes, Ma'am."

From that point on, neither of us said a word, at least not a coherent one. Edward worked hard to restrain himself but our unyielding desire for each other added a certain sense of urgency to our actions. I wish I could say I was as confident as Edward in bed, but it was a place I always found myself feeling clumsy and awkward. But his reaction to me dissolved every insecurity I ever had. At least for that night.

Afterward, as he traced the outline of my face with his fingers, I began to drift off to sleep. And as I did, I realized that somewhere between first feeling his hand pressed against my thigh and lying next to him afterward, wrapped naked in his arms under the down comforter, I'd found a state of nirvana that transcended anything I had ever known.

I was rattled from a sound sleep by the ringing of my cell phone. I had left it on the nightstand, and after a moment of fumbling about, I managed to answer it. I turned on the speakerphone in the process and decided to leave it so as not to accidentally disconnect the caller.

"Excuse me, but what in God's name is going on there?" It was Sarah.

I rolled over to find Edward sitting up in bed, reading the paper. He looked over the top of his reading glasses at me and smiled.

I asked Sarah what would have been an obvious question if I had been willing to turn away from Edward and look at the clock. But I was too preoccupied with his beautiful brown eyes to move.

"What time is it?"

"Eight o'clock." She said.

"Good morning Sarah. What's goin' on?"

Edward had taken his glasses off, leaned over, and started kissing me while I desperately tried to listen to Sarah. He made it difficult and I wasn't awake enough for such a challenge.

"C.C., both Henry Baker and Phoebe Foster have already called me this morning. Along with the Washington Post, The Willow Creek Herald, The Richmond Times-Dispatch, and about fifteen other media outlets."

"Um, why?"

"Henry wants to return the money, Phoebe wants to sell her part of the winery, and according to the press, you're getting married and in charge of Thomas Hall." She was talking at lightning speed, and I was having trouble keeping up with her rant. All I could think about was how sore I was. The night before had been heavenly, but I used muscles that I don't think had ever been used quite like that, and my body had not yet recovered from the damage caused by my attacker either.

"Wait a minute. That's too much at once this early in the morning. Start again and speak slowly. Take one thing at a time."

"Well, Henry asked me for the exact amount he had taken over the last two years because he needs to replace it as soon as the will's gone through probate."

"Yeah, we're going to take care of that between the two of us. He won't be allowed to make withdrawals anymore. I'll be signing off on everything." Edward's hands moved slowly across my body as he playfully nibbled on my neck. "Edward, I'm on the phone!"

"What is Edward doing there this time of day? Oh my God, you slept with him last night, didn't you?"

"Yeah." I think I surprised both of us with my casual response. "Hold on."

I knew Edward was enjoying playing with me, and I gave him an evil grin. He nibbled his way down to my breasts as if I would be his breakfast. "Do you mind? This is winery business."

I could hear an audible gasp come out of Sarah's mouth with each word. "Oh! My! God!"

"Um, Sarah, Edward and I are getting married."

Edward looked up and smiled. It was the first time he had heard me say it and the sound of it coming from me pleased him. He went back to nibbling on my body. He was driving me absolutely crazy and I was getting a case of the giggles on top of it.

"Cut that out!" The other end of the phone was quiet. "Sarah?"

"I guess it's true then. You're engaged to Edward and in charge of the winery."

"I didn't realize the news would travel so fast. I should have called you last night, but I was, well, busy. Why did Phoebe call?"

"Her lawyers needed some figures about the winery. Something about her wanting to sell her shares. Is it okay to release those numbers?"

"Yes, but do it the way the numbers will look after Henry puts the money back. Call Zachary O'Keefe if you have questions about how the shareholding works. Henry and I are the only ones who know about the withdrawals and I'd like to keep it that way. I'm probably going to get in trouble for asking, but can you make the whole thing look like a loan and that Henry repaid it?"

"Sure. That shouldn't be too hard. But C.C., I'm surprised this is the way you want to handle this. Of course, it seems like everything in your life is a surprise to me right now."

"Henry has the money from his inheritance now to pay what he's taken and no real harm's been done. It's a family matter and I'm handling it."

"Wow! The Bakers sucked you in quick, didn't they?" I didn't like the tone of Sarah's voice and her comment stopped Edward dead in his tracks.

"What's that suppose to mean?"

"Nothing."

"Sarah?"

"They just have a 'family above all' philosophy that I find a little disturbing."

"It's no different than any other family." Edward looked at me and smiled, then continued on his breakfast adventure that was my body. He had reached the edge of my scar from the broken bottle and gently kissed his way around it.

"I'd disagree, but it seems like your whole world is changing and I'm having trouble keeping up. Is there a theater program for this Broadway play?"

"It is a little crazy, isn't it?" I said.

"A little?" Finally, laughter came out of the usually happy Sarah, but her voice remained serious. "C.C., just remember what I told you about men like Edward, okay?"

"I'm still not sure I understand, but okay. Has Michael heard about all of this yet?"

"Yeah, he's standing right here and you're on speakerphone."

"Why didn't you tell me that earlier? Michael, I am so sorry."

It was only then that I heard Michael holding back laughter. "It's all right. I'm good, but I've gotta admit I'll never get used to hearin' you say you were too 'busy' last night to call."

"Okay, I'm completely embarrassed now. So unless you need anything else from me, I'm going to hang up."

"I think that's it. We should probably get together soon though and crunch some numbers so that you know where things stand with the winery's finances."

"Sounds good," I said. "Plan it for lunchtime, and we'll grab a bite to eat before going over it at your office."

I hung up the phone and turned my attention back to Edward. But the light in the room made me uncomfortable. I had found solace in the dim light and shadows the night before and didn't care for the exposure the morning sun brought with it. I stood up and simultaneously wrapped myself in the top sheet of the bed, walked across the room, and pulled the large curtains to the patio closed. Upon returning, I turned out the light on Edward's side of the bed. He turned it back on, and when I sat up to reach for the light, he stopped me.

"I want to see you."

"I like the dark."

"You like to hide in the dark," he said.

"I'm not hiding. I just like the dark." The truth was I had always been self-conscious and if I couldn't see my body, neither could he. He reached over and switched the light off.

"We'll work on the light issue later. But tell me something, what did Sarah mean 'men like me'?"

"Oh." I didn't really understand it, so I didn't know how to explain it. "Nothing important. Just girl stuff."

"Good, because I like girls. Especially this one."

He playfully swept me back, all the while minding my ribs. When he kissed me, his lips tasted like coffee. I had never acquired a taste for it but liked the flavor on his mouth. He had only kissed me but anticipating what would come next caused my breathing to become shallow, making my chest rise and fall like waves along the sand. He slid his hands to my breasts just as we heard someone open the front door.

"Hello? Is anyone home?" It was Phoebe.

Edward was a man who didn't like to be interrupted and was annoyed with the way his plans were unraveling. "Damn it. Doesn't anyone knock around here? I'll get it. You stay here."

I wasn't aware that he had taken off the t-shirt and sleep pants he was wearing when I first woke up, but he had stripped them off at some point. He threw his clothes back on and went out to the living room to talk with Phoebe. I got up and slowly headed toward the shower. My ribs still hurt but not quite as much as the day before. I grabbed what was probably the quickest shower of my life, threw on yoga pants and a t-shirt, and went out to join them.

"Good morning Phoebe. Who are you selling your shares to?"

Edward walked up behind me and kissed the back of my head.

"What? How did you know?" She asked.

"I have my ways." I laughed as I confessed. "Okay, so Sarah Abbott's my best friend and I just got off the phone with her."

"Well, let me see the ring again and then we'll talk."

I showed her the ring smiling and she grinned.

"It's impressive big brother."

"Thanks, but what happened to my morning plans?" He wrapped his arms around me and began to plant kisses down the side of my neck, using a single finger to pull on my shirt, exposing more skin.

"Some of us have a winery to run, or did you forget?" I smiled at him and took his hand off my shirt edge, entwining his fingers in mine. I looked back at his sister. "So, selling your shares?"

"I know Dad just left them to me to be fair, but I have no interest in the winery except to be here on the weekends. I don't want to get mixed up in the business of it."

"Well, Vivian owns the property, so being here shouldn't be a problem."

"Exactly. When I talked with Mom last night, she suggested I sell my shares to you."

"Me? Really?" While I was happy she'd thought of me, I would have thought she would have wanted to sell her shares to Henry or Edward.

"Absolutely. Are you interested?"

"Yes, of course. I mean, if I can afford it. See what the lawyers and accountants come up with for numbers and let me know what we're talking about."

"With the current state the winery's in, it shouldn't be much. Hell, Phoebe may have to pay you to take them." Edward commented as he headed toward the kitchen to put on some fresh coffee. But before he reached the threshold, he stopped and turned back to the two of us. "But Sweetie, if you want it, it's yours. Sis, let me know how much and I'll have a check cut for you."

I shook my head and let out a small sigh. Living with Edward was going to take some getting used to. For a brief moment, I considered arguing with him about spending money on me but then thought better of it. Phoebe wanted to sell her shares, Edward was willing to buy them for me, and most importantly, it kept the winery in the family. The fact that Edward would be happy that I would let him do this for me was just an added bonus.

Once he was out of the living room Phoebe's face became very serious and focused. "Cassandra, there's one more thing. Whoever killed Dad and tried to kill you wasn't joking around. I'm sure you were just in the wrong place at the wrong time but if you go digging they might try to kill you again. My brother is way too happy and I don't want to see anyone else die at Thomas Hall. So do me a favor and just lay low. It would be nice to have a sister-in-law I actually like."

"What? You don't like Darla?"

Phoebe looked at me and we both burst into laughter.

As Phoebe and I laughed the whole house shook as if we were in a glass snow globe that had been picked up off a shelf. Edward ran from the kitchen to find

Phoebe bracing herself between the arms of the overstuffed chair she was sitting in and me on the floor leaning against the wall I had been thrown into. As Edward helped me to my feet and looked at both of us his question summed up all of our thoughts. "What the hell was that?"

At first, I thought there'd been an earthquake, but simultaneously, the three of us smelled the burning of wood, bricks, and shingles. Not knowing where it was coming from, we ran out the front door. I turned and looked around. Edward's house seemed fine but a large billowing black cloud rose from behind the one-story home. Edward and Phoebe ran to the back of the house to get a better view. There was no way my body was going to let me run. When I caught up with them, they were standing in amazement as the roof of Phoebe's vineyard cottage collapsed into the house, from which the black smoke and tall flames rose.

Edward turned to look at me and when he did I saw the panic form in his eyes. Now both Phoebe and I seemed to be in danger and he knew he couldn't protect us. "Cassandra, go in the house, call 911, get anything out you can't replace, then get out of there!"

I gladly followed Edward's orders. I went back into the house, grabbed my cell phone and medicine from the nightstand, and called 911 as I grabbed my carry-on from the closet. I threw my purse, passport, and medicine into it as I explained to the emergency operator what was going on. I put on my tennis shoes and fleece jacket and headed towards the door. Edward came in as I was at the door frame. He ran back to the bedroom, threw on some real clothes and shoes, and grabbed his briefcase. He moved at such a rapid pace that I was only a few steps out the front door when he came out behind me.

I knew exactly why Edward was in such a rush to clear out of his house. House fires like the one destroying Phoebe's home spread fast. And it was a blustery morning.

As the family stood in awe, we watched the firefighters pour an endless stream of water from the truck's hoses onto Phoebe's house. Alex paced back and forth, furious that the firefighters refused to let him check on the commercial wine cellar as it sat directly below the burning home. Everyone reassured him the cellar would be fine, but he wanted no part of it. Poor Alex was two seconds away from a nervous breakdown. His mother had spent the night at his house after the reading of the will and had been trying to calm him, to no avail.

I wasn't as worried about the cellar as I was the vineyard. We were surrounded by vines that had been there for decades and if the fire spread in the wrong direction it could all be gone in the blink of an eye. I could already see the newspaper headlines, "Vineyard Burns to Ground on New Owners' First Day." The firefighters were kind enough to honor my request to hose down the nearby fields. It was only a preventative measure and it did not guarantee their survival but it was all I could think of to do.

It was obvious that Alex and I had very different opinions in the order of winery importance. I felt like he could always make more wine and he was not as concerned with the vines as they could be replaced. He argued the wine in the cellar could never be duplicated. However, even facing our worst fears for the winery, we respected each other's point of view.

Detective Brian Hayes arrived and we stood next to one another as we watched the scene continue to unfold.

"Brian, do you think there's a connection between this and Senior's death?"

"I would be shocked if there wasn't."

I sighed and thought about everything I had experienced at Thomas Hall. "Did you ever get the feeling that death, destruction, and mayhem follow you everywhere you go?"

"Can't say I have, Ms. Martin. But something tells me you can."

"Unfortunately, yes. And please, call me Cassandra."

"You know, I think it's time I hear the whole story from you. I've heard bits and pieces but I have a feeling there's a lot more to this that I should know."

"Where do you want me to start, with Senior's death?"

"No, how exactly did you end up at Thomas Hall Winery?"

"That's a long story."

Brian looked back over the burning house and then at me. "I think we have the time."

It was nearly one when I finished telling Brian everything that had happened, starting with my arrival at Michael and Sarah's and why I had decided to take the time to travel. We had relocated to the sunroom of the main house where we were safely away from the fire and firefighters but could still see the sad event unfold, although nearly everyone had chosen to focus on what I was saying as opposed to watching Phoebe's vineyard home burn to the ground. I had collected quite a captive audience and Victor brought all of us iced tea at about ten-thirty, but I was starting to feel a little light-headed as I neared the end of my story.

"Brian, I hope this doesn't sound rude, but could we continue this a little later."

"Sure, but you should write a book. I've never heard of such an adventure in my life." The detective stood to let himself out, presumably to check on the progress outside, and took a long look at me. "Are you feeling all right? You look a little pale."

Vivian, whose life was crumbling fast around her due to last week's events, was still attuned to everything going on around her, including my current state. In a flash, she was sitting beside me. Edward was across the room on the phone with his glasses sitting low on his nose and a stack of files on his lap. He swiftly set the files aside, took off his glasses, and hung up the phone without saying goodbye. He made his way quietly across the room.

"Sweetie, what's wrong?"

"I'm just a little weak and tired."

Vivian chimed in with a question that would resolve everything. "Cassandra dear, when was the last time you ate something?"

I had to think about it. We had not had breakfast when the house went up in flames and Edward and I skipped dinner last night in order to feed a different kind of hunger. "I guess lunch yesterday."

"Sweetie, you didn't eat lunch yesterday, remember?" Edward was right. I had been so wrapped up in what Darla said I skipped lunch altogether, only politely playing with my salad.

"Oh yeah, I guess it was breakfast yesterday then."

"No wonder you're lightheaded." Despite the stress Phoebe was enduring, she was genuinely concerned for me. She stood up and walked over to Edward and me. "Only my brother would fall in love with someone who forgets to eat."

Phoebe bent over and kissed the top of my head, then Edward's. She walked out of the room and headed outside.

Vivian looked at me. "Edward, why don't you take her up to your room to rest and I'll have Victor bring up some lunch."

I had never been in Edward's suite at the main house and was surprised by what I saw when we entered. It was decorated in a nautical theme, á la teenage boy. The sitting room contained a sofa, coffee table, desk, and an entertainment center with a flat-screen TV, surround sound speakers, DVD player, stereo, and three different video game systems.

There was only a half wall between the sitting room and the bedroom. In the bedroom was a king-sized bed and bookcases filled with pictures, trophies, certificates, books, toys, and model airplanes. I understood why he preferred to stay here as opposed to the villa. This was home.

"Welcome to the Edward Suite." He led me back to the bed to lie down, but before I could even take my shoes off, Victor tapped on the open door's frame and walked in with a huge tray.

"I didn't know what the two of you were in the mood for, so I brought a bit of everything." He set the tray down on the coffee table and walked to the door. "Call down to the kitchen if you need anything else."

Victor hadn't brought a little of everything, he had delivered the whole kitchen. There was fresh fruit and vegetables, grilled chicken, hamburgers, fresh-cut French fries, pasta salad, deviled eggs, and chocolate cake. It looked like he had pulled together an impromptu cookout for us.

Edward and I lounged on the sofa and shared a long leisurely lunch. We didn't talk much but it was nice to have a quiet moment together. We hadn't had a moment like it since the fireworks on the night of the Harvest Ball. It was the one thing we hadn't had the time for since that night, yet we both knew the quiet moments like these were vital to the well-being of our relationship.

The food was, as always, delicious. The chicken was tender and mouth-watering and the vegetables were fresh and crisp. The cake was so decadent I knew I would be stuffed by the time I finished my slice. And I was.

Edward had been insistent that I lie down and rest after lunch, although I thought it was completely unnecessary. When I woke up an hour later, it was clear that he was right and that I needed the rest. I sat up and looked into the sitting room, fully expecting to see my soon-to-be husband hard at work, pulling together the details of the upcoming merger. What I saw was something completely different. I found the CEO of a multi-billion dollar corporation playing video games. He was deeply entrenched in God of War. He had changed into a pair of sweats and an old t-shirt. He was wearing his glasses and looked like he was about twelve years-old.

It was then I knew I could marry him. Until that moment I had only seen him as a CEO, a sexy Greek God, and a confident man. He had the money, class, and power to have any woman he wanted, and few would be crazy enough to refuse. But the overgrown boy in the next room, the one playing video games, was someone real, someone attainable. He was everything. And he was mine.

I watched him play a few seconds longer before I said anything. "Working hard?"

"You're awake." Edward finished the level he was playing and saved the game.

"I didn't mean you had to quit. You can keep playing if you want."

He stood up and walked to the edge of the bed, laid his glasses on the nightstand, and ran his fingers through his hair. "Guilty pleasure."

"I thought that was supposed to be me?"

"No guilt with you Sweetie, just pleasure." He sat on the edge of the bed. "Feeling better?"

"Much better. Lie down with me."

"I don't need to be told twice to crawl into bed with a beautiful woman." He climbed under the covers and gave me a long lingering kiss. I looked into his eyes and smiled.

"What's with the smile?" He asked.

"What do you mean?"

"It's one I've never seen before."

"I think you'll see it more often than you know," I said.

"Why's that?"

"Because I love you." I had never said it out loud before. But there it was.

"I know." The smile on his face canceled the arrogance of his statement. I knew he was glad I said it.

"I know I'm not good at saying it, but I really do mean it."

"Cassandra, I've known you were in love with me since the day of the Harvest Ball. When we were in the study, waiting for Dr. Rice, there was a moment when—"

"I remember, trust me. Was it, I mean, is it, that obvious?"

"To me, yes. But does it matter?" He leaned over and kissed my neck. "I love you too, Sweetie."

We leaned back into the soft mattress and within seconds we were both naked. Last night had been passionate and wanting, but this was slower, softer. We kissed, talked, made love, laughed, and kissed some more. The only word I could use to describe the afternoon's encounter was bliss. He made me feel like a goddess, wrapped in the arms of a god.

As he traced my naked body with the tips of his fingers, I began to giggle.

"I didn't know you were ticklish, Cassie."

He lightly tickled my thighs, causing me to playfully squirm. I tried to talk through my laughter but gave up until we were done giggling, kissing, tickling, and rolling around under the covers.

"Honey, do you realize that twice now you've called me Cassie?"

"I did? I wasn't even aware of it. When do I do it?"

"When we're in bed."

"Does it bother you?" He asked.

"No, it's just the only other person that ever called me that is dead."

"Tony? Your parents?"

"No, someone else."

"You want to tell me who?"

"Not really. I just want to enjoy now and the answer to your question is a sad one."

"That's fine," he said. "I'm glad you don't mind. I'm not sure I could consciously stop."

"No, I think I kinda like it."

We were still lying in bed, naked, wrapped in the sheets, talking when there was a tap at the door.

"Edward, I've come to check on Cassandra." It was Vivian.

We looked at each other and I'm sure my eyes got as big as saucers. I wrapped the sheet around me and scurried to the bathroom as Edward threw on his sweats and answered the door.

I looked around the bathroom. It was similar to the one in the Elizabeth suite except the bathroom was connected to Edward's walk-in closet.

"Clothes, thank God," I said to myself as I walked into the closet. There was no way I could go out and face Vivian in a sheet. I rummaged through the closet and found a pair of flannel sleep pants and a t-shirt. While I put them on I could hear Edward and Vivian's conversation on the other side of the wall.

"How's Cassandra? Is she feeling better?" Vivian asked.

"She seems to be. She should be out of the bathroom in a minute."

"You really love her son, don't you?"

"I fell in love with her the first time I met her." The tone of Edward's voice was one of complete contentment.

"But does she really love you? I don't want to see you in the same boat as Henry."

"Mom!"

"I know, I know, she's nothing like Darla. I just worry about my children," she said.

"Did I tell you she called and scolded me for setting up an account at Zoe's shop?"

"No. Does she know you're the silent partner of that business?"

"No, but get this. She told me if she had known, she wouldn't have spent so much. Mom, Cassandra didn't know how much I was worth until *after* I gave her the ring. Even then she questioned whether or not I could afford it."

Vivian began to laugh and I decided it was as good of a time as any to make my entrance.

"Hi." I felt a little sheepish walking in the room. She had to have known I was in there getting dressed since my clothes, bra, and underwear were scattered across the bedroom floor.

"Feeling better, dear?"

"Oh, yes Ma'am. Lunch was lovely. Thank Victor for me please. A little nap afterwards did a world of wonder too. It's strange to spend the whole afternoon in bed though."

Edward hugged me from behind and kissed the base of my neck. "We should do that more often."

"Edward!" I could feel my face getting hot and had a sudden urge to smack him. I couldn't believe he said that in front of his mother.

"Don't worry about it dear. I've never seen my son so happy. But I came up to see if the two of you would like to stay for dinner." Vivian gave me a motherly look. "I want to make sure you eat again today."

Edward and I looked at each other and then I looked at her. "Would it be terrible to say, I'd rather eat up here, alone with Edward tonight, than sit downstairs with the family?"

"Not if you happen to be working on grandchildren for me."

Edward replied. "Then we'll be eating dinner up here."

Chapter Seventeen

EDWARD HAD BEEN ON the phone with Kelly for over an hour. The phone rang just as we finished breakfast and it hadn't occurred to me until then that Edward had been away from the office for over a week. When he arrived at Thomas Hall in the early hours of the day last Thursday, he had planned on being back in D.C. first thing Monday morning.

He was working at his desk in the living room of his house. I had grabbed a couple of books from the library at the main house and found a comfortable spot on the sofa to read about winery operations in order to research my new job. But I was really eavesdropping on the issues Edward was having with the merger he was working on in the days just prior to his dad's death and my beating. As I listened to Edward talking to his assistant I realized that he needed to get back to work.

"Kelly, I can't leave right now. I don't care what they want from me." He was about to blow a multi-million dollar deal and while he would not think twice about it, I did not want to be responsible for it. I stood up from the sofa and walked over to the desk. Edward was speechless when I took the phone out of his hand.

"Kelly, it's Cassandra. Give me a minute to talk some sense into Edward. He'll call you back." I hung up the phone and turned to Edward, who sat motionless, with his mouth wide open. "What are you doing? If Kelly says you're needed at corporate, then you're needed at corporate. You should go back to D.C. and take care of business."

"No, I don't want to leave you here alone until we know who's doing these things."

"Why? I'll be fine."

"I don't think so. And besides, if I leave you here alone I just know you're going to go snooping around, trying to figure out who's doing these things."

"So what if I did? No harm ever came from following the truth."

"Cassandra, you're going to get yourself killed if you do that!"

"That's ridiculous."

"Are you saying that I'm ridiculous?"

"No. But you've got to go Edward. You've put too much time and energy into this deal to let it go now." I walked back over to the sofa and had a seat.

"Fine, then you're coming with me."

"What am I supposed to do in Washington?"

Edward smiled. "You'd make for good eye candy. It might soften up the board of directors there."

"I can't go with you until the winery's buildings and cellars are declared sound and you know that! But you need to handle your own business too!" I was aware that my voice was getting louder and louder with each sentence, but for the first time in my life I really didn't care. I was determined to convince him I was right.

"I told you, I'm not leaving you alone until I know you're safe!"

"You're being stubborn!" I said.

"No, I've got to stay here and take care of you! First someone turns the house upside down, then they kill Dad and try to beat you to death, and Phoebe's house yesterday was no accident. It's not safe for you to be alone!" I couldn't tell if he was still yelling at me or becoming frantic recalling the events of the last week.

"I'll be fine. Whoever's doing this isn't doing a very good job. I mean, I haven't left, I'm not dead, and despite her house being burned to the ground, Phoebe is fine as well."

"I'm not going anywhere. This is looking more and more like these things are being done by someone here at the winery and I'm not letting you out of my sight. Especially now that I realize you plan to try to find Dad's killer."

"That's just absurd!"

"No, damn it!" Edward pounded the desk with his fist out of frustration. "I'm protecting what's important to me. You better get used to it, because this is what I do!"

I stood up, walked back over to the desk, and got in Edward's face as I spoke. "Well I don't need you to protect me! I hated it when Tony would hide behind that excuse!"

"Did you just compare me to Tony?" He pulled at his hair and ground his teeth together. "I am nothing like him."

I knew I had crossed the line bringing up Tony during an argument. "I didn't compare you to Tony, I just said –"

"Why are you being such a child?"

"Did you just call me a child?" I was so angry I wanted to scream and did. "Well, at least I'm not a stupid Neanderthal who's refusing to use the brains God gave him!" I grabbed my cell phone off the desk, walked over to the door, and put my shoes on.

"Where are you going?"

"I don't know. Maybe your Mom's house."

"We're not done talking about this!"

"Yes, we are. I'm beginning to feel like I'm just another acquisition and merger." I swallowed hard to hold back the tears that would prove how much this argument was upsetting me. "Call me when you're ready to behave like half of a real couple." As the words left my mouth I finally understood exactly what Sarah tried to warn me about.

"There is no way in hell you're going anywhere!" He walked to the door and stood between me and the door frame, grabbed my wrist, and pulled me close to him.

The terror in my eyes must have spoken volumes. Our faces were only a few inches from one another and I was staring straight into his eyes. "Let. Go. Of Me. Now."

Edward looked at where his hands had landed and knew he had crossed a line with me that he had no business even being close to. He pulled his hands up and away from mine, holding them up like a robbery in a bad western, and stepped away from the front door.

I turned and walked out the door and rushed to the main house, where I knew I would not be alone.

I had always rung the bell to the main house and waited for someone to answer, but this morning I walked in like I owned the place. Vivian was in the sitting room, reading the paper when she saw me wandering aimlessly in the foyer rubbing my temples with my fingers.

"Cassandra, I didn't know you were here."

I stood frozen, I didn't know what to say or do next. She could tell I was distraught over something.

"What's wrong my dear?"

"I think I just ruined my relationship with Edward." I looked at the grandfather clock in the foyer. It was only ten-thirty in the morning. "Is there any tequila in the house?"

"That bad, huh?" She got up and I followed her down the hall to what the guys called the Gentleman's Quarters. "I call this The Man Cave."

It had a pool table, big screen TV, leather furniture, and an oak bar. It was dark, musty, and smelled of stale cigars. Vivian walked behind the bar, pulled out a bottle of Patron and two shot glasses. She poured each glass full and had a seat on the stool on the other side of the bar. I followed her lead and she looked at me.

"Tell me what happened."

"We got into a huge fight."

"I figured that my dear," she said.

"I called him a stupid Neanderthal."

Vivian laughed out loud and handed me a shot of Patron. I downed it and set the empty shot glass on the counter. "He'll get over it."

"That's not the worst part. I compared him to my late husband."

"Where's the insult in that?"

I took a deep breath so I could get it out all at once. "Tony used to hit me when he was angry, and he spent a lot of time angry."

"Okay, why did you compare Edward to him?" It was obvious Vivian didn't like the idea of her eldest child being compared to someone who abused their wife.

"He's being controlling, just like Tony used to be. 'You can't do this! I forbid you to do that. You're going to do this.' And then, and then, he called me a child!"

"Calm down Cassandra. You need to understand. He's used to being in charge."

"Well, I'm not an employee he can just boss around."

"I'm certain he knows that." She slid the second shot across the bar, but I slid it back.

"One's probably enough." I took a deep breath and blew it out. "I'm not as sure he knows that as you are."

I laid my head on the bar and closed my eyes. I was a little surprised that Vivian downed the other shot, especially considering the time of day.

She put her hand on my shoulder. "Why don't you go lay down upstairs and relax. You'll feel better in a bit and Edward will have calmed down. Then you can go back to Edward's and work this out."

I stood up and moved to the door. "What if he doesn't want to?"

"Trust me my dear, he will."

Vivian and I walked down the hall and to the bottom of the stairs. I turned and looked at Vivian. "Is it okay if I rest in the Elizabeth suite?"

"Of course. I just figured you'd take Edward's room."

"Not today." Edward's room contained happy memories for me and I wanted to be mad at him, not fall in love with him all over again.

I climbed the stairs and had just turned the corner, out of sight of the foyer and the stairs when I heard the front door open. I could hear Edward's footsteps as he walked over to his mother. I stopped and listened to the conversation unfold downstairs.

"Where is she?" I expected him to sound angry, but he didn't. He sounded sad and sheepish. "Where is she Mom?"

"I just sent her up to rest. She looked exhausted."

"I need to talk to her." I could hear his footsteps as he started to move but Vivian must have stopped him.

"Edward, let's sit for a second."

"Not now Mom."

"Right now." Her tone was that of a mother about to ground her teenage son. I could hear them walk across the room and hoped I could still hear their conversation from where I stood, still out of their sight. I was lucky they chose to sit in the only two chairs that were positioned near the front of the foyer. "Edward, I don't think now is the best time to talk to her. She's quite upset, both with you and herself."

"She shouldn't be mad at herself. She was right. I've been behaving like the CEO of a corporation and not her husband." There was an awkward pause. "What is it Mom?"

"You can't treat her like a child."

"What did she say?" I could hear the sheepishness being replaced with annoyance.

"She didn't say anything except you called her a child and you were being controlling. I know you love her, but she can't help the fact that she's more than twenty years younger than you. It's not fair to throw that in her face when the two of you have an argument."

"But she was being childish." I took a step toward the staircase but froze when Vivian responded.

"Because you were treating her like a child. You can't tell her what she can and can't do. She's a grown woman."

"Did she say that?"

"No, Edward, I did. If you're going to marry her you've got to treat her like your equal or it won't work."

There was a stretch of silence and I wished I could see what was going on. I wondered if the conversation had come to an end.

"Oh, so that's what she meant," he said.

"What dear?"

"Right before she left to come up here she told me to call her when I was ready to behave like half of a real couple. I didn't understand it then, but I think I get it now." There was a long pause and I was about to head to the Elizabeth Suite when Edward asked his mom a question. "You really think I should leave her alone for a while, don't you?"

"I think if you go up now, it will end in another fight. You're both just too emotional right now."

"I'll take your advice then. Hell, if I had taken Cassandra's advice this morning, we wouldn't be like this. And it turns out she was right, I've got to go to D.C. and handle this merger. Ask her to call me when she wakes up, will you?"

"Wait a minute. This was about work and she was being the sensible one? Edward, dear, I have one word for you: flowers. Considering the circumstances, most women would be begging for you to stay, but she's giving you the go-ahead to handle business and you pick a fight? Better make that lots and lots of flowers. Oh, you can plan on some groveling too."

"Mom, I don't grovel. Ever."

"If you love her, you better start warming up to the idea."

"If that's what it takes, I guess I'll have to learn."

I heard her tell him to drive safely as she walked him to the door. I was glad he realized he was being an idiot but wasn't sure whether or not it was a good thing he was so dense when it came to relationships. I turned and walked down the hall to Edward's suite, laid across his bed and cried until I fell asleep.

The first two thoughts that popped into my head when I woke up a few hours later were, Holy Mother of God, I've got a winery to run and this relationship with Edward's a mess. Since I didn't want to talk to Edward about the morning's fight yet, I picked up my cell phone and dialed Alex's number.

"Talk to me."

"Hey Alex, its Cassandra."

"Good afternoon boss! What's up?"

"Have I ever mentioned I hate cheerful people when I'm in a lousy mood?"

"You won't today. The building inspector was here and the cellar is solid and good to go. He did suggest a few reinforcements, though."

"Thank God. We'll get the reinforcements started in the next couple of weeks. I guess you can be cheerful then, but just his once." I was still lying across the bed when I dialed Alex. While we were talking I got up, walked over to the bar, and grabbed a bottle of water from the frig.

"Well get used to cheerful, at least until the end of my contract."

"Look, I know you were held by the police for something you didn't do, but you're not really thinking about leaving are you?"

"Don't know yet. It depends on the new boss. Have you heard anything about her?"

"Very funny. Seriously though, don't leave. I don't know enough about viticulture to be in charge of what I've just been handed. I need you here."

"That sounds very promising. Maybe we should discuss this over dinner."

"Did you forget? I'm also engaged to Edward."

"Okay, not so promising for me, but still I have no intention of leaving Thomas Hall. Especially since I own part of it now."

"Good. So I called to find out what I'm supposed to be doing right now. I'm clueless about what to do next." After struggling with the bottle top I finally opened it, took a sip of water and set both the top and the bottle on the nightstand.

"Well, why don't you take some time to recover? I hear you nearly died. Everything is running along smoothly. If I need you, I'll call you. Is this a good number for you?"

"Yeah, it's my cell and the only way to reach me by phone."

"Okay Boss. I'll call if anything comes up. Why don't we meet sometime next week and we'll start with an overview of what goes on each month of the year here at the winery. If you want, we can then meet periodically and I'll try to break down each month for you in more detail. As a matter of fact, I'll write up a month by month breakdown and send it over a little later. That way you'll have an idea of what we're going to be talking about."

"That would be great. I need to learn as much about Thomas Hall Winery as quickly as possible. I wouldn't want to agree to anything that would drive it into the ground."

"Don't worry, I won't let that happen. See ya soon."

I laid back down on the bed and stared at my phone. I didn't want to call and apologize to Edward, but I wanted to hear his voice. After some thought, I decided I wouldn't, under any circumstances, apologize for anything, but I would call him.

"Hi."

"Hi. Hold on a second." I heard him ask whoever was in the room to excuse him as he needed to take this call in private. "Still mad?"

"Not at you, just my behavior," I said. "You?"

"I feel like an idiot."

"I shouldn't have compared you to Tony. It was cruel. I'm sorry." It had only taken me ten seconds to apologize. I was way too much of a pushover when it came to him.

"I shouldn't have grabbed you like that, especially after you compared me to Tony."

"I know you'd never do it on purpose. But, Edward, I can't handle you doing that. If it happens again, well ..." I didn't want to finish my sentence and my stomach churned just thinking about it.

"Just say it, Sweetie. It's okay."

"It's a deal-breaker. I won't marry you."

"I know. I'd be disappointed in you if you didn't feel that way."

I didn't know what else to say on the subject. Was there anything left to say?

"Cassandra, are you there?"

"Yes."

"I'm sorry."

"Me too. You're really not a stupid Neanderthal."

"Well, I behaved like one." He exhaled. I think he was as glad as I was the discussion we just had was pretty much done.

"Who were you talking to?"

"Kelly. And I don't want to hear a word about my being back in D.C. It's killing me, not being at home with you."

"You've never referred to your house at Thomas Hall as home before."

"Because until now, you didn't live there." He sounded stressed as he continued talking. "Look, I did something and I hope it's okay. If you hate the idea, you can dismiss them, but I hired B&B to guard you until I get back. I just want to try to keep you safe."

I hated the idea of a bodyguard following me around like a puppy, but I knew it was important to him.

"That's fine. I know you're just trying to protect me." I paused for a moment. I had to ask the question, although I was not sure I wanted to know the answer. "Edward, when we were arguing this morning, did you ever think that maybe we shouldn't get married?"

"No. Did you? I mean up to the point of me trying to force you to stay."

I did something I hadn't expected I would do. I lied. "Of course not."

There was a long stretch of silence between us. Sarah had told me once that she knew when I was lying. It was something about how I would say things. I never bothered trying to figure it out. Had he?

"What is it, Edward?"

"I just don't know if I can figure out how to split my time between here and there."

"We'll figure it out."

"I guess," he said.

"You don't sound convinced."

"No, you're right, we'll figure it out. I just didn't think it would be this hard."

There was more. I could feel it in my bones. "And what else?"

"I'm just aggravated with this deal. I'm about ready to chuck the whole thing out the window. Hey, how did you know there was more?"

"Why are you ready to chuck it? You've worked really hard on this acquisition."

"The board members of this company agreed to sell the business to me but now they want this and that. They're like a bunch of spoiled children and it's driving me nuts. Any ideas?"

I couldn't believe he asked me for corporate takeover advice. The man needed serious mental help.

"Well, are they worried more about the money or their employees?"

"That's the problem, both."

"Are the board members financially able to buy back all the common stock from its shareholders?"

"No, that's why they want to sell to me. This economy has left them all broke."

"Well, here's what I'd do. Tell them this is your offer, take it or leave it. But if they choose to leave it you will buy up the other shareholders' stock, run them off the board, then close each location one by one, leaving all their employees with no jobs."

"Whoa, that's pretty hardcore. I never pictured you as the cut-throat business type."

"I'm not. I didn't say you had to follow through, but they don't know you won't, do they?"

"Good point."

"Well, you can sit there and listen to the 'whiner babies' all day or you can be back here with me if I'm what you want."

"Only if you're naked, Sweetie."

"Men!" Edward laughed at my response and I joined in.

"I tell you what, let me call you back in fifteen minutes," he said.

After we hung up, I decided it was time to go home. Home. The word stuck in my head. Less than three weeks ago I had no home, no family, and no career. And now it was all in place. It was as if it had been waiting for me at Thomas Hall all along and all I needed to do was just show up.

I put the shoes on I had kicked off before my nap and headed downstairs where Victor met me at the bottom of the staircase.

"Miss Martin, going back to Edward's?"

"Yes, but I should probably thank Vivian first. Do you know where she is?"

"She went to go visit Senior's grave. She took a bottle of champagne with her, so I don't expect her and her driver back for some time."

I felt terrible. I had stormed into her house unannounced and spilled my problems to her. Completely forgetting she had buried her husband only three days ago. Victor sensed my feelings of self-aggravation.

"I must tell you, you and Edward have definitely been helping her keep her mind off of Senior's death."

"By constantly running to her for help."

"I've discovered people usually want two things in life, to be loved and be useful. When they stop feeling both, that's when their spirit starts to die."

"I suppose."

"Why don't I pack up some dinner for you? It's nearly five o'clock."

"That would be lovely. Thank you, Victor."

I followed him back to the kitchen where the chef was busy finishing up the evening's meal. He asked the plump gentleman to pack up enough food for three.

"Three?"

"Something for Bubba and Brick too." I didn't bother asking how he knew Edward had hired them to protect me. I was learning not to question how anyone knew anything at Thomas Hall. The place was a well-oiled machine of organization, efficiency, and communication.

"Good idea." I sat at the kitchen table and Victor poured us both a glass of iced tea before he joined me. "Victor, I hope I'm not prying, but did you get the situation with your son handled?"

I drank my tea as he answered my question.

"No, you're not prying. I appreciate your concern." Victor smiled. "I did get it handled. Of course, after taxes and my son's problem, there's not much left."

"I'm glad it worked out that you could help him. Hopefully, he won't allow that to happen again."

"I hope so too. He says he's clear with the loan sharks and bookies. I'd like to see him join a gambling support group, but he won't."

"Loan sharks are dangerous people. I'm glad he's clean of that kind of company."

Victor tilted his head and raised an eyebrow at me. "And you know this how?"

"Let's just say my late husband's family has some experience with them. Make sure he keeps his account closed."

"It's just a shame that someone had to die for it to get resolved."

Victor's comment struck a chord with me that caused made me nauseous. Could he have killed Senior?

When I left the main house I had enough food for a small army. When I saw Bubba camped out by the front door, I remembered why. Once we were back at the villa, I convinced Bubba to eat something with me. And boy could he eat.

Edward hadn't called back after dinner. He told me not to go snooping but he never said anything about working out who the killer was on paper, so I rummaged through his desk in the living room and found an unused steno pad and pen and took a seat on the sofa. I needed to map out my thoughts on everything going on at the winery and Senior's murder. I started with the fingerprints on the weapon to come up with a list of suspects. Then I looked at what their motives were, if they had alibis, and any other factors, to try to pinpoint the killer.

Obviously, I could eliminate both Senior and myself. He was dead and I couldn't beat myself that brutally. Edward didn't do it either. He was with me until I went to the basement and on the phone while the killer beat me to a pulp. Michael and Sarah not only had no motive but were both in D.C. at the time of the murder. Dr. Rice was at the hospital seeing patients and while Vivian had recently come face to face with Senior's mistress, there was no way she had the physical strength needed to beat me up. That left Darla and Henry.

I knew Henry had been embezzling and Darla was cheating on Henry, but that was all I knew. Did they have motives or alibis? Were they in on it together? Henry just didn't seem like the type. Something wasn't right. Maybe I was thinking too hard. It could have been someone whose prints weren't on the weapon. All they would need to do was wear a pair of gloves.

I kept thinking about the red high heels. Did I really see them the night of the murder or was I so desperate to find something else that I dreamt them up? Could I trust my own memory? I was getting nowhere fast, so I gave up on the shoes and went back to brainstorming on potential suspects whose prints weren't on the murder weapon.

Alex had a motive but an alibi as well. If Alex felt like Senior was running the winery into the ground, he wouldn't have needed to kill him. Alex was young and talented and any winery would be lucky to have him. It was obvious at the reading of the will that Alex did not know Senior was his father, but the two had a genuine fondness for each other, even when they argued. As for Jennifer, although I heard the argument between her and Senior, I had trouble believing that she was the murderer and furthermore that she would frame her own son for the crime.

Would Victor kill Senior knowing he would get the money to help his son? I didn't know. Victor loved the Baker family, but your own family always comes first. Killing Senior would have been out of love, maybe even for both families.

No more suffering for Senior and the financial problems of his son would be solved. But to kill so violently and to attack me as well, seemed out of character for Victor.

I was getting nowhere fast with these thoughts, so I gave up, closed the notepad, and slipped it into the desk. As I closed the drawer, I thought about Victor again. I just could not imagine he would do it, but he had the means, multiple motives, and definitely the opportunity. I pulled out Brian Hayes' card and dialed the number.

"Hayes here."

"Brian, it's Cassandra Martin. Is now a bad time?"

"Nope, just put the kids to bed."

I looked at the clock. "I didn't realize it was so late. I should have waited until morning to call."

"No, actually this is good. It's quiet once the twins are asleep. And besides, you're never dull to talk to. What's up?"

"I'm not sure. But something odd about Senior's murder keeps popping up."

"What's odd? I'm at such a loss I'll take anything and it sounds like you're a smart woman."

"It's Victor. He had means, motives, and opportunity."

"Victor? You mean the Baker's butler?"

"Yes."

"Oh God, please don't tell me the butler did it." I could tell he was holding back laughter. "If you do, I might have to shoot myself just to keep with the 'Agatha Christie-ness' of it all. Oh, speaking of Agatha Christie, in the future, if you and Edward are going to make out in the balcony of the movie theater, move back a little further so you're completely out of sight. I was at the movies the night of Senior's murder. I wish I could say my date was as exciting."

I could feel my face turning beet red. "Okay, I'm going to lock myself in the house forever now." I heard Brian laugh on the other end of the line and couldn't help but to laugh a little myself.

"Seriously though, what makes you think Victor is involved in this?"

I went on to explain what I knew and everything Victor had said to me. When I was done Brian only had one question and the tone of his voice had changed from joking to dead serious.

"Cassandra, would Victor have known about the money he was due to inherit?"

"Victor knows everything that goes on at Thomas Hall."

"You might be on to something. I'll check it out and let you know, but in the mean time I want you to stay out of this. Whoever is doing these things won't stop until they get the results they want and one of those results is you with no pulse."

"That's what Edward keeps telling me."

"Then maybe you should listen to him."

"I'll try."

"Good. Let's keep this between just the two of us. I don't want anyone at Thomas Hall to know where the investigation is currently at. I'm certain the murderer is someone who is there every day. And the less the staff and residents of Thomas Hall know the better."

When Brian and I finished our conversation it was ten o'clock and Edward still hadn't called. I knew he wouldn't after ten. I thought things had taken a turn for the better before we hung up, but maybe they hadn't. Maybe I just so wanted things to be right between us that I had only convinced myself that things between us were better when they weren't. I didn't know what to think about anything anymore. All I knew was that I was in pain.

The stress of the day had intensified the pain of my broken ribs. And while I was beginning to physically recover from the attack, I still needed something for the pain if I was going to get any rest. I took half a Percocet and turned to Brick who had relieved Bubba from his post at nine.

"I'm exhausted. I'm going to bed. If you want to watch a movie or some TV, help yourself. I'm a heavy sleeper so it won't bother me. There is plenty of food in the refrigerator too, if you get hungry."

"Thank ya Ma'am. I'm fine with the TV off though. I wanna be able to hear anything unusual. I might take you up on the food a little later though." He smiled briefly and as I turned to walk away he said, "You let me know if ya need anything now, all right?"

"I will. Thanks."

I picked up the book from the coffee table I had intended on reading that morning, walked back to the bedroom, and crawled in the bed. But my mind was too full to concentrate on learning something new.

After reading the same line four times, I gave up and closed my eyes. I thought about everything that had happened over the last couple of weeks. The crazed series of events was a lot to take in and it left me with two questions. Why would someone who lived at Thomas Hall want to destroy me or the Baker family? And what kind of future did I really have with Edward. Or if I even had one at all.

Chapter Eighteen

It was seven in the morning and I was ready to throw my five and a half carat engagement ring out the window. Edward never called me back. I had taken the first step in patching things up by calling him the day before and he had the nerve not to call me back. I wasn't calling him again, he would have to call me.

On the bright side, when I stood to get out of bed I realized I was not in horrible pain. At the hospital, you are asked to rate your pain on a scale from zero to ten. Zero being no pain, ten being the worst pain of your life. I started with a pain level of nine the day I was admitted into the hospital, and it had been steadily decreasing. But today, without drugs in my system, I woke up at about a three. It was good to move around in mild pain and not agony. I knew I wouldn't be completely better for a couple of more weeks but I finally felt like there could be an end in sight to all the pain pills I needed to take.

I walked out to the living room expecting to see an empty house. What I found was delivery person, after delivery person, bringing in house plants, flowering plants, and fresh-cut flowers. I stopped the lady supervising the massive move. It turned out she was the owner of the florist in Willow Creek.

"Excuse me. I think there's been some sort of mistake. I didn't order any flowers, let alone all of this."

"Are you Cassandra Martin-Baker?"

I couldn't help but to smile at the word Baker stapled on the end of my name.

"Yes, I'm Cassandra."

"These are for you. All of them." She smiled. "Mr. Baker must really be in the dog house to be doing all of this. I think I'll have to close the shop until I get another flower shipment tomorrow."

"Do you need some to make any orders with? I wouldn't want to be a problem for your business."

"That's sweet, but I'll be fine." She reached into her pocket and pulled out a card to go with the flowers and her business card. "This is my card if you have any questions about what the different flowers are or how to care for them, feel free to call me. And this is from Mr. Baker."

When the last of the floral extravaganza delivery team had departed Brick looked at me.

"He must have made you really mad."

"We had a moment yesterday." Brick found my response humorous and laughed.

"Well, I'm gonna go do a perimeter check 'round the house and make sure everything is clear. I'll be back by the door in a moment."

Brick left and I opened the envelope.

Sweetie, I'm sorry. I'm a world-class idiot. I love you. Marry me.
Forever Yours, Edward

It was the sweetest apology I had ever received and the most extreme as well.

I still didn't want to call him but he left me no choice. I had to. So I picked up the phone and dialed.

"Edward Baker's phone." It was Kelly. I was mildly surprised that Kelly answered his phone. While she was his assistant, Edward always carried his cell phone with him.

"Hi Kelly, its Cassandra."

"Hey, Edward told me he needed to talk to you regardless of what's going on here."

"Is there something going on?"

"I'm not sure. Yesterday afternoon he called me and said to get all the major players on this deal in the boardroom now. He walked in and yelled at them, called them all a bunch of four-letter words, and told them the deal on the table expired at four p.m. today. Then he screamed some more and told them if they didn't sign it he was going into hostile takeover mode and he would destroy the company, pulling it apart, bit by bit. Then walked out of the room and locked himself in his office for about three hours. When he came out he was like his old self. Cassandra, I've worked for him for fifteen years and I've never seen him lose his cool like that during a merger." He had done what I had suggested but took it to the extreme, in typical Edward fashion.

"I think it might be my fault. We had a pretty big fight yesterday."

"That explains it."

"Explains what?"

"Last night, as we were all leaving the office, he made a comment to me that seemed a little off the cuff. He said this company might have cost him everything he loved and if it did, he would tear it apart."

"What's he doing now?"

"He's in a board meeting, but I'm walking in right now and handing him the phone."

"Don't interrupt him." But she didn't listen. I heard her say to Edward that I was on the phone. He excused himself and I heard a door close behind him.

"Hey, Beautiful." He sounded more like the man who dropped his cup of coffee the first morning of Crush Weekend.

"Nice card. I think I already addressed everything on it though."

"I just wanted to be sure you could live with a Neanderthal," he said.

"About the flowers. The gesture's nice but maybe a few less next time. It kinda looks like an Amazon rainforest in here."

"I didn't know what your favorite flowers were, so I ordered them all."

"Orchids and roses, but that's not important. How's the merger going? I heard you had a little temper tantrum yesterday."

"How did you know that? Doesn't matter. It worked. We're signing at noon. I should be back tonight."

"Edward, how are we going to do this? Is splitting our time between two places really going to work?"

"Now you're the one sounding unsure."

"Yeah."

"Don't worry, you said it yourself, we can do this. We're just going to have to plan it, together." It was the one word I needed to hear from him: together.

"We'll need a calendar at the house then."

"I'll have Kelly put one in my briefcase."

"You should get back to work, so you can get home." I wanted Edward to hold me, kiss me, love me. I'd become spoiled in the short time we had spent together and missed having him so close.

By mid-afternoon, I was pacing around the house aimlessly. I couldn't stand to be still any longer, so I went for a walk. Or should I say Bubba and I went for a walk. It seemed B&B changed shifts at nine. Bubba was the day man and Brick worked the nights. Edward and I had needed them way too much lately. When hired for twenty-four hour bodyguard service, Bubba would show up at about a quarter before nine in the morning. The guys would spend about fifteen minutes bringing each other up to date before Brick left. Then twelve hours later, Brick would arrive, they would repeat their rendezvous, and Bubba would go home.

In a single week, the weather had turned and a sweatshirt and jacket in combination were barely enough to keep me warm against the cold, strong wind that tore across the vineyard. I would need a winter coat soon. I hadn't owned one in over a year and I wasn't excited about living somewhere I would need one. Bubba didn't have on a coat at all and I wondered if he was one of those crazy people who actually liked the cold.

We turned left out of Edward's place and took the path to the production building. I poked my head in and said hi to the guys. Alex was knee-deep in the lab and Henry was trudging through paperwork. The phones were ringing, and the whole place looked like a disorganized, jumbled mess. While there was a desk for a receptionist or secretary, it was vacant. I made a mental note to talk to the guys about hiring a receptionist to help out as soon as possible.

I went into what used to be Senior's old office. It was a massive room that was neatly split into two functioning parts. The half furthest from the door housed a massive conference table and chairs. The window on the far side of the table allowed for a second-story view of the main production room, where the stainless steel vats rose from the ground and the bulk of the harvested grapes were transformed into wine.

The side closest to the entrance was a beautifully decorated office with views of the vineyard, an elegant tasting bar and matching cherry wood desk. Strategically placed throughout the room were chairs, barstools, small tables, and even a sofa. I guess it would be my office now.

As I walked across the giant purple and green oriental rug, which hid the industrial flooring, I realized the room was just as Senior had left it the last time he had stepped foot in the office. His laptop, although turned off, was open, and a stack of papers and messages were laid across the desk. An empty coffee mug was next to the messages, stained with brown rings inside.

I sat in the chair behind the desk and thought about all that had happened over the last couple of weeks. I wondered what my parents would have said about all of this. I knew Dad would have hated that I was about to give up an academic career for winemaking and would have completely lost it when he realized Edward and Fred were the same age. Mom would have liked it all, though. I could almost imagine her convincing Dad it would be fine. She'd tell him I was happy and that you can't live your child's life for them and that Edward would take good care of me. For the first time since I arrived at Thomas Hall, I missed my parents.

Bubba and I hadn't walked very far from the production building when we spotted Darla. She was walking down a path that only led to and from one place, Alex's house. She was smoking a cigarette as she walked. Her hair was a mess, and her clothes were wrinkled, but she had on high-heeled shoes in true Darla nature. And to top off the whole picture, she looked pretty pissed off.

There was something about Darla I just didn't like. After that moment in the wine cellar when she frightened me, I was uncertain what she thought of me and how she felt about my marrying Edward. Still, she was a Baker, so no matter how scary I thought she could be, I wasn't about to be rude. I stopped to face her, and Bubba waited a few steps behind.

"Hey, Cassandra. You're pushing yourself too hard. You look like hell." I wasn't in the mood for her bitchiness, so I ignored her.

"No, I'm just too restless to stay in bed anymore. I needed to get some fresh air and exercise."

"Who's the walking wall?"

"That's Bubba. Edward didn't think I was safe until the killer was caught, so he hired Bubba & Brick to keep an eye on me."

"Brick?"

"He works the night shift."

"Where are you walking to anyway?" She said as she dropped the end of her cigarette onto the ground and put it out with her shoe.

"I'm not sure, back to the house, I guess."

Darla's expression softened and she smiled. "Why don't you join me at my place for a drink? We have a full bar."

I had no desire to spend any time alone with her. I looked at my watch; it was already four forty-five. "I think I'm going to have to pass. Edward should be home soon."

"Oh, come on, it's just for a few minutes. If we're going to be sisters, we should start getting to know each other better. Besides, you know he'll call your cell if he gets to the house and you're not there." She seemed very eager to have me join her and I felt as if I'd been backed into a corner.

"I don't know about a mixed drink with all the meds I've been taking, but I'll join you anyway if you'd like."

"Great," she said.

We were standing in front of Henry and Darla's house when we started talking, so we walked up the sidewalk and into the house. Bubba checked each room and told me he'd do a perimeter check and wait on the porch. I felt uneasy about the whole thing but didn't say anything to Bubba. I couldn't. Darla was now glued to me and I wasn't going to tell Bubba I was afraid of Darla with her standing next to me.

The outside of Henry and Darla's place looked similar to Edward's home, but the inside was a completely different story. It was lavishly decorated, to the point of being ostentatious. There must have been a million dollars tied up in furniture, paintings, lamps, and sculptures. Darla walked over to the bar and fixed herself a drink and I settled for a bottle of water. "Follow me back to the bedroom. You can sit while I change."

The bedroom was even more outrageous than the rest of the house. In addition to the furnishings, there were tons of designer clothes and fur coats. There were at least four furs that I could see, and who knows how many more were hanging in the closet. One fur, the newest, I presumed, was still in the box. I ran my hand along its collar.

"Nice fur."

"Yes, I love them. Every time Henry and I reconcile, he buys me a new one."

"Really," then jokingly, I added, "All I get are flowers when Edward and I fight." Of course, I knew all I would have to do if I wanted one was mention it to Edward and the coat would show up on the front doorstep the next day.

I sat at Darla's vanity table and looked at the perfume and make-up while we talked. I noticed a pair of diamond earrings laying haphazardly in one of the table's compartments. They looked strikingly similar to mine, and I was surprised she owned a pair of earrings like that. She always wore big, dangling earrings. Her taste in jewelry ran in two sizes: Big and bigger.

"You mean like the entire florist that was delivered this morning?" She had obviously seen the delivery truck unloading. "I know he's got more money than anyone in the family, but what do you see in him besides his money anyway? I would have said he's a cheapskate, but after the rock he bought you, maybe not." She pulled out a fresh set of clothes and started to change.

I had full intentions of answering her question, but Darla continued to ramble on.

"Maybe I should have married Edward instead." I never knew she had taken an interest in Edward but was more concerned for Henry's well-being.

"Don't you love Henry?"

"I love being a Baker. You met my mom at the hospital, right? Do you know how hard it was growing up as the middle of five children with a deadbeat dad and a single mom working rotating shifts at the hospital? I never had any new clothes. I always had to help care for my younger brother and sister, was bossed around by my older brothers, teased at school, and never had anything nice. Then I met Henry. Even in high school, he was such a gentleman. He'd buy my lunch, carry my books, and surprise me with little gifts. When I wanted to go to the homecoming dance, he even bought my dress. So I let him fall in love with me. And now, I am the queen of my castle!" She spun around and threw herself onto the bed backwards, stretching her body out as if she were going to make angels in the snow. "I love being pampered like this." She sat up and smiled at me.

Pampered? Pampered! Oh my God! The earrings! The red high heels! All of the pieces fell into place and I instantaneously knew who killed Senior, but why had Darla tried to kill me too? I had to get out of there, but how? Bubba was parked in a chair by the front door and I was inside the house. I thought fast and came up with an escape plan. I tried to look nauseous and frail and then bent over in pain.

"Cassandra, are you okay?" She stood up and walked over to the vanity table. I slowly stood as she reached over and put her hand on my arm.

"It's just my ribs. I guess I have tried to do too much today. I hate to be rude, but I think I should get Bubba to walk me back to the house so I can take something for the pain and rest."

"I have a better idea; why don't I get Bubba to run back to Edward's and get your pills for you and you can rest here." There was something about her smile that I found disturbing. It was like the look on her face the night we were in the cellar after the will reading. I was in real danger with this woman, but I knew I had to keep calm if I was going to get out of there alive.

"I'll be right back. Why don't you lay down?" She scurried out of the room.

Now what? It only took me half a second to pull my cell phone out of my pocket and dialed Edward's cell. I would have called 911, but instinctively I knew I'd never be able to explain where I was or what was happening fast enough. I'd have to leave that call for Edward to make.

"You've reached the voicemail of Edward Baker. Leave a message, and I'll call you back."

I sat the bottle of water I was drinking on the nightstand, laid down on the bed, and waited for what seemed like an eternity for the beep.

"Edward, I know who killed your dad and I'm –" I heard the clicking of Darla's high-heeled shoes as she walked back down the hall. "Darla was sweet enough to insist that I rest here until I feel better."

Darla walked back into the room and looked me over from head to toe, raising an eyebrow as she listened to me speak. I pretended I was listening to Edward speak on the other end. I didn't want Darla to know I called Edward and got his voicemail. So after pausing, I continued the conversation with myself.

"No, Edward, I'll be fine." Darla turned and smiled at me. One of those smiles I was certain was inspired by the devil himself. "Darla's taking excellent care of me."

"I will. Bye." I pressed what I thought was the end button and put the phone back in my pocket and looked at her. "That was Edward. He said to take good care of me and he'll be back at Thomas Hall as soon as he can."

"Oh, I'll take care of you." She said sarcastically and took a long look at me. "You look like crap. I'll get you another bottle of water and see if Bubba is back yet." She returned a couple of seconds later and handed me a fresh bottle of water and a pill. However, it wasn't my pill. It couldn't be. Bubba couldn't have made the round trip between the houses that fast. In addition, the Percocet I had been taking was a small, white, round tablet and this was a light blue and purple capsule with a lavender band around one end.

"Take that and I'm sure you'll feel much better." She said.

There was no way that pill was going into my mouth. I wasn't sure what it was, but there was no doubt in my mind that no good could come of this. I looked at Darla, then at the pill again. I took a deep breath and tried to summon a little bravery before speaking.

"Well, go ahead." She insisted.

"Darla, there is no way I'm taking this." I sat the bottle of water on the nightstand and stood up." I don't know what it is, but it's not mine."

"Oh, you will take it." You could hear the evil saturate her voice as she spoke. "You don't have a choice."

As I looked at Darla, I saw a shadow in the doorway behind her. I couldn't quite see who it was at first, but I didn't want to stare. I wanted Darla to think we were alone.

"But I do." I took the capsule in my hand and pulled it apart, allowing the contents to spill into the thick carpet that covered the bedroom floor. As she watched the tiny granules fall, I watched her expression change from calm and confident to angry and frantic.

"You stupid bitch!" She screamed. "You think you're so smart. Now there's only one way to do this!"

I glanced over at the doorway again and got a better look at the shadowy figure. It was Henry. He held his finger up to his mouth, signaling me not to say a word about his presence. I paused for a moment, trying to decide if I should keep my mouth shut or keep talking. I opted to keep talking. "To do what?"

Darla walked over to her dresser as I spoke, pulled a Derringer .25 automatic from the top drawer, turned, and pointed it at me. I could feel my whole body tremble and my palms began to sweat. I had experienced many things, but being held at gunpoint was not one of them. My legs felt rubbery and I sat on the edge of the bed to keep from falling onto the floor.

"To get rid of you once and for all." She said. "See, the pill I just gave you wasn't Percocet. It was Penicillin. That would have been so much easier for me. Less mess, less explaining. From what I understand, you would've been dead in about fifteen minutes. Now, well, I guess it will just have to be this way." She flung the gun around before pointing it back at me.

"Why?" She rolled her eyes at me and then began her rant when I asked.

"You were in the wrong place at the wrong time, at least the night I killed Senior." I looked over to see a much more visible Henry in the doorway with a single tear falling off his face. I wished he wasn't standing at the door. Hearing her admit to killing his father had to be heartbreaking for him.

"Then you went and inherited part of the winery and insisted that Henry pay back the money he took. That really pissed me off. And to top it off, you just annoy the hell out of me! 'Poor, sweet Cassandra.' 'She's all alone in the world.' 'She's so polite.' 'We all love Cassandra so much.' I couldn't take it anymore. Everybody loves you. Hell, even my husband likes you better than he likes me!" Darla took a single step closer to the bed. "You know, I thought you'd leave after I ransacked Edward's place. I was certain you'd run off with your little mouse tail between your legs. But no, you had to stick around and make things difficult. Then when you walked in on Senior before I had a chance to leave the scene, I had to resort to all of this."

I glanced at Henry again. He was braced against the door, running his hand through his hair. He was falling apart as he listened and I wasn't confident he would be of much help to me. Where was Edward? Had he even gotten my message or understood it? Henry and I both needed him, desperately, and now.

"You know, this winery was supposed to be mine and Alex's."

"Alex?" I questioned.

"I told Henry I broke it off with him, but I didn't. I figured Henry and I would reconcile; I'd set him up with some drunken pictures with a hooker, divorce him, and live happily ever after with Alex, the money, and the winery. But then Alex told me that he was done with me. So I guess I'll just wait and see whom I find to share it with. All of this *will* be mine and I'm not going to let a little slut like you blow it all for me."

Regardless of what questions I asked, she seemed to be telling me the answers threefold. While I was scared to death of how this could end, I decided I'd better keep talking in hopes of buying time in the event Edward had understood and was on his way.

"Darla, why did you blow up Phoebe's house?"

"I overheard her and Vivian talking about selling her shares to you. I couldn't let her do that. Of course, the bitch got out of bed and was gone before the gas tank under the water heater caught fire." She paused for a long minute and I watched the anger build in her eyes. "Enough! You're stalling me. No more questions."

"If I'm going to die anyway, just tell me one more thing. Why did you kill Senior?"

"Fine. The old bastard wouldn't bite it. Five years ago was supposed to be Senior's last Harvest, last Christmas, and so on and so on. I got tired of waiting. And if I had to hear about not giving him any grandchildren one more time, I would go insane!"

I had to say it. I just could not let her think she had completely controlled his death. "You know, the coroner said Senior would have been dead within a week or two. You probably saved him a lot of pain."

She walked over to the edge of the bed and pistol-whipped me across the face. The cold, hard barrel of the gun stung my cheekbone and I could feel my skin start to swell around my eye socket.

"You can't be serious. That sorry son-of-a-bitch drove me to this for no reason?" She was less than a yard away and took aim, pointing the barrel directly at my face. "Too bad for you, though, because now you –"

Henry barged into the room, pushing her back and wedging himself between the gun and me. "Darla! Enough!"

Darla was speechless. It took her a moment of thinking before she partially lowered the gun and asked, "Henry, what exactly did you hear, my little cup-cake?"

"Everything. How could you? My Dad, Phoebe, and now Cassandra!" The volume of his voice grew along with his despair. "I gave you everything! And, and, you never loved me, did you?"

"Oh, Cupcake, you know you're special."

"Don't Cupcake me!" I had never heard Henry sound so confident. "Darla, give me the gun. No one has to die here."

She flung the gun around in her hand as she gestured toward me. "She does."

"No, she can't. She's the only woman my brother has ever really loved. You haven't got a clue what it's like to truly love someone, do you?" I was surprised to hear what he was saying. While it was all true, I knew how hard it was to see the ugly truth about the people you love.

"I love you, Henry. I really do."

"No. You cheated on me. You shamelessly lied to me. You killed my father. And now, you're trying to destroy Edward by using her as a pawn in your sick game!" He turned his body in my direction but never took his eyes off of Darla. "Cassandra, I know you and Edward fought yesterday. He called me and we talked. You need to know that whatever happens here, he loves you. He loves you more than life itself."

I thought about what Henry said, whatever happens.

If I died, I knew that Edward loved me. I was certain of it. But I wanted one more chance to tell him how much I loved him. He taught me what it meant to be truly loved, truly cherished, and I'd never even thanked him.

Henry turned back, completely focusing his attention on his wife. "Now, Darla, give me the gun."

"I can't; if I give you the gun, Cassandra will live. If she lives, you'll lose me forever." He took a step closer to Darla.

"If she dies, I'll lose you forever too."

"Henry, you wouldn't testify against me, would you?" There was a silence that seemed to last an eternity. I carefully studied both of them. Darla was hanging on the edge of what little sanity she had left, wondering what Henry would say. Henry stared at her and took a long, deep breath.

"Darla, either way, you're done. You killed my father. There's a price to pay for that." He looked at me. "Cassandra, I want you to get up and walk out of the house."

I was terrified as I followed Henry's instructions and stood to leave. Darla looked at me wide-eyed in disbelief. Henry saw an opportunity. I knew he didn't want to see anyone else get hurt. He grabbed the gun in Darla's hand and she fought him. I watched as they went back and forth, pulling at the gun until they were a few inches apart and the weapon was buried between them.

I don't remember hearing the gunshot. I'm sure it was deafening as the three of us were standing within a couple of feet of one another. But everything unraveled so quickly that I only remembered the ringing in my ears and the events that followed. When I looked at the two of them, the only thing I saw was blood. Lots and lots of blood.

"Henry, are you okay?" I grabbed him by the shoulders and turned him toward me. When I did, the gun fell from his hand and dropped to the floor. His clothes were soaked red to the point of saturation. "Oh God, Henry! Say something!"

But he didn't say anything. He stood, motionless, trance-like, as though he had been frozen in a block of ice.

I looked at Darla. I let go of Henry and bent over her slumped, lifeless body and, in the process, blocked Henry's view of her. She was on the floor, leaning against the nightstand with a hole in her chest. The blood was still flowing out of her like a waterfall. I checked her pulse. She was already dead and nothing I could do would revive her, so I left her as she was. It seemed that death was the karmic price for all the harm she had caused.

The gun laid on the floor next to my feet. I carefully placed it in her hand, putting her finger on the trigger. Henry didn't need to pay for Darla's horrible behavior. No one should feel the death of a loved one was their fault. I lived with that ghost every day and would not wish the same curse on anyone, especially Henry. I looked back at him.

He was in the same position I left him in, still motionless and covered in Darla's blood. I stood up, and when I grabbed his arms, he snapped out of his shock-induced trance and into a complete panic.

"I killed her! I killed her, didn't I?"

I pulled Henry to hold him, but he collapsed to his knees, taking me with him. I held him like a mother consoling her child, rocking him back and forth. "No, Henry, you didn't kill her. She killed herself."

He looked over at her and saw the gun in her hand.

"Oh God, Cassandra! She's really dead, isn't she?"

I heard knocking on the door and someone yelling. It was Edward. "Open the door." He must have already been on the corporate helicopter when I called, heading home. It made sense. The only time he didn't answer the phone was when he was in the air. "Darla, open it now!"

The next thing I heard was Bubba beating down the door. I could only imagine Edward's sense of panic when he ran into the bedroom and saw me in yet another pool of blood. His terror-filled eyes met mine and they locked. I don't know for how long, but we both knew how close I had come to dying. He had listened to almost everything on the voicemail of his cell phone. I had accidentally hit the speakerphone button trying to hang up after leaving my cryptic message.

I turned to Bubba. "We need to get Henry out of here now."

Bubba nodded in agreement and lifted Henry off me, literally carrying him out of the house. When I looked down, I was soaked in Darla's blood. My clothes, hair, shoes, and skin were all coated in bright red liquid. I wasn't going to let myself faint. Not this time. Henry needed his whole family, including me, and Edward needed to see that I was okay.

Edward reached down with both arms and lifted me off the floor, all the while looking at my blood-soaked clothes. The first time he set me upright, my knees buckled. I felt lightheaded and nauseous. I feared I might faint regardless of my desire not to. He lifted me a second time, and I found my footing along with the determination not to pass out.

"None of this blood's yours, is it?"

I shook my head as I answered. "No, but if I'm not out of these clothes and in the shower in the next five minutes, I'm pretty sure I'm going to throw up."

He breathed a sigh of relief and that sexy grin crept up onto his face. "I think I can have you naked and in my shower in less time than that."

Chapter Nineteen

The next morning was dark and the rain that started the night before had yet to cease. I was glad to be in the house and had no intention of leaving Thomas Hall. The temperature in the house laid fact that it was cold outside and beginning to feel more like winter and less like fall. Virginia was like that. Fall seemed to only last a couple of weeks and it had arrived unusually early that year.

I was lying in Edward's arms with the doors locked and the shutters and curtains drawn. Edward had started a fire in the fireplace and brought our tea and coffee to bed. The light from the fireplace was just bright enough for Edward and dim enough for me. Soft music played quietly on the bedside clock radio.

"Sweetie, how did you figure out it was Darla? I've known Brian a long time and he's damn good at his job. The only reason he doesn't go to work for a bigger city is because of the twins. What did you know that he didn't?" While he spoke, he stroked my hair and pushed it behind my ears.

"I kept going back to the murder weapon. I knew something wasn't right with those pruning shears, but I couldn't pinpoint it. Then, when I was at Darla's, she commented how she loved being pampered. It reminded me of something she said at the spa."

"What did she say?"

I took a sip of my tea before I continued. "I think her exact words were, 'I don't do grapes.' I thought it was interesting because Zoe assumed we were all in the fields at some point. Darla never went out to harvest with us, but her prints were on the murder weapon. Of course, the earrings and her confession made it easy."

"Wow. I don't think any of us could have put all of that together to name Darla as the killer."

"Well, I was the only person at both of those discussions and to find the earrings in her vanity, so it would make sense that I would need to be the one to figure it out." I handed him the teacup and he set it on the nightstand.

"Well, that makes sense."

"Edward, I'm tired of talking about Darla." Last night, after our shower, Edward insisted to Brian that I rest before giving him my statement of what happened. Brian agreed and took the time to finish what needed to be done at Henry's place.

However, rest wasn't what was on my mind. After the longest, hottest shower I ever remember taking, I spent the next hour in bed with my fiancé. Making love with Edward was anything but restful, but it did leave me calmer. And the calmness helped when it came time to relive the events earlier in the evening.

Brian suggested taking my statement at our house at Thomas Hall. He expressed concern about my health and recovery and thought it unnecessary for me to make the trip to Willow Creek. It took nearly three hours to go over everything that happened with Brian concerning the investigations of both Senior and Darla's deaths. I gave him a necessary minute-by-minute account of the events in Henry and Darla's house. I knew that sooner or later, my fingerprints would show up on the gun, so I embellished my story slightly, commenting that I had seen Darla's gun on the dresser and picked it up while exploring her room. When we were done, I was relieved to be in my own living room, as it was after eleven when Brian left and Edward and I slipped into bed.

Edward leaned over and kissed me just under the eye that the hit from the pistol had left black and blue. He cupped my cheek with his hand and leaned my head against his chest.

"That's fine, Sweetie. I'm tired of talking about her too. Anything on your mind?"

"I talked to my uncle earlier this morning while you were on the phone with Kelly."

"Really?" I could tell by his voice that he was smiling, although I never looked up and he continued to stroke my hair.

"Yeah, I called to tell him about our engagement, but it seems he already knew."

"I called him the day I put the ring on your finger and asked for his blessing."

I couldn't believe he called and asked for Fred's blessing. That was really old-fashioned, even for me.

"What did he say?"

"The same thing he said when I called to ask his permission to date you. He gave me his blessing but reminded me that he'd kill me if I ever broke your heart."

We both laughed. I liked the sound of our laughter mixed together. Edward leaned my head to the side and nibbled on my ear as he whispered, "So, my love, when do you want to get married?"

"I don't know. I've always liked the idea of holiday weddings, maybe Christmas or New Years?"

"What year?" I thought the question was funny and laughed, although it was barely audible. I knew I had made it clear in the beginning that I wanted a long engagement, but the things Darla said about outliving Edward stuck with me. I shifted my body position so I could see his face.

"I was thinking this year."

His eyes lit up like fireworks and by the time he released his lips from mine, I knew everything I needed to know about his feelings on the subject.

"What happened to a long engagement?" He asked.

"Last week made me realize that life's too short to wait. And yesterday, there was a moment when I thought I might never get –"

"Cassie, stop." His voice cracked as he spoke. He knew where I was going and the thought tormented him.

"No, I need to finish. I thought I'd never get the chance to tell you, show you, or thank you for loving me. I don't ever want to be in a position again where I wish I had the chance to finish something left undone with you. I want to marry you and I want to do it this Christmas." I realized I sounded demanding and found myself verbally retreating. "But we can wait if you want."

"No, no, this year's fine with me." Edward smiled. "We could have a Thanksgiving wedding."

"Have you seen what's on the winery's schedule in November? There is absolutely no way."

Edward laughed and then brushed the back of his hand across my unbruised cheek with that soft romantic touch that always made me melt. "Dad was right, you know. You really were meant to be a Baker."

"Speaking of Bakers, we should go up to the main house later and check on your brother," I said.

"Do you think he's going to be okay? I've never lost a spouse before. I don't know what I'd do if I lost you." I found it amazing that he was already referring to me as his wife. We weren't married yet.

"Edward, Henry's going to be miserable for a while. Regardless of what she did, he loved Darla, and her death's going to be painful for him. It'll get easier, though. The best thing we can do is be supportive. We'll go to the funeral, say kind things about her, and help your mom host the reception afterward. It will be a long process for Henry, but he'll be okay. It'll just take time."

"For a while last night, Henry thought he had shot her. Be it accidental; he was certain it was his fault."

I took a deep breath as I thought about the moment he realized Darla was dead. "I know. But it's important that he realizes he didn't do it. I don't think Henry could live with himself if he believes he killed her."

"I guess I just don't understand the confusion. Her finger was on the trigger. I saw it."

"It looked that way, didn't it?" As soon as the words came out of my mouth, I wondered if I should have said anything at all and bit my bottom lip as I stared at the comforter on the bed.

Edward lifted my face to his, looked deep into my eyes, and stared for a long, lingering moment. Then he kissed me like he had never kissed me before. It was a kiss that told me he loved me, not just because I loved him, but because I loved his family too. I was aware he knew, without me even saying the words, exactly what I had done. It was a secret we'd both take to our graves, a Baker family secret.

The End

Acknowledgments

First, I would like to thank Joyce Norman and Joy Collins for introducing me to the world of publishing. I could not have asked for better guides.

Next, I would like to thank my beta readers. This group of extraordinary women gave me the kind of feedback that made me a better writer. Betty Bryant, Katy Hines, Lynn Whitt, and Stefanie Lewis. I owe each and every one of you so much.

And last, but certainly not least, I would like to thank Miss Ebbie Rice. Who not only suggested I write a romance novel, but is the only person I have ever known who inspired me to create a character based on some of their most wonderful characteristics.

Also By Beth Sorensen

The Thomas Hall Series
Crush at Thomas Hall – Book One
Divorcing a Dead Man – Book Two
Waiting for Time to Tell – Book Three

* 9 7 9 8 9 8 6 1 1 3 3 6 4 *